Song
of my
Soul

Song of my Soul

Ginny Aiken

Revell
Grand Rapids, Michigan

© 2004 by Ginny Aiken

Published by Fleming H. Revell
a division of Baker Publishing Group
P.O. Box 6287, Grand Rapids, MI 49516-6287

Second printing, October 2004

Printed in the United States of America

Library of Congress Cataloging-in-Publication Data
Aiken, Ginny.
　　Song of my soul / Ginny Aiken.
　　　　p.　　cm. — (Silver Hills trilogy)
　　ISBN 0-8007-5875-7 (pbk.)
　　　1. Colorado—Fiction. I. Title. II. Series: Aiken, Ginny. Silver Hills trilogy.
　　PS3551.I339S66　2004
　　813'.54—dc22　　　　　　　　　　　　　　　　　　2004001245

Scripture is taken from the King James Version of the Bible.

Let the saints be joyful in glory: let them sing aloud upon their beds. Let the high praises of God be in their mouth.

Psalm 149:5–6

1

Adrian Gamble wasn't his name, but it was the one he was willing to use.

He led his horse down Hartville's main street, taking note of the sights and sounds it offered. On either side, solid buildings replaced the ramshackle structures he'd expected to find in the mining town. Evidently, the residents had found a good enough living here and decided to stay. They'd established permanent homes and businesses and looked to be thriving.

Perhaps he'd live long enough to do the same.

As had become his habit, he glanced over his shoulder and to either side, checking to see if any familiar faces followed in his wake. He prayed every minute of every day for the Lord to keep him safe from his pursuers.

He hoped out-of-the-way Hartville and its established mining company would provide a measure of anonymity.

A wooden sign in the window of a plain, whitewashed storefront on the right side of the street told him he'd reached his destination. Douglas Carlson, attorney-at-law, did business within.

"Good afternoon," he said to the bespectacled and serious man he found shuffling papers in a cabinet just inside the door. "I'm looking for Mr. Carlson."

"You've found him. And you are . . . ?"

He bit his tongue to keep the dangerous name from popping forth. "Gamble," he said instead. "Adrian Gamble, and I'm here to finalize my purchase of the Heart of Silver Mining Company."

A flicker of interest showed from behind the glass lenses as the lawyer extended his hand. "Pleased to make your acquaintance. I've been looking forward to this day."

Adrian returned the firm clasp. "So have I." *But for very different reasons.* He ignored his irritating conscience, aware that subterfuge was his only choice at present.

"Please, follow me." Douglas gestured toward the open doorway at the left side of the room. "My secretary had to go to Denver for a family funeral, but she prepared all the documents you need to sign. I have them at my desk."

The attorney closed the door to the simple, attractive office and pointed to the comfortable-looking leather armchair in front of his neat desk. "Do take a seat."

Adrian sank into the chair. "Ah, it's a pleasure to sit in something other than a saddle after riding a ways."

"There's a reason trains are such popular means of travel from practically any part of the country."

Adrian didn't take the bait. He had no intention of revealing his departure point or explaining his reasons for avoiding crowds. "So you say everything is in order."

Douglas's eyes again gleamed, this time to broadcast that little escaped his notice. Adrian would have to remember that in the future and guard his tongue.

"Everything from the deed to the property to the general store and its inventory, as well as the Harts' former home and all its furnishings. You only need to sign and assume the reins."

Adrian allowed himself a satisfied smile. "I'll also need to gather the two boxes I shipped ahead in care of the company. Would they still be at the train station?"

The lawyer pushed a pen-and-inkwell stand toward Adrian and handed him a sheaf of papers. "No. I decided it made more sense if everything was delivered to the general store, since the porters know to take all mining company supplies there."

With conscious effort, Adrian avoided signing the wrong name on the deed. His man in Virginia had assured him that he would be the owner of the mine and all the other company property despite signing as the stranger, Adrian Gamble. The man he once was no longer existed.

"There," he said. "What's next?"

Douglas stood. "As I said, all you need is to move right in—to your new home and business. Both are ready."

"You did indeed take care of everything. I'm much obliged."

The lawyer shrugged and reached for a brown overcoat hanging from a hook on the frame of a tall mirror near the door. "If you don't object, I'd like to show you around."

"First I must find a livery."

"Of course. Amos Jimson's stables are right around the corner, and you won't find a finer man or better place to keep your animal."

Adrian followed his guide. He'd achieved a major goal and wanted to celebrate, but the wariness that had replaced his once easygoing nature prevented him from even the slightest lowering of his guard. His life depended on his vigilance.

The stables were as clean and well tended as any Adrian had ever seen. And the owner? Amos was another matter altogether.

"Where you hail from, son?" the large black man asked in a kind voice.

Adrian gave the reply that had served him well for a while. "Oh, from just about everywhere."

"From just about everywhere, you say." Canny smarts lay behind the slow, molasses-rich southern voice. "And precisely whereabouts is everywhere?"

"Back east."

"I see. Back east." The livery owner's perusal turned to scrutiny, and Adrian began to chafe under its intensity. Then Amos added, "An' just what brings you to Hartville?"

"Give the man a chance to catch his breath, Amos." Douglas evidently knew the livery owner well. "He's just ridden into town, and from the looks of him and his horse, he's been on the road for a fair spell. This is Adrian Gamble, the mine's new owner."

Still more interest lit Amos's smile. "Mm-hmm. Looks like we'll have us plenty time to get us better acquainted, won't we, Mister Adrian Gamble? I don't figger you'll be travelin' *everywhere* for a spell. Running the Heart of Silver takes a toll on a man's time."

"I'm not afraid of work—never have been. I know I've taken on a large responsibility, but I trust the Lord will make me equal to it."

Again the wise brown eyes narrowed, and the lines at their corners, lines surely gained over years of life's experiences, deepened. Adrian felt as though his drawers were flapping open in the brisk Colorado wind.

"Glad to see you're a God-fearing man, Mister Gamble. Always good to know another brother on the straight and narrow road to heaven."

He squirmed. He hadn't fooled Amos for a second. And he wouldn't be taking him up on his roundabout invitation to get better acquainted either. "I must be on my way, Mr. Jimson. Pleasure meeting you."

Amos laughed. "Is it now? Well, we'll soon see, son, how much pleasure you'll be finding in Hartville. At least you'll know for the next while where you hail from, now won't you?"

Adrian spun on his heel and headed out the wide entry to the stables. Douglas took several loping steps and caught up with him seconds later.

"I'm sorry about that," he said, gasping. "Amos is incorrigible. He survived the hell of slavery and figures he's entitled to say whatever's on his mind. Sometimes he goes a mite far."

"A man has a right to speak as he wishes." Adrian cast a sideways glance at his companion. "And to keep his counsel, too."

Without missing a step, Douglas met Adrian's gaze, acknowledging his meaning.

"He certainly does." The lawyer then waved toward the substantial structure they'd reached. "And the general store's a good place to be mindful of that. Not much that happens or is said here stays within these four walls."

Adrian paused on the steps to the boardwalk right in front of the store. "Surely you're not saying I have a gossiping busybody in my employ."

"Heavens no," Douglas said. "Phoebe Williams is a hardworking woman, not given to excesses of any sort. And as a pastor's widow, she's the soul of discretion."

Adrian forced his shoulders to relax. "I'm glad to hear that. I can certainly use an efficient and sensible manager at the store."

Douglas cast Adrian a sharp look. "Excellent. The whole town has worried about Mrs. Williams's future. No one knew your intentions for the store, and she depends on her wages."

"I hope no one's thought I'd come to turn folks out on the street. I don't intend to make many changes—if any—to what seems to be a well-managed operation."

"Well," Douglas said, "there is something you might want to consider. You've a sizable number of Chinamen working the mine, and the situation might be growing troublesome. You'll have to watch for—"

"Oh! Dear me, Douglas," exclaimed the tiny, gray-garbed

dynamo who barreled into the attorney. "I had no idea you were out here. Did I hurt you?"

The woman's question brought a smile to Adrian's lips.

Douglas laughed. "Letty, you're no bigger than a minute. Of course you didn't hurt me. And if you had, what then? Why, I'm sure you'd patch me up right quick."

He turned to Adrian. "Allow me to introduce our intrepid physician, Dr. Letitia Morgan—"

"Dr. Letitia *Wagner*," the petite woman interjected.

Adrian arched a brow and extended his hand. "A most progressive town, Hartville."

The doctor's chin rose as she took his fingers in a firm clasp. "As they all should be, Mr. Gamble."

Her use of his recently acquired name gave him pause.

She noticed. "I'm afraid your fame precedes you, sir." At his alarm, she chuckled and waved. "Nothing to worry about though. It's merely a matter of small-town reality. Everyone knows most everyone here. You see, before she left, Mrs. Hart gave us enough particulars regarding the sale of her late husband's holdings to satisfy the rampant curiosity, and your name was one of those particulars. We've been expecting your arrival these last few days."

"I see." As his heart beat a wild tattoo, Adrian renewed his determination to guard his privacy.

With a bob of her head, the doctor smiled, patted Douglas's hand in a friendly way, and started down the boardwalk in the direction from which he and Douglas had just come.

She paused and said over her shoulder, "Do keep in mind, Mr. Gamble, that my clinic is on Willow Lane, just a few houses down from Silver Creek Church—in case you're in need of my services, of course."

"Of course." Was the good doctor someone of concern?

"Letty is the most generous and caring woman in town."

Carlson held the store's door open for Adrian. "Besides my dear wife, you understand."

Adrian grinned. "Ever given thought to politics, counselor?"

The lawyer laughed as they stepped inside. "Call me Douglas, and no. I just favor living longer. My Randy happens to be Letty's closest crony, and I have a healthy respect for those two. Alone they're impressive, but together they're nothing short of formidable."

Adrian blinked at the contrast in lighting. "Perhaps there's a good reason for a man to remain a bachelor."

"Life would be too dull if I had to live it alone. Randy and our new little Emma Letitia—after the good doctor, you see—are God's greatest gifts to me."

Pain stabbed Adrian in the deepest part of his heart. He'd said farewell to his family forever. He'd had to do so to ensure their safety. The hole created by the knowledge that he'd never again see Mother; his brother, Stuart; sweet Priscilla, the youngest of the three; and Aunt Sally was a deep, ever-aching wound.

"Hello, Mr. Carlson," a woman said, her voice melodic and sweet.

"Good afternoon, Phoebe. I've someone here I'm sure you're anxious to meet. This is Adrian Gamble, your new employer."

Although Adrian's eyes hadn't yet adjusted to the darkness, he didn't need perfect vision to recognize fear. The woman's sharply indrawn breath said it all.

When the shadows around him cleared, brightened by a gas lamp, Adrian made out a feminine form next to a long counter. Tall and well proportioned, Phoebe Williams seemed stunned by his presence in the store.

"I'm pleased to meet you," he said in his kindest voice. He remembered Douglas's concern for the widow's livelihood. "I've heard excellent things about your skills. I hope you'll do me the honor of continuing in my employ."

13

Evidently, he'd said the right thing. The tightness of her shoulders and neck eased just enough to let her nod.

"I'd be much obliged, Mr. Gamble," she said. "I hope everything is to your approval, but if it's not, please let me know, and I'll take care of those changes you wish to make."

To his delight, his eyes finally cooperated. Although pale, Phoebe Williams looked quite unlike what he'd expected. From Douglas's description, he'd thought the preacher's widow would be much more timeworn and gray. Instead, she looked scarcely more than twenty, with soft blue eyes and honey-colored hair pulled up into a soft knot on her crown. Her simple cotton blouse buttoned up to her throat, and a small cameo brooch held it closed. Her hands, clasped at her waist, looked more like those of an artist than those of a shopkeeper. Although not beautiful in the classical sense, Phoebe Williams was attractive and undoubtedly the most feminine creature Adrian had ever seen.

He was intrigued.

Realizing Douglas and Phoebe still awaited his response, he repeated his earlier sentiment. "I'm not one to make hasty or unwise changes, so I won't disrupt what appears to be a smooth-running operation. I'm certain the store's success is in no small measure due to your excellent influence."

He turned to Douglas. "Lead the way to the house, counselor. I'm afraid the trip has got the best of me. I'm looking forward to washing away the road dust and crawling into bed."

Douglas nodded and headed for the door. In Adrian's last glimpse of Phoebe, he noted the heightened peach tint of her cheeks. "I look forward to working closely with you here at the store, Mrs. Williams."

Something he said must have flustered her, because she blushed a deeper shade of apricot and nodded, her knuckles whitening as she tightened her clasped hands. Then she smiled, and Adrian felt as though the sun had just come over the eastern horizon for the second time that day. Her smile made him think

14

physical beauty inconsequential as it illuminated her features from within, bringing them a certain softness and a warmth that reached him where he'd been too cold for a long time.

She glowed with something he lacked, something his words had just given her.

Hope.

It glowed from the lovely widow's face, and Adrian knew he had to watch himself. Phoebe held the future in her graceful hands, while his future had died on a train nearly a year ago. Without his identity and with killers on his trail, he had no hope, nothing to offer, no future in sight. He certainly had nothing for the too-appealing Phoebe Williams, nor even for himself.

His life had come to an end on the day he killed another man.

"Did you meet him, Phoebe? Did you?" Young Julia Miller, cheeks flushed, brown curls bobbing, dodged the makeshift seats around the pot-bellied stove in the Heart of Silver Mining Company's general store.

Phoebe Williams bit her bottom lip. She sent her friend Letty Wagner an anxious look and handed her the parcel of homeopathic remedies she'd ordered from the Luyties Apothecary in St. Louis, Missouri.

"I did," she said.

Julia, full of youthful fervor, fairly quivered in anticipation. When neither Phoebe nor Letty spoke further, she frowned. "Well? What do you reckon?"

Again Phoebe looked at Letty, who shook her head. She shrugged. "I reckon I know nothing more than you do."

Julia's exuberance deflated. "Oh."

Phoebe smiled at the girl's crestfallen expression. "Was there something your mother wanted, or did you just come to visit?"

Julia blushed. She tangled the fingers of one hand with those of the other, then scrubbed the palms of her hands on her skirt. She shifted her weight from her left foot to her right. "Well, I'd just delivered a load of fresh laundry to one of her customers, and . . . well, I thought you might know more about the new owner."

"Nothing, dear," Phoebe said with a sigh. "I don't know a thing beyond what Mrs. Hart said at church three weeks ago before she went back east. She had to sell the mining company after Mr. Hart went to his eternal rest, and Mr. Adrian Gamble bought everything. He's here in town now."

Julia leaned against the gleaming oak counter, eyes sparkling with curiosity. "Well then, what do you reckon he'll do with the store? My ma says no eastern swell's going to want to fuss with it. He likely only wants more of what he has—silver, and plenty of it."

An icy lump landed in Phoebe's middle. "I'll have you know the store does a solid business and turns a tidy profit," she said to convince herself as well as Julia. "I wouldn't ever let down my Father in heaven or my employer on earth by lazing about instead of working. I assure you, this store is no loss to its owner. Besides, he said he wouldn't disturb our smooth-running operation."

Before the girl could gather her wits, Letty stepped in. "Haven't you something more fruitful to do than chatter, Miss Julia Miller? I'd think your mother could use help with the laundry."

Julia winced and lowered her head. "Yes, ma'am, I reckon she could. I'll be heading home, then. Afternoon, Dr. Morgan . . . er . . . Mrs. Wagner . . . Oh, botheration. What do I call you now you're right and wedded?"

Letty struggled with a smile. "You may call me Dr. Wagner or Mrs. Wagner, Julia. Now do hurry on home. If your mother doesn't need you for the wash, then she can certainly use you to help keep your brothers in hand."

A mulish expression replaced the young woman's abashment, but she marched back up the store's central aisle. "I'd as soon scrub the skin clear off my knuckles on a rusty old washboard, Dr. Wagner."

The cowbell on the establishment's half-glass door jangled in Julia's wake. Phoebe tried to breathe a sigh of relief, but she realized no relief could be found. Not yet.

"Has your husband learned anything about the new buyer?" she asked her friend. "Has he prepared a story about Mr. Gamble for his newspaper?"

Letty patted Phoebe's hand. "Don't fret. Eric has no more information than the rest of us do, but I doubt the new owner will close the store. Surely he knows it does a hearty trade, and I'm certain he also knows he must keep his miners supplied and content. Keeping the company store open and successful is a sensible and wise proposition."

Phoebe nodded without much conviction. "I know what he said, but I can't be sure of a stranger. I don't know what I'll do if he does close it down. Now that my dear John is gone, I've no one else—"

"Hush now. You're not at all alone. You have brothers and sisters at Silver Creek Church."

Phoebe stiffened her spine and held her head high. "I could never let myself become a burden to anyone. The good Lord called John to join Pastor Stone as his junior, and He must have had a reason to bring me here, too. But why He let the mine shaft cave in and take my John—"

"Plus Mr. Hart and a dozen and a half miners, too."

Phoebe winced, chagrined by her uncharacteristic self-centeredness. "I'm so sorry. I can't seem to take my eyes off myself these days. Of course I'm not the only one who lost someone dear that day. It's just . . ."

"That you feel your own loss most deeply. Especially since you'd only been married a brief time."

"I'm so glad you understand, you being a newlywed and all." Phoebe made herself don a smile. "Thirteen months and two weeks is all we had, to be precise."

The memories of happy times rushed to her mind, times

she still couldn't revisit. They were much too sad to remember when she no longer had John's loving presence at her side. She pushed the images away and tried to put words to the feelings inside her.

"That's what makes it so hard, Letty. I can't know what the future holds. I try to trust the Father, but He's kept His counsel so far. He must have something for me." She looked around the store, at the floor-to-ceiling shelves replete with every conceivable necessity—and a few items not so necessary, too. "I can't imagine life without greater purpose than selling flour, calico, tin pans, salt mackerel, crackers, pickles, and tea."

"Oh, but it *is* an important task. Hartville needs this store. The miners depend on its reduced prices to replenish their supplies, and the rest of us appreciate the convenience it provides. I'm sure the Lord has a purpose for you, and He'll reveal it in His own good time, even if storekeeping happens to be it. Do think of the ministry in service."

Phoebe frowned, certain that storekeeping wasn't a purpose—not in the way she meant. "I must say, I'm praying He doesn't take too long. I tremble each time someone mentions the sale of the mine."

Letty gathered the remedies Phoebe had wrapped in brown paper and placed the package in a large basket over her arm. "I daresay I risk sounding as though I'm offering only platitudes, but do try not to fret until you know for certain what Mr.—Oh, what was his name?"

"Gamble." Phoebe could never forget the name. Too much depended on the man who bore it. "Adrian Gamble is his name."

As she skirted the stove on her way to the door, Letty nodded. "Trust in the Lord, Phoebe, and wait on Mr. Gamble. I'm certain neither shall leave you destitute."

Oh, Lord, I certainly pray that is the case.

Phoebe remembered something she'd wanted to ask her friend. "Will we see you at the quilting circle tonight?"

Letty opened the door and set its bell to jangling. "I can't understand why all you expert needle women continue to invite me. I can't sew a straight line even when you've drawn it for me." She shook her head, smiling. "But it's a lovely way to spend a few hours, so I will be there—unless someone's baby decides to come along right at that time. It's a daily hazard for a doctor, you understand."

"Of course."

Letty stepped outside, and Phoebe stayed behind the counter. Life teemed with hazards, and Phoebe knew too well their consequences. Widowhood was a true calamity for a young associate preacher's wife. With no one to count on and nothing to fall back on, she lived at the mercy of others.

She prayed mercy had a home in Adrian Gamble's heart.

2

Phoebe spent the rest of her day thanking the Lord for His mercy. She'd decided to take Adrian's words as God's answer to her prayers. And she'd determined to keep Letty's words about her ministry at the store in mind and to take them to heart.

Now she looked forward to tonight's activities. The Hartville ladies' quilting circle gave her the opportunity to visit with the friends she'd made during her brief residence in town and helped to ease her loneliness.

She started attending the cheerful events shortly after she and John arrived in the spring, never imagining how much those hours would come to mean to her. She'd never envisioned a future without him at her side.

As soon as they'd disembarked the train, Adele Stone had welcomed her, enveloping her in a warm embrace and involving her in the many activities at Silver Creek Church. Pastor Stone had greeted her husband with equal enthusiasm, glad for an assistant in his church's ministry. She and John had felt certain they'd found their mission field.

Soon after their arrival the condition of the miners, especially that of the quiet Chinese who lived in the shantytown at the far end of town and whose work had them scurrying in and out of the mine shafts, had begun to trouble John. Many of these men were sent back into old, well-mined passages to glean what scant scraps of ore might remain, a job the regular miners wouldn't do. Others packed explosives in places where the brawnier western men couldn't fit.

During one of her husband's secret forays to look into the Chinamen's working circumstances, the worst had occurred. Not only had a group of the foreigners perished in the cave-in, but the accident had also taken John's life. Mr. Hart, most aggrieved by John's efforts on behalf of employees to whom he scarcely gave thought, had followed her fiery spouse into the mine and lost his life as well.

Phoebe sighed as she let herself out of the former storeroom at the rear of the company store where she now lived. The Stones had wanted her to move into the manse with them, but efficiency carried the day. Living behind the store made more sense.

She shivered in the chill of the late fall evening, grateful for the warmth in her tidy quarters. She drew her Shaker-made woolen cape tighter around her shoulders and smiled. Few would consider the plain chamber a home, yet she'd managed to make herself comfortable within its four walls. As an orphan raised by the Shakers in North Union just outside Cleveland, she'd learned to prefer simplicity to excess.

"Hands to work and hearts to God," she remembered Eldress Clymena saying. Phoebe still found that instruction infallible.

When she opened the door to the church's fellowship hall, the numerous welcoming calls warmed her heart.

"Look who I brought for you tonight," Randy Carlson said, holding out a well-swaddled bundle. "Little Emma Letitia loves her honorary Aunt Phoebe's singing, and since she wouldn't go to sleep, I decided she should come with me to keep Douglas from fetching me just as I settled into my quilting pace."

Phoebe doffed her cape and hung it on a hook by the door. She rubbed her cold hands to warm them lest she chill the little one, held out her arms, then cradled Emma to her breast.

"She's precious, Randy," she said, breathing in the intoxicating fragrance of infant child. "It's a pleasure to hold her."

"Of course it is," Randy said with a wink. "You haven't held her fussy little self all day long."

"I've come to disagree with more of the Shakers' views of the faith than those I agree with," Phoebe murmured, making sure her voice didn't startle the baby, "but I found that the wealth of loving arms in the children's dwelling made caring for little ones much easier. Those practical, efficient ways provided us with enough Sisters to watch the children so that a fresh pair of arms could always spell the tired ones."

Randy's green eyes gleamed with curiosity. "One of these days you'll have to tell me more about your time with the Shakers. It sounds so . . . exotic and strange. I don't understand any of it—it sounds plumb crazy, if you ask me. And yet, since that's where you come from, why, then it can't be *all* bad."

Phoebe smiled at her friend's backhanded compliment and swayed side to side to soothe little Emma. "It wasn't at all bad. Shaker life is quite satisfying. Everyone is welcome and does hard, necessary work, and there's never cause for loneliness. It's the other, their way of worship and their strange teachings about Christ, that led me to leave."

The baby began to fret again, whimpering and waving her little fists. "You're right though," she added. "This isn't the time to consider such weighty matters. I'd much rather sing this dear one to sleep."

Phoebe walked off to a corner, humming one of her favorite Shaker hymns. Once she had a measure of privacy, she sang the lyrics, lovely words of God's love. She praised the Father and ministered to the child with such wholehearted attention that the room's growing silence failed to register.

By the time she came to the end of the next song, however, she couldn't miss it. All the women had left their quilting by the wayside to focus on her. She blushed, uncomfortable at drawing so much notice to herself.

"Don't stop," Adele Stone said. "You have a voice that makes me think I'm hearing one of the Lord's own angels. Please, dear, do go on. We can all benefit from your words of praise and a bit of thoughtful silence."

A concurring chorus brought more heat to Phoebe's cheeks. "Oh, but we didn't come here to listen to me. We came for the fellowship and the sewing and . . ."

Gentle insistence brought her words to a halt.

"Don't stop now," Letty added. "My little namesake is likely to object, and you don't want her fretting again, now do you?"

Phoebe glanced down at Emma Letitia, who stared back at her with wide-open gray-green eyes. How could she refuse? Not when this tiny bit of the Almighty's miraculous creation asked her to continue.

She closed her eyes to better pretend it was Sunday morning, that she stood in church, that the choir would accompany her, that everyone would join in and praise and worship the King of Kings.

After one more Shaker hymn and three other better-known ones, she stopped. "I need a pause," she said. "I'm parched."

Randy stepped up to retrieve her daughter, who was now deep in peaceful slumber. "Thank you so much, Phoebe. Emma favors your singing just as well as the rest of us do."

As the redhead headed back to the quilting frame, bursts of fire flashed before Phoebe. She closed her now-blinded eyes tight and groaned.

"Wynema Howard, shame on you! You must stop this sneaking up on folks. Why, you're likely to give someone apoplexy with your camera antics, and then where would you be?"

"Of course I won't give anyone apoplexy," her good friend replied in her brisk voice. "I'm just recording life for posterity."

Phoebe decided to let the matter go. The young photographer

seemed to put stock in her warning, however, because she folded the tripod and placed the contraption in its black case.

With a proud tilt to her head, Wynema clapped her hands together, ridding herself of the dust of her art. Her brown eyes glowed, and the bun on her head slipped farther down one side, sending a shower of straight tendrils over her eyes.

She gave the strands an impatient gust of breath and said, "Someday my likenesses may make their way into a big-city newspaper. You might even become famous, what with your voice."

Phoebe shuddered. "I can't think of anything more dreadful than strangers wanting to look at me, to learn more about me, to hear me sing. You listen to me good, Wynema. Please, don't go giving my photograph to the newspaper. I don't want even a scrap of fame."

Phoebe turned to Letty, who'd come to her side and held out a steaming cup. She took a sip of the sweet, mulled apple cider. "Thank you."

"Mrs. Stone used the mix of spices you suggested," Letty said. "And I must admit it's the best cider I've ever tasted."

"Shaker herbs are unparalleled, and the Sisters learned to use them in the most ingenious ways. It's Eldress Clymena Miner's recipe I gave Mrs. Stone."

The pastor's wife placed an arm around Phoebe's shoulders. "And the ingredients as well. I agree with you. The quality of the herbs and spices you helped me order is more than satisfactory. Pastor Stone has nothing but praise for my meals these days."

A sniff and a harrumph announced Miss Emmaline White-hall's approach. The town's schoolmarm and librarian rarely had anything good to say. Phoebe had learned to greet her with polite words and then step far from her vicinity. To her regret, she had nowhere to go this time.

"I don't cotton to consorting with lunatic heretics," Emmaline said and gave Phoebe a pointed glare. Her long, thin nose flared with obvious indignation.

"Why, Emmaline!" Adele Stone returned the glare with a reproving stare of her own. "The good Lord calls us to Christian charity."

"He also admonishes us against casting pearls before swine, Mrs. Stone. I'm afraid those heathenish Shakers quite fit the bill, what with worshiping that Mother Ann and communing with dead folks."

Phoebe bit her bottom lip, chagrined by the memory of similar attacks while she'd lived with the kind Shakers. The sect, much maligned by the Emmalines of the world for over a century, had suffered from the criticism—though it wasn't wholly undeserved, as she well knew. Phoebe had always recognized the error in various Shaker religious teachings, but the Lord called His children to love and witness to those in error, that none should be lost but all be saved. Attacks didn't fit into the Gospel message.

As she went to respond, Daisy, the good doctor's young protégée and an aspiring reporter at the *Hartville Day,* called out. "Will no one work on this quilt tonight?" The girl's hazel eyes telegraphed a message of understanding to Phoebe. "Last I heard, the missionaries in China still need warm blankets."

The strain in the room melted as the women returned to the vast frame that held the piece under construction. A beautiful pattern in blues, grays, and muslin creams illustrated the piecing talents of Naomi Miller. After she lost her miner husband when he partook in a drunken brawl with a bevy of fellow workers, the industrious Naomi eked out a living for herself and her three children by washing laundry for unmarried miners and hiring out her exquisite stitching skills.

Once she finished a top, the sewing circle paid for her work, then took over. The ladies would sandwich soft, clean cotton fill between the pieced top and a backing fabric that matched. They'd then baste together all three parts, bring out the quilting frame, and stretch the whole of the future quilt taut enough for the fancy stitching to start.

"Don't pay Emmaline any mind." Daisy's hushed voice startled Phoebe with her nearness. "Everyone knows she's a mean old biddy and more sour than any lemon."

Aware of the girl's troubles in the past, Phoebe studied her serious expression. "You don't mind her rudeness?"

Daisy shrugged. "I'm used to the town's proper folks looking down on me. I minded more when Doc Letty took Emmaline's vitriol because she wanted to help my friend Mim and me. Emmaline made a great deal of trouble then."

Phoebe glanced at Letty, who, despite her lack of talent, had again taken up her needle, determined to master the craft. "As cheerful as she is, I can't imagine the doctor letting anyone steal the joy inside her."

"Oh, everything turned out fine. And she even gave stuffy old Mr. Wagner a good shaking up. Why, he's almost like regular folks now, and they've only been married six months or so."

The two erstwhile outcasts took their places around the quilt and turned their conversation to a more general vein.

Soon, though, Phoebe became the center of attention once again.

"Do tell, Phoebe," Naomi Miller urged. "How do you find the new mine owner?"

The question struck Phoebe as odd. "I don't find him one way or the other at all. He arrived in town, Mr. Carlson brought him to the store, and I haven't seen him since."

Julia's mother waved away Phoebe's response. "Oh, you know that wasn't what I meant. What's he like?"

"Why . . . I'm afraid I wouldn't know, Naomi. I scarcely saw the man for five minutes, maybe ten."

Naomi leaned over the edge of the frame and glanced around, as if to divulge a great confidence. "I've heard say he's as rich as cream and more comely than an angel."

Phoebe followed Naomi's perusal of the stitchers, hoping

someone would speak, change the topic, anything, but it became altogether obvious that everyone was waiting for her.

She drew a bracing breath. "I . . . well, as I said before, I wouldn't know."

She bent over her needle and the blue square before her, hoping her fellow quilters would follow her lead and resume their business. Talking of others made her most uncomfortable.

Emmaline sniffed. "There's no call for playing coy, Phoebe. Goodness knows you have eyes in your head. Do tell. Is he as comely as dear Naomi says?"

Phoebe's cheeks warmed and she stuck her thumb. "It was fairly late in the day when they came to the store. I didn't take much notice of the gentleman in the dark."

Oh really? Phoebe's conscience often raised its head at the most inappropriate moment.

"We-ell, sugar," Dahlia Sutton said in her syrupy southern accent, "of course he's rich. A body can't just up and buy a whole big mining company with but a penny or two. And my sweet mama didn't raise no fool. Even if the darling's uglier'n a stump, why I'll have y'all know, I've set my cap on him. Can't y'all just see little old me as the rightful mistress of that lovely, big old Hart mansion?"

Phoebe's stomach gave a strange twinge. Dahlia was beautiful indeed, with lush black curls spilling in an artful frame around her delicate face and a figure that mirrored a perfect hourglass. Each time the banker's daughter took a stroll down Main Street, the miners and other males who happened upon her followed her progress with avid admiration in their eyes.

Still, Phoebe hadn't been altogether truthful a moment ago. Yea, the store had been a mite dark, but not so much that she hadn't gotten a good look at Adrian. Although not quite as tall as Douglas Carlson, he likely topped out at a solid six feet in height. His wide shoulders and broad chest suggested great strength, and his chiseled features added to his masculine pulchritude. The

27

angles in his face didn't quite add up to a handsome whole, but his appeal came from that very rough-hewn imperfection. Mr. Gamble intrigued her, and the unexpected, haunted look in his dark eyes tugged at something deep within Phoebe's heart.

"Y'all just wait," Dahlia added. "Wedding bells'll be ringing by Christmastime for us. Papa always says that when I set my mind to something, why, there's just no stopping me. I mean to live in that mansion—it's just plain meant for me."

Phoebe kept her thoughts to herself. She hoped her expression didn't betray her. The mansion might be meant for Dahlia, but she suspected the very interesting Mr. Gamble was not. At least, she hoped he wasn't.

She feared Hartville would soon witness a most unbecoming spectacle, as the wooing of the newcomer by the well-heeled banker's spoiled, southern belle child would surely be. Phoebe doubted the mine's new owner was the sort to swallow Dahlia's lure. What remained to be seen, indeed what she hoped to learn, was just what sort of man Adrian Gamble really was.

Her middle gave an unfamiliar, tingly little hop as the thought took hold.

❦

"Good morning, Mrs. Williams," Adrian said as he closed the door behind him. He waited for his eyes to adjust and took in the savory, tangy scent of the store. The still air carried the smell of cooking spices, but he also sensed the presence of a pickle barrel hiding somewhere among the varied necessities. Once he could see again, he studied his surroundings.

Phoebe, up on a ladder, looked over her shoulder. "Good morning, Mr. Gamble. If you'll kindly wait a moment, I'll be down to help you."

"Take your time," he urged as he continued his perusal.

Stacked high over his employee's head, a variety of tin pans gleamed in the low light. To her left, colorful blankets lined four more shelves. To her right and near her high-button-shoed feet, tins of sardines, link sausages, oysters, and salmon vied for shelf space with bottles of vinegar, tomato catsup, and piles of plates, cups, saucers, and bowls made of sturdy white stuff.

Across the way, bolts of cloth filled an entire section from floor to ceiling except for the uppermost shelf, where cans of castor oil and turpentine competed for primacy with containers of chewing tobacco, snuff, and cigars.

An assortment of oak cabinets labeled "J. & P. Coats" ran the length of the counter, each one furnished with two, three, or five sliding drawers of differing depths. Rows of tables piled high with denim pants, overalls, socks, hats, pairs of brogans tied by the laces, and other assorted ready-made garments lined the front aisle. A pair of wooden chairs, a keg stamped "Nails" and another stamped "Horseshoes," as well as a small bench surrounded the bulging stove. Adrian suspected that at certain times of day, a group of regulars held court there to discuss the town's doings.

"If you would like, I do have the time right now to show you around," Phoebe said on her way to his side.

"I should have an idea what sort of wares I peddle, shouldn't I?" he asked and gave her a wry smile.

Her lips curved, and again he witnessed the transformation. Phoebe Williams glowed from within each time she allowed herself a smile. He felt the urge to elicit as many as he possibly could.

"I couldn't agree more," she said. A graceful hand gestured toward the counter. "Why don't we start here? The cash box is in the top drawer, and I always keep it locked."

She slipped a hand into a hidden pocket in her skirt and withdrew a small brass key. "It doesn't leave my person. I'd be guilty of gross carelessness if I did otherwise."

Her earnest demeanor needled him to tease her. "And I suspect you'd rather just about anything else befall you than that you should be careless."

"Why, Mr. Gamble, I'd be mortified," she said, her blue eyes wide with alarm. "Besides, how sensible would that be? A woman employed in a position of trust must always strive for efficiency and common sense."

She had common sense to spare, but did she also have a sense of humor? Something in Adrian challenged him to find out. But not today. Not until she knew him well enough to let down her defenses.

"Admirable virtues in a lady," he said.

"In an employee," she countered.

He nodded acquiescence, then pointed to the oak cases atop the counter. "What do these curious little cabinets hide?"

"Threads, sir, the finest available. Our lady customers appreciate quality supplies. Mr. Hart felt we should offer as many comforts from back east as possible in the hope of encouraging more men to bring their womenfolk to town."

As Adrian pulled out a drawer, the cowbell on the door clanged and firm footsteps came in their direction.

"I do declare, Phoebe Williams," a young woman exclaimed in a voice replete with the flavor of the South. "I can't seem to keep myself in embroidery floss. Do say you've received more of the lovely mauve I so favor, dear."

Adrian took note of the new arrival's brunette beauty. He also noted she didn't incite any curiosity in him. Not like the Widow Williams did.

"I'm afraid you've exhausted my supply, Dahlia," Phoebe said. "And I don't expect another shipment for a week or so."

The southern belle stamped her dainty black-booted foot. "Living on this forsaken, uncivilized mountain does present unimaginable tribulations for a lady, now wouldn't you say, Mr. Gamble?"

Adrian arched a brow. Her coy and forward manner gave him pause. "I'm not one with an opinion, ma'am. I've been in town but a day."

"Dahlia," she practically purred and lowered long lashes over her snapping black eyes. "My name is Dahlia Sutton, and I'd be delighted if you'd call me by my given name."

He gave a brief nod, then turned back to Phoebe. Her even features now bore an odd expression—was it exasperation? Dismay? Adrian couldn't know, but his store manager didn't seem to warm up to Dahlia any more than he did.

"I see what you meant," he said, "when you mentioned that the store does a fair business in threads."

Phoebe nodded but said nothing more.

Regrettably, Dahlia didn't follow suit. "Surely, you're accustomed to much grander establishments . . . Adrian." Her black eyes slanted toward him, her fair cheeks tinted with attractive rose.

Her efforts to charm merely amused him. "I've been to establishments of various sorts."

The cowbell clanged again. A brassy blond woman marched right up and slapped her hand flat onto the counter. "Give me a pound of lard, half a pound of sugar, a dozen eggs, and a bottle of good mustard, Phoebe."

Adrian frowned at the graceless demand but took note of Phoebe's gentle nod.

The latest arrival addressed him. "I presume you're the new owner here."

"You presume correctly, madam." He took the hand she extended and pressed it lightly. "Adrian Gamble, at your service."

"I'm Naomi Miller, and I'd like to offer my laundry services, sir. I charge reasonable rates, and anyone can tell you I do good work."

"I'll keep that in mind." Although they were discussing a simple business matter, he had the uncomfortable feeling that Naomi was measuring him for . . . who knew what?

"Now, don't be bothersome, Naomi dear," Dahlia chided. "What Mr. Gamble here needs is a good wife, not a washerwoman."

"He'd do well to find one with more to commend her than scant years of experience, a pretty face, and her daddy's dollars."

Good heavens! Were they about to fight for him right before his eyes?

Adrian shuddered. He'd never been witness to a more distasteful spectacle. Sheer terror in his gut, he cast wild looks around the store but found no easy means of escape other than by the main entrance. To get there, he had to get away from the women on either side of him.

He glanced at Phoebe and had his answer to an earlier question. It seemed the lovely, gentle widow did indeed have a sense of humor. Unfortunately, his predicament was its current fuel.

A hand clasped his forearm, and his every instinct told him to tear from its grasp and run for the door. Only the manners his dear mother had taught him kept him from doing so.

To his regret.

"Shall we, Adrian?" Dahlia said. "I'm sure we can find us somewhere more pleasant to become better acquainted than this too-public store. Tell me, sugar, where are you from?"

That brought reason crashing through Adrian's mortification. He took Dahlia's small hand in its light purple glove and gave it a brief clasp.

"I'm afraid I don't have the time for such a . . . pleasure right now, Miss Sutton. I've a great deal to do in order to become familiar with the mine's workings. I fear I must leave you and return to those very pressing matters."

"B—but—"

He didn't wait for her sputters to congeal into an objection. He clapped his hat back onto his head and headed outdoors. Without looking back, he knew Phoebe's smile had just widened, her eyes brightened, and her cheeks colored to the warm shade of peaches.

He'd have to find an opportunity to incite the transformation again soon—very soon—and not at his expense.

3

Later that evening as Phoebe washed the supper dishes, the cheerful chatter of her friendly shadow, Wynema Howard, Hartville's unconventional lady photographer, followed her every move.

"*I* would never cast myself like an old braided rug at the foot of *any* man, no matter how fat his money clip might be," the young woman stated, her brown eyes bright with indignation behind her thick spectacles. "A modern woman no longer needs the likes of Mr. Adrian Gamble to be someone. That's what I like about you, Phoebe. You're a sensible, independent woman—like me."

Phoebe smiled and continued drying her few utensils.

Wynema paused long enough to draw breath. "That fool Dahlia—whoever heard of such a ridiculous moniker anyway, I ask you?"

Phoebe placed the thick yellowware bowl she used for rising dough on the shelf next to the red-painted water pump. "I'm certain her mama and papa have."

Wynema stood and began to pace. Her severe white blouse, plain-as-soot black skirt, and heavy brown brogans displayed her disinterest in feminine fripperies. The young woman marched from Phoebe's neatly made bed to the apartment's back door, then across to the Stones' discarded woodstove, and finally to the cabinet where Phoebe stored her few pans.

She spun and faced her hostess. "Anyway, that silly chit gives womanhood a bad name. *I'm* not here in Hartville to catch me one of those crude miners for a husband. Are you?"

Phoebe chuckled. "I hardly think so. I came to Hartville because I already had a husband—he brought me. I'm unmarried because he died, if you'll recollect."

Wynema's freckled features lost their crossness. "Oh, Phoebe. Please forgive my loose tongue. See why I had to come out west? Mama always said I was a disgrace to the family with what she called my 'refusal to be civilized.'"

"Don't fret, Wynema. I couldn't forget my widowed state no matter how hard I tried, and discussing John's passing, while it still makes me awfully sad, no longer distresses me. Not now that I know Mr. Gamble is willing to keep me on at the store."

Wynema's delicate chin went out. "I should hope so! Why, you're the man's greatest asset. If I were the wagering sort—and you know I'm not—I'd bet that, were you to go to that filthy, noisy, smelly, dusty mine of his, you'd have it running most efficiently and with a minimum of soiling in no time at all."

Phoebe sank onto her bed, laughing at her friend's nonsense. "I doubt even Mother Ann Lee could persuade a mine's dirt to depart, no matter how many sweeping 'gifts' she was supposed to have bestowed from the other side of the veil. The misguided Shakers insist she once did in odd visions and dreams."

Wynema shuddered. "Didn't all that dead-folk stuff just plumb rub your nerves all raw? I couldn't have lived around folks talking with their dear departeds night and day."

"It was odd. But I went to North Union after I turned ten. I'd met Jesus before arriving there, and I trusted Him to watch over me. Besides, the Shakers don't spend their days communing with those on the other side. Most of our time was spent on common, everyday chores and much of the rest in prayer and praise."

Wynema patted her cheeks with her palms. "I do declare, Phoebe Williams, nothing flaps you."

"I wouldn't be so certain. I was plenty flapped, as you call it, while waiting for Mr. Gamble's arrival. I didn't know but that I'd slept my last night in my cozy corner of Hartville and would be turned out on the street the moment he appeared."

Wynema discounted Phoebe's fears with a wave. "Even if that had been his intention before getting here, he would simply have had to change his mind. No businessman would fail to notice your worth once he stepped foot into that store. I should know. I'm a businesswoman, as you well know."

"Where did you leave your contraption?" Phoebe asked. "I rarely see you without that great black thing you use to do your picture taking."

"I left it at my studio. Contrary to what Mama always said, I did listen when she insisted one shouldn't drag work along when one goes on a social call, even though I think that's foolish. I feel called to capture every last bit of life on God's earth—social occasions and all."

The younger woman's assessment of their unceremonious visit had Phoebe stifling another laugh. "I'm sure she'd be proud if she could know."

Wynema's expression grew even more animated. "Do you really think so? I wish . . ."

Phoebe stood and placed a comforting hand on a slender shoulder. "Yea, I do think that, were she still alive, she'd be pleased with all you've accomplished. Even if she did object to your . . . bluestocking ways."

"She did—object, that is." Wynema pulled out her heart-shaped pocket watch. "Mercy me. Would you look at the time of night? I'd best be off. We both need to be up at the crack of dawn. We businesswomen can't waste our days lolling around in bed past a certain hour. We have things to do, goals to reach, important things to accomplish. We're not anything at all like the silly, clingy, weaselly Dahlias of the world."

Wynema donned her heavy black woolen ulster, a dreadful thing that dwarfed her fine-boned frame. She then crammed a man's black derby atop the slapdash mahogony bun off-kilter on her crown and hugged Phoebe.

"You're so kind to feed me on a regular basis," she said. "I know I'm a nuisance at times. I'm blessed to call someone like you my friend."

Phoebe chuckled again, something she often did in the young woman's presence. "As outrageous as your pronouncement might be, I couldn't have you starving from your lack of cooking gifts. You're thin enough that I fear one of our sturdier gusts of wind will someday pick you up and dump you somewhere in the middle of Denver."

Wynema's eyes flared with excitement. "That wouldn't be wholly intolerable. I'd soon set the town ablaze with my brilliant photographing 'gifts,' as you call them."

"Get on with you. You're incorrigible, but I love you dearly. Friends don't see each other as a nuisance, and I treasure your company. Besides, we have work aplenty for you here in Hartville."

A sober look gave Wynema's features sudden maturity. "Regrettably, the more tragic sort of photography takes more and more of my time these days."

"You don't say?"

"Oh yes. A week scarcely goes by that Sheriff Herman doesn't call me to take the likeness of a criminal or, worse, a corpse."

She opened the door, and a blast of Colorado's icy air slapped them both.

Phoebe removed a forest-green wool shawl from the Shaker pegboard she'd installed about five feet high on the walls and wrapped herself in its warmth.

Wynema went on, evidently unaffected by the weather. "You're fortunate you're shielded from the worst. You're at the very end of the tamer part of town. But I tell you, there's plenty of danger in Hartville. And I'm not speaking of mining accidents. Gunfights break out over the smallest things all too often. Winter is the worst time of year, and it's coming right at us."

Phoebe bit her bottom lip. Then she shook her head. "I don't understand all the hurt people seem bent on heaping on each other."

"That, Phoebe, my dear friend," Wynema said as she stepped out onto the stoop, "is because you haven't a wicked bone in your body. You're too tenderhearted, and you'd give your bed to the first hoodlum who spun you a hard-luck yarn. That's what got your John killed, you know, his wanting to help those Chinamen who work at the mine. Pastor John knew things weren't quite as they should be for them, and he wanted to set them right."

She pointed at the moonless sky. "Most souls look like that, pitch black, and they're meaner than a mama bear whose cubs have just been taken. The Good Book says there's more evil than good in men, and I've seen it's true. You just haven't had to see it."

Phoebe shuddered. "I thank the Lord I haven't. I don't know what I'd do if I were to stumble onto that kind of sin." Right then the Shakers' protected way of life bore a hefty new appeal. "I surely hope I never have to meet a hoodlum or, even worse, a killer. I pray the Lord will keep me from that."

"I hope He answers your prayer," Wynema said without much conviction in her voice. "If anyone deserves to avoid that fate it's you." She stepped down onto the packed dirt walk behind the store and smiled back. "Will I see you at church tomorrow?"

"I wouldn't miss a service, and you know it. Good night."

"Likewise."

As the sound of Wynema's footsteps faded into the night, Phoebe closed the door. She fought against the urge to move her solid oak table against it and instead took up her Bible. Of course she'd be at church the next morning. She loved to worship the Father with other like-minded folk.

Another shudder racked her. Tonight, tomorrow, and every day thereafter she'd offer extra-fervent prayers. Surely the Lord would hear her plea to keep her safe from the kind of men Wynema had just described. Cruel, violent killers.

❦

A killer on the run had no right to try to fit into a normal kind of town. Adrian slammed the ornate walnut door behind him as he stormed into the fussy Hart mansion.

He couldn't even carry on a conversation. True, he'd been uncomfortable for other reasons, too, but he'd had to run before he unwittingly revealed things he couldn't. His life depended on his silence.

Although he was a Christian, had made peace with God a long time ago, and knew where he stood with the Father on all accounts, he didn't feel ready to leave this world. Not as long as he sensed he had yet to accomplish all that the Lord meant for him to do.

Strange way for a man to feel, especially one who'd taken another's life.

In the oppressive silence of the mansion at the edge of town, overwhelming exhaustion assailed him. He wanted nothing more than to collapse, let down his guard, but he feared he couldn't. For one, that constant vigilance had saved his hide a number of times in the last year.

For another, there was nowhere a man could rest in the whole blasted place.

Adrian had never seen a greater glut of accoutrements. Every conceivable kind of gewgaw littered every visible surface in every last corner of the house.

The settee, although generous in size, wore the slickest satin damask upholstery known to mankind. He'd sat there after returning from the Silver Belle restaurant the night before. To his dismay, no sooner had his behind hit the dark plum cushion than he'd found himself on the ornate black, ivory, maroon, and navy Chinese rug, feeling sillier than he remembered ever feeling.

Then there was the matter of the beds. The house boasted five bedchambers, each one appointed in the same fashion as the rest of the place. He'd expected to have his pick of sleeping quarters, and he did. When he'd retired on that first night in town, however, he'd discovered yet another of the Hart mansion's peculiarities.

Layers of pillows, poufs, scented sachets, lace, satin, silk, and who knew what other kind of stuff lay in artful piles on each of the beds. By the time he'd dug his way down to a plain cotton-dressed pillow and mattress, he'd found himself floundering in a sea of the fluffy froth.

He'd had to face the mess the next morning with no idea how it all went back together again. He seemed to have the same effect on the whole place, no matter where he went.

All that . . . that fashionable elegance stifled him. He didn't think he'd feel any more bound behind steel bars than he did by the satin cords of these so-called amenities.

His thoughts would horrify Mother.

He took another look around the parlor.

They might, and then again, they might not.

Eleanor's touch was light and sensible, making her home a welcome haven for her family.

"Home," he whispered, bracing for the bittersweet pang that came all too often. The lovely old Virginia spread boasted beauty, quality, and luxury, but one never really noticed it, probably because of its mellow subtlety. The house and property had been in the family for ages, as had most of the treasured pieces displayed inside.

The now-familiar gnawing bit again at his heart. He'd never see Whitelawn again. Or Mother. Or any of the others.

He'd had to cut all ties, if for no other reason than to do his duty by them. He'd vowed to Father, right before he went to be with the Lord, that he'd protect the family, even with his own life. That was what he'd done.

Doing the right thing had never been so difficult, so painful. So dangerous.

Running from everything he knew and loved for their sake was his only choice. Still, if he made the slightest mistake, it might indeed come to giving his life.

He had, after all, taken another's.

It shouldn't come as a surprise that those who'd been affected by that death wanted to bring him to their version of accountability. A life for a life.

Especially since by taking his, they would exact retribution and avoid accountability. By killing him, they meant to save themselves.

Sunday morning saw him groomed and cleaned and in his best suit, seeking an empty spot in one of the pews at Silver Creek Church. The attendance surprised him. Adrian wouldn't have thought a mining town's residents to be particularly devout. Evidently, he'd been wrong.

He breathed in the familiar scent of melted wax and lemon polish. It seemed churches everywhere wore the same fragrance, and he smiled. As he surveyed the gathered faithful, he took note of Dahlia Sutton in the front right-hand pew. To the left and halfway to the back, he observed the washerwoman as she scolded a pair of fidgety boys on one side of her. A young woman sat at her other.

These days even a Sunday worship service was fraught with great danger.

"Gamble," a man called from his right.

Adrian spotted Douglas Carlson beckoning him. At the

lawyer's side sat a vibrant redhead, undoubtedly his formidable Randy, a sleeping infant in her arms.

"Thank you," he murmured.

"Think nothing of it." Douglas shook Adrian's hand. "Can't have a newcomer stand through a service. Even though you didn't call attention to yourself when you first walked in, someone would have noticed you. I'm glad I was the one."

The redhead leaned across her husband. "Good morning," she said, a generous smile on her pretty, freckled face. "Douglas has spoken of you, and I'm pleased to make your acquaintance. I'm Miranda Carlson, but I'd rather you call me Randy—everyone does. And I do want to welcome you to Hartville. You must join us for supper sometime this week. We can't have you feeling out of place in your new town."

Fortunately for her, she didn't know just how out of place he really was.

An organ chord rang out, and the whispers died down. A group of navy-robed men and women approached the altar and stopped to its left. In the front row of the choir, he saw a familiar face.

Then the music started in earnest. Phoebe launched into song, alone, her voice clear and sweet, needing no one else to carry the hymn. Notes like the purest silver flowed from her lips. Joyous praise soared and filled the church, her words a most sincere form of worship. Adrian couldn't tear his gaze from her.

She'd intrigued him from the moment they'd met. But now her singing touched something deep in his heart, a place that for a long time had been empty and cold. A craving grew—the need for fellowship, a connection to another human being, some form of contact to erase the months of loneliness he'd suffered. Even after the rest of the choir joined their voices to hers, Adrian could still identify the pure, gleaming sound of Phoebe's song.

He stood with the congregation, sat with them, and acknowledged the beginning of Pastor Stone's message, all without really registering any of it. His gaze remained on Phoebe, his heart still ringing with the echo of her expression of love for her Lord and Savior.

"And so, dear brethren," he finally heard the pastor say, "it is to such forthright openness that our Father calls us. Walking with Him brings us into the presence of the Light of the world. We must allow Him to shine through us. We must seek to be as windows in every way—our words, our actions, and especially in our relations with one another. Evil, deceit, and rottenness cannot survive in the cleansing light of God's eternal truth. So make sure you let the Father's Word illuminate your daily walk."

Adrian wished he hadn't taken his attention from his talented storekeeper. His jaw ached from clenching his teeth. He'd always lived his life as the good pastor exhorted his flock to do. He'd never been one for subterfuge or guarding his every word, action, or stance—until the day his life ended.

Although he continued to exist, he felt as though his life had come to an end that fateful day. What kind of life did he have now? One of darkness, filled with deceit, without a soul with whom to share his days, his successes, or—more often—his failures.

A man who spent his days looking over his shoulder couldn't share anything. Simply being in his presence could cost a friend his life. The utter loneliness threatened to crush him, a man who'd once been sociable, gregarious, joy filled, and outgoing.

The man he'd had to become still felt as foreign, as ill fitting, as if he'd donned a bearskin or a medieval jester's suit. He feared his true nature would make a spontaneous appearance at the worst possible moment and overcome his cautious restraint.

The rustle of the departing crowd broke through his dismal thoughts. He stood and asked the Lord's forgiveness for his inattention and inability to join in corporate worship.

"Good day, Mr. Gamble," Phoebe said.

Adrian hastened toward the aisle where she stood, knocking a hefty hymnbook from the pew in the process. He bent, gathered the tome, and replaced it. His cheeks heated.

That spark of humor again filled her blue eyes. To his chagrin, the smile he so craved to see had reappeared at his expense. "Good morning, Mrs. Williams."

He joined her in the aisle and accompanied her toward the door. "Allow me to congratulate you on your lovely singing voice," he added, hoping to redeem himself in her eyes. He'd never before been this awkward, not even as an unpolished youth.

She lowered her gaze as her cheeks took on the now-familiar shade of peach. "Thank you."

"Adrian, darling," Dahlia called.

He turned and saw her steaming toward him with such determination on her features that she put him in mind of a runaway locomotive. Without the slightest care for Phoebe's presence, the southern miss, swathed in purple and jet and exuding a cloud of cloying scent, swept right up to his side.

"I do declare," she went on, "it's a pure pleasure to see you again. Do let me introduce you to my dear mama and papa."

At a loss for words, Adrian recognized how a deer felt when it found itself in the path of a hungry hunter.

Dahlia pierced his stupor with yet more forward action. "Come, Adrian, darling," she said, linking a possessive arm through his. "Mama and Papa are at the door chatting with Pastor Stone. I do so want to make the proper introductions. They'll surely be tickled to meet you."

Like a sheep led to slaughter, Adrian went with his handler, casting only a backward glance at the woman with whom he would rather have stayed. In that momentary glimpse, he saw Phoebe shake her head and shrug in helpless laughter. The sound reached his ears, and he thought of Christmas bells.

Dahlia executed the introductions. Her frowning father glared at their linked arms. Her mother, on the other hand, cooed and fussed in a manner that belied her patrician elegance and insisted with her daughter that Adrian join them for Sunday supper. She simply wouldn't take no for an answer.

"I'm afraid, Pauline," the pastor's wife hastened to say, "Mr. Gamble has a prior engagement. You see, he's agreed to join Pastor Stone and me for the noonday meal."

Adrian dragged his arm from Dahlia's clutches and gave Mrs. Stone a grateful grin. To Pauline, whose pout rivaled her daughter's, he said, "I do, however, thank you for your kindness, ma'am. Perhaps another time."

Dahlia's pout flipped right back into a smile. "Why, of course, you silly darling. You always have a standing invitation to our humble little old abode. Doesn't he, Papa?"

"Enough." Mr. Sutton's brows drew down in an ominous line over his dark eyes. The chastened Dahlia sidled closer to Pauline. The banker said to Adrian, "Allow me to apologize for my womenfolk's atrocious behavior, young man, and please consider yourself welcome at the Hartville Savings and Trust Bank anytime."

Adrian thanked the man but didn't sigh his relief until the Sutton troupe had descended the church steps and ascended a black buggy waiting at a nearby hitching post.

"Might I offer a word of advice, son?" Pastor Stone said.

"Of course, sir. I welcome the words of anyone who imparts such inspired wisdom from the pulpit as you do." *Inspired though mostly ignored, and utterly discomfiting at present.*

A silvered brow arched high, informing Adrian he hadn't gotten away with his bit of irony.

"There are more men than ladies in town," the pastor said. "But most miners leave their wives in Silverton or Ouray and some even as far as Denver, thinking the larger towns more appropriate for women's gentler natures than Hartville. That leaves a number of our ladies to fret over their lack of marital prospects. Should you not aspire to a speedy trip up the aisle, son,

I urge you to overcome your abundance of gentility. Otherwise, someone like Miss Dahlia will have you at that altar back there before you have a chance to blink."

Adrian gritted his teeth. "I have no intention of wedding, not sooner nor even later. I'm not cut out for marriage and family life."

Mrs. Stone tsk-tsked. "Dear me. You're awfully young to make such a dire pronouncement. Surely you don't intend to spend your long, prosperous life without a special someone with whom to share it, do you?"

How could he respond to these two kind souls? They'd be horrified to learn he didn't expect to have any future at all.

He cast about for words to extricate himself from this latest awkwardness without revealing more than he should and turned back toward the altar, seeking the oak cross behind the plain wooden pulpit for inspiration.

Phoebe stood a handful of pews away inside the sanctuary. She couldn't help but have heard the conversation. His heart lurched. He didn't want to renounce the future. He wanted to anticipate it with faith, to seek God's guidance on his choice of a spouse, to pray for a family and about putting down roots.

He wanted to make Phoebe laugh at more than just his misfortune.

The sudden flash of fire to his right caught him off guard.

The single thing he'd known could not happen had just taken place. A camera had captured his likeness. Concrete evidence now existed. Someone could prove he hadn't died, as he'd worked so hard to establish. Someone could show his photograph—even innocently—and despite his current lack of fancy sideburns, mustache, and goatee, his pursuers might identify him.

Hartville wasn't the safe haven he'd hoped for after all.

He sought Phoebe's face, his eyes blurred by sparks spawned by the flare. Before, he'd only feared for his life. Now he also feared for his heart.

She was the sort of woman a man cherished. He couldn't let himself come to know her better in even the slightest, most casual way. A man more dead than alive couldn't risk falling in love.

Not when death lay just around the corner, beyond the town limits, or even a mere reproduced likeness away.

4

The next time Phoebe saw Adrian, he sat behind the counter in the store, wearing a white shirt with the sleeves rolled up to reveal strong, tanned forearms, and gray trousers held up by blue and white suspenders.

"Good morning," she said, surprised to see him on the premises this early. She had wakened a scant half hour earlier and didn't usually open the store for business for yet another hour.

"Morning."

His brief response raised her curiosity. What was consuming his attention?

Phoebe stepped up to the counter and saw the open transaction ledger, Adrian's large finger running down the columns. She frowned. "Is there a problem?"

He looked up. "No. Quite the contrary. Your record keeping is simple and clear and completely up-to-date. The only thing I don't see is any notation about wages paid to your assistants."

"Assistants?"

"Well, of course. This is a fairly large emporium, and from the numbers in this book, you turn a substantial trade. The store is cleaner than even pure smelted silver, and everything is laid out in perfect display. It must take quite a few folks to maintain such order, not to mention the cleanliness."

Phoebe laughed. "You won't be finding any such notation, because I'm your only employee here."

His eyes opened wider. "But you couldn't possibly do it all. Not without help."

She walked around the stool where he was perched, reached for her navy apron, and knotted its ties at her back. "I do appreciate your taking notice, but it isn't that difficult. Not if you put your hands to work and your heart to God."

Her much-prized Shaker broom still leaned against the far end of the counter where she'd left it the day before. To avoid revealing her nervousness, she took it up and began her daily sweeping.

"Besides," she said when the silence grew long, "Mother Ann said Christians should work as if we might die tomorrow and only had this chance to do things right, and as though we might yet live another thousand years and the fruits of our labor were needed to endure all that time. Everything should be done with perfection as our goal. And she also assured her brethren that there was no dirt whatsoever in heaven."

"Who is Mother Ann?"

A glance revealed Adrian's bewilderment. Phoebe braced for the inevitable reaction once she revealed where she'd learned of the long-dead sect leader.

"Ann Lee founded the Millennial Church of the United Society of Believers in the Second Appearing of Christ. You know them better as Shakers."

She wielded her broom with even greater vigor than usual. When Adrian didn't respond, she risked a peek. He hadn't moved from the stool but stared at her, a look of interest on his face.

At least he hadn't made a nasty remark.

The swish-swish of her broom filled the silence.

"Well?" he asked. "Is that all you're going to say? It's hardly fair to make tantalizing statements and then leave a fellow hanging without further explanation."

Phoebe stopped sweeping, clasped both hands on the broomstick, and faced her employer. "What exactly do you want explained?"

"Everything."

"Oh, Mr. Gamble," she responded with a smile. "I'm afraid I'm unequal to that task. I couldn't begin to explain half the mysteries of this world."

He grinned. "And you wouldn't be working in a mining town's general store if you could, now would you?"

Phoebe paused to remember Letty's words about purpose a few days before. "I don't know. The work is satisfying. I do it as worship, to thank the Father for providing for me, and I try to see it as a ministry. Folks here have needs I can help meet, and not just with merchandise."

His eyebrows rose in query.

"See the seats around the stove?"

"I've stumbled over them already."

"Well," she said, "at about four every afternoon, a group of older miners comes in, and they gather 'round to talk over their day. They're lonely, and the store is a kind of home to them."

When he nodded but didn't speak, Phoebe resumed her sweeping. Once she'd completed the circuit of the store, she gathered up the debris she'd collected and disposed of it in the barrel she kept in the back hallway.

She came back into the store, closed the door and returned to the counter, again stepping behind it. "If you'll excuse me, Mr. Gamble, I need one of the catalogs on that shelf to your right."

"Adrian," he said and scooted the stool closer to the display case.

"Excuse me?"

"Please call me Adrian."

Heat filled Phoebe's cheeks. "I—I don't think I should. It seems dreadfully disrespectful. You're my employer."

"It would be more disrespectful if you went against my wishes —as your employer, you understand."

She drew a deep breath. "Very well, sir. If you insist."

"I do. And I also insist on a further explanation of that Mother Ann's odd sayings."

With a shrug, she gathered the J. & P. Coats catalog, went around to the front of the counter, opened it to the embroidery flosses, and kept her eyes focused on the page.

"There's really not that much to explain," she said. "Shakers see work as worship because they believe the millennium has come, that heaven is here now, and that it's up to them to make it manifest. Everything one does must be worthy of heaven on earth, to reflect God's kingdom."

"Awfully lofty standard. And does any Shaker attain heavenly perfection in his work?"

"Many say their clever instruments and fine furnishings do."

He arched a brow. "What about the dirt? How would she know just what is in heaven and what is not?"

Phoebe drew the line at explaining Shakerdom's more un-orthodox spiritualist teachings. "That's not something I care to discuss. But I do favor cleanliness and order. They're far more sensible and efficient than soil and slovenliness."

When she glanced up to see what effect her refusal to respond had had, she found, to her dismay, that Adrian looked even more interested than before. She again stared at the list of colors the thread manufacturer offered and hoped he'd decide to busy himself elsewhere. Perhaps he had something to occupy him at his mine.

His presence in the store was difficult to ignore. Not just because he'd usurped her usual spot, not even because he hadn't left the stool any of the times she'd had to go behind the counter, but rather because he was there. Phoebe had never been quite so aware of another human being. Not when she'd lived at North Union among the many Shakers who made up the village's large Center Family nor even while she and John had shared a home.

That didn't sit well with her.

As attractive as Adrian was, Phoebe wished he'd leave. A mischievous smile widened her lips. Perhaps Dahlia would find herself in need of additional colors of floss. Phoebe had never seen a man more discomfited by a woman than Adrian had been in Dahlia Sutton's presence.

"Tell me," he said, still planted on her stool. "How do you come to know so much about Mother Ann?"

It always came to this, and Phoebe should have been used to it by now, but it seemed she'd never reach a point where others' censure about her past wouldn't bother her.

"I lived ten years with the Shakers from the time I was ten. I left when I accepted that I couldn't sign the Covenant and become a Sister. I don't believe in Christ as they do."

Adrian dropped his chin on his fists, propped his elbows on the counter, and studied her even more intently than before. "That's fascinating. Not everyone is fortunate enough to see what's behind a group like that."

She lifted a shoulder. "Not everyone wants to see more than what they think they know."

"How so?"

"As kind and generous and hardworking as the Shakers truly are, they have certain beliefs and practices that most folks in the world outside don't understand and certainly don't approve. Those outsiders then assume that everything Shaker is evil and hateful. But they're only people—misguided in certain matters of faith—but people still."

"Ahem!"

Phoebe spun, her heart beating wildly in her chest. "Emmaline! I didn't hear the bell. I didn't even know the door was open. It isn't store hours yet."

The schoolmarm gave her a slit-lidded look. "Interesting

indeed." She went to the shelf where Phoebe kept the stacked stationery supplies and school slates.

Phoebe straightened her neat apron, patted her smooth hair, wiped her clean hands on a length of toweling, and closed the catalog. Still, Emmaline didn't move.

"Is there something in particular you need?" Phoebe asked.

"I can find the chalk myself, I'll have you know." Emmaline gathered a rectangular, green-printed box, then approached the counter, a simpering smile on her thin lips. "Mr. Gamble, I presume?"

The hunted look reappeared in Adrian's eyes. Phoebe shook her head and smiled.

He yanked his pocket-watch chain, popped open the lid, and glanced at the timepiece. "Ah . . . er . . . yes." He leapt from Phoebe's stool and rounded the counter, giving Emmaline a wide berth. "And running distressingly late, Mrs . . . ?"

The spinster drew herself up to her full height and pursed her lips. She sniffed. "It's *Miss,* sir, Miss Emmaline Whitehall."

"A pleasure to make your acquaintance, I'm sure." He skirted the keg of nails by the stove. "But I really must be off. A great deal of work, running a mine . . ."

The door closed with the jangle of the cowbell. Phoebe strove for a more suitable, serious expression. "That will be nine cents, Emmaline."

Her customer opened her purse, counted out the nine coins on the counter, then snapped the strings to close the bag. "Talking Shaker talk again, I see. Can't seem to *shake* the heresy, can you? And you so pious at church in the choir and all."

Lord Jesus, grant me the grace to cope with this woman.

As she always did, Phoebe chose to ignore Emmaline's venomous words. "Here's your chalk, and I hope you have a wonderful day with your students. Children are such a joy, aren't they?"

Emmaline peered down her long, narrow nose at Phoebe. "It's most obvious you've never had contact with youngsters.

They're evil and uncivilized and must be handled with a firm and resolute touch."

Again Phoebe turned to her Lord and asked for forbearance.

"Well, I hope they're pleasant for you today."

"That will never happen. It's not in their nature to be pleasant, not until they're made to face the error of their ways."

The schoolmarm opened the door with an abrupt tug, sending the cowbell crashing against the glass. Phoebe hoped the expensive pane wouldn't break, not so close to the coming snows.

"I'll have you know," Emmaline offered in parting, "I've an excellent method for breaking the wayward will of children and instilling in them the fear of the Lord. You'd have done well to have a Christian woman like me in charge of your upbringing rather than those madly twitching, dead-folk-loving, lunatic Shakers."

Phoebe collapsed on her stool, trembling from the control she'd had to exert on herself. Through the store's wide front window, she watched Emmaline march across the street. A deep sense of gratitude filled her.

"Thank you, Father," she prayed, her voice low and fervent. "It's by your grace and mercy that there aren't more Emmalines around. And please, keep me always mindful of the words I speak."

꽃

Hours after Emmaline's departure, Phoebe still felt the sting of the woman's poison. Not, however, as much as she suspected the schoolmarm's charges did. She pitied the town's youngsters. In all her years of either living or working at the children's dwelling house in North Union, she'd never been subject to harsh treatment, nor had she ever seen the Shaker Sisters who raised and trained little ones dole it out. She didn't know a Shaker child who'd turned out more sin-filled or evil than any other.

At least Adrian hadn't been present for Emmaline's diatribe. It had been mortifying enough to withstand on her own, but to have him witness such an attack . . .

The cowbell announced a newcomer's arrival. Phoebe looked up, surprised, since she rarely had customers after two o'clock and before the invasion of the stove crowd.

The sight of the Chinese woman wending her way down the aisle sparked Phoebe's curiosity. The Chinese miners shopped at the store, and she knew that not all of them had perished with John, but she'd never seen one of their women in town. She'd heard that most stayed in California, or if they came to Colorado, they stayed in Denver, not here in Hartville.

A thin wail alerted Phoebe to the bundle in the woman's arms. She had a baby with her.

"May I help you?" she asked, smiling.

"John Williams?" the girl—for she couldn't have been much older than perhaps fifteen—asked. "You know?"

A pang crossed Phoebe's heart. "He was my husband, but he died months ago. What do you want with him?"

"Died? Dead?" Fear widened the girl's almond eyes and etched a fine line across her smooth brow.

"Yea. In the mine."

She gasped and clutched the baby closer. A tear appeared in one dark eye. By now Phoebe had also grown alarmed. What did this woman want with John? How had she known him?

"My man, Li Fong," the girl said with a sob. "He write. Say John Williams good man. Help him and friends."

Phoebe's apprehension drained away. "Yea, he did try. I don't know how much he actually accomplished before his passing, but he did try to help the men."

"You know Li Fong?"

Phoebe shook her head, dread in her middle. "I'm afraid I know very few of the men in the mine. They come here to shop, but they don't all give me their names."

54

The girl drew herself to her full, though petite, stature. She tipped up her rounded chin and squared her shoulders. "You help Mei-Mei. I Mei-Mei. You find Li Fong. He boy need him." She held out the infant, who objected to such treatment with a howl.

What could she say? What should she do?

She offered a quick prayer for guidance and chose to offer hospitality.

"Here, Mei-Mei." She led the girl to one of the chairs around the fat iron stove. "Please make yourself comfortable. Would you like a glass of water? Oh! Perhaps a cup of tea?"

Once seated, Mei-Mei seemed to lose all the bones in her slight body. She sagged into the chair and held the baby to her chest. She closed her eyes and didn't respond to Phoebe's question.

When Phoebe realized how pale her unexpected guest had gone, she went to Mei-Mei's side, afraid she might drop the child. "Here, let me hold him. You look about done in."

She took the little one without any resistance from his mother. She didn't think the girl had any more life left in her, a fact that became understandable when she took a good look at the infant. Li Fong and Mei-Mei's son was no more than a month, perhaps six weeks old. The trip from Denver was fairly difficult, but if she'd come from California, then surely she was half dead.

Phoebe came to a decision. "Mei-Mei, I have a perfectly good bed sitting empty in my apartment right here behind the store. You need to rest. Please let me welcome you to my home and help you regain your strength."

Pride made the girl try to resume her earlier posture. She failed. If she was going to get any rest at all, it was up to Phoebe to see that she reached the bed.

"I'm going to put my arm around you, and you're going to lean against me. Then we're going to go slowly to that bed."

As she slid her hand around the girl's waist, Mei-Mei stiffened and gave her a startled, frightened look. In her gentlest tone of voice, Phoebe continued to offer reassurances until she felt the girl's thin body ease. At that point, she helped her guest rise and led her to the apartment behind the store.

After tucking Mei-Mei and the baby under her blue-and-white quilt, she put a kettle of water on her wood stove and gathered cups, spoons, and her best canister of tea. She also sliced bread and cheese and wiped an apple on her apron. Mei-Mei needed more than a bracing drink.

When she turned back to her guests, a lump rose to her throat. Mei-Mei held her son to her breast, where he suckled, his tiny fist waving gently under her chin. A tear slid off her chin and fell onto the little hand.

As she watched mother and child, Phoebe allowed herself to consider what she suspected was the awful truth. Would Mei-Mei have ventured all the way to Hartville with a newborn child if her husband had been writing or sending his pay?

She feared she was in the company of another woman widowed that same horrid day.

ॐ

Where could Hart have kept the mine's paperwork and records? Adrian had searched the mansion, including the library and the massive desk inside it, and had come up with nothing. He'd gone to the mine, but that, of course, was just a hole in the side of the mountain.

He hated feeling stupid, but he feared he'd have to swallow his pride and ask Douglas. He also hoped the unmarried women of Hartville found plenty to keep them indoors. He had no desire to dodge their attentions at the moment.

He left the mansion and headed for the center of town. He kept his gaze on the road just a few feet beyond his steps, determined to avoid a conversation. His new plan was to become the hermit of Hartville, notorious for his lack of social contact.

It was the only way to avoid the trap of saying the wrong thing to the wrong person at the wrong time.

He passed the Silver Belle, the only restaurant in town, and the scent of roasted poultry wrested a rumble from his stomach. That was one form of human contact he wasn't likely to give up. If forced to feed himself, he'd have to resort to canned victuals from his general store. And goodness knew that was a dangerous place to go.

As he approached the store, he couldn't keep from glancing in its direction. Phoebe stood outside on the wooden sidewalk, a tin pail in one hand and a rag in the other, intent on shining the front window within an inch of its life.

Drawn by her straightforward simplicity, he stepped up onto the walkway. "Is there nothing more to spit and polish inside?" he asked.

She dropped the pail, and the liquid inside splashed the hem of her skirt. She didn't seem to notice. "Mr. Gamble! Please don't sneak up on a body like that. You might scare someone to death someday."

"I'm sorry. I didn't think I was particularly quiet. My boots make quite a bit of noise on these boardwalks. Perhaps you were too deep in thought and didn't hear me."

She blushed. "You could be right. I *was* thinking. Is there something you needed?"

It couldn't hurt to ask, even though Adrian doubted Phoebe would know the whereabouts of the mine's records. "Do you know where Mr. Hart carried out his business?"

"Why, in the mining company office, of course."

Of course. "And exactly where would I find that office, if you'd be so kind as to tell me?"

She pointed skyward.

His gaze followed her digit. All he saw was the soffit of the overhang above the boardwalk. "Where?"

"Upstairs, Mr. Gamble. Where else?"

"Where else, indeed. And how would I get up there?"

She shook her head and opened the door, her pail forgotten for the moment. He gathered the vessel and followed her into the store. A burst of male greetings hailed their entrance. They weren't directed at him.

"Phoebe girl," called a grizzled old coot, "d'you have any more of them salty crackers I fancy?"

"A new barrel arrived just yesterday, Petey. I'll fetch some for you in a moment." She reached for Adrian, took hold of his arm, and led him forward. "Gentlemen, this is Mr. Gamble, the mine's new owner."

The sudden silence deafened him. Four pairs of eyes, mostly rheumy, subjected him to minute scrutiny. He hoped he measured up. An easterner probably inspired little respect from seasoned men like these, but to his surprise, he found himself wanting to earn it.

"Evening, men." He held his hand out to Petey. "Call me Adrian, please."

With a nod, the miner stood, held out a hand dingy from years of extracting ore from the rock. "I'm Peter Towers, but most folks hereabouts just call me Petey. I'd be much obliged if you did the same."

That was a start. "I'll be glad to."

After shaking hands with the other three, Hal, Quinto, and Mack, Adrian turned down the invitation to join them. "I haven't yet been to the office, and Mrs. Williams has kindly offered to take me there. I will, though, keep your offer in mind for another day. Enjoy your free time."

He met Phoebe at the door in the rear of the room. She smiled. "You were wonderful with them. Mr. Hart would clear them from the store each time he found them here. He had no patience with their long-winded yarns or even their presence around the stove."

"Why? Do they cause trouble? Do they chase away other customers?"

Phoebe gestured for him to follow her through the doorway, and he found himself in a narrow hall. To his immediate left he saw the stairs, a spiral iron monstrosity he suspected discouraged visitors. To his right, he saw two doors. "Where do they lead?"

"The one at the back of the hall leads to the washroom," she said, averting her gaze, "and the one at the end of the hall leads to my . . . home."

"You live here, too? Why didn't you tell me before?"

A blush tinted her cheeks. "I really haven't had the chance. The matter hasn't come up in our conversation." She squared her shoulders. "Do you object?"

"Not at all. It strikes me as a wise arrangement. You certainly don't have far to go in the morning."

She nodded, and he got the impression that he'd eased her worry just as he had when they first met and he asked her to stay on in her job.

"It's a most efficient arrangement," she said, "and one that suits me very well. Now, you'll forgive me if I don't accompany you upstairs, but that steep and narrow metal staircase isn't suited to my skirts."

He gave her a wry grin. "I'm wondering if it's suited to any person at all."

"Mr. Hart liked his privacy."

"I can see that. And did he value neatness and efficiency as well as you do?"

"I'm afraid I wouldn't know." She smiled. "But I'm sure you'll soon find out. Good luck, Mr. —"

"Adrian, remember?"

She lowered her lashes. "Adrian. Do let me know if you need help. I'm not sure there's anything I can do, since I've never gone up there—"

"And probably have no desire to even now."

She chuckled. "I'm happy down here. And now, if you'll excuse me, I'll return to my stove regulars."

As she slipped back into the store proper, Adrian experienced a pang of envy. The regulars didn't know how lucky they were. During the hours of operation, she graced them with her company. He wished he could aspire to spend time with her as well. Instead, he had to be satisfied with heading up to work.

In spite of the interest he'd initially felt in owning a silver mine, he found himself wishing for more mundane pleasures. A simple smile, a gentle voice, a soft touch. Normal things for a normal man.

More's the pity. There wasn't a single normal thing about Adrian Gamble, owner of the Heart of Silver Mine.

He wished there was.

5

"Good night, gentlemen," Phoebe called out to her stove regulars as they made their way down the steps outside. "Don't forget to bring back that new harmonica tomorrow, Hal. I'd like to hear more of your tunes. And, Quinto, please wear a muffler. That cough of yours is a mite worrisome. "

The lanky Hal nodded, a grin spanning his face. At his side the dark, craggy Quinto made a comment Phoebe couldn't hear and then slapped his crony with his hat. Hal returned a shove, and Petey and Mack hastened to insert themselves between their two squabbling pals.

Mack collared Quinto and dragged him along behind. "We'll be seeing you right abouts four or so tomorrow, Miss Phoebe," he said. "Just as we always does. You just keep that old stove of yours burning and we'll keep setting 'round it every old day."

When it felt mannerly to go back inside, Phoebe closed the door behind her, locked up, and hurried to her apartment.

Nearly two hours had passed since the last time she'd checked on Mei-Mei and her baby boy. They'd both slept then, but she doubted they still would.

"Lord Jesus," she prayed, her hand on the doorknob, "I know you brought them here. What I'm not so clear on is just what you want me to do with them. I scarcely have enough to scrape by on my own, and I'm afraid Li Fong is dead. Please show me the way."

In the Almighty's silence, Phoebe stepped into the room.

෮

Despite her anxiety, Phoebe went ahead with her plans to attend the quilting circle's session later that evening. Mei-Mei had indeed been awake when she'd entered the apartment, but the girl had only wanted tea and another few morsels of food. The babe had nursed and then fallen asleep in his mother's arms. Sleep had overtaken Mei-Mei only moments later.

Fearing for the little one's safety, Phoebe had emptied one of her bureau drawers and lined it with a length of soft toweling. After she'd replaced the infant's damp diaper with a new one pilfered from the store, she placed him in his makeshift bed.

Mei-Mei would see him on the floor at her side the moment her eyes opened.

Now, as she approached the church fellowship hall, Phoebe heard the quilters' usual chatter. She smiled, marveling at the normalcy of it all in the face of the odd turn of events in her life. She couldn't quite explain why, but she felt it advisable to keep the arrival of Mei-Mei and the child to herself.

Inside the vast room, Phoebe took off her woolen cape and hung it up. Only then did she notice the newly spawned silence.

She also found every eye glued to her.

The urge to flee engulfed her, but summoning all her courage, she stepped farther into the hall. "Hello . . ."

Her greeting seemed to break whatever spell had befallen the women. The conversations took on an artificial intensity and sparkle, and their sewing donned a frenetic determination that bothered Phoebe perhaps more than the scrutiny had.

"Oh, for goodness' sake." Daisy sprang from her chair at the quilting frame and hurried up to Phoebe. "Don't pay them any mind, do you hear me?"

62

When Phoebe nodded, Daisy went on. "They're all itching to ask you about Mr. Gamble. Why, if they were a passel of cats, they'd all likely be dead by now."

"But I can't tell them anything more than what they already know. Besides, can't they leave the poor fellow to get settled in peace?"

Daisy snorted. "The ones who are married are dying to get him hitched up with their individual favorite candidate among the ones who aren't. And the odd one who's not got wedding bells in mind just wants to know every last little detail about him."

"To what purpose?"

"Curiosity's all I can figure. I think the best thing's for me to interview him for the newspaper. That way they can read to their hearts' content and leave him to his business."

"Why, Daisy, that's a brilliant idea."

"What's a brilliant idea?" Letty asked, coming in the door right behind them. "I had a miner's leg to patch up before going home to make sure my brood was well fed and tuck the youngest ones into bed."

"It never ceases to amaze me how you can doctor everyone and still mother five children," Phoebe said.

Love glowed in Letty's silver eyes. "It's a pure joy—they're a pure joy. I love them as well as if I'd borne them, and my Eric is the most devoted papa. We're both so thankful the Lord blessed us with our ready-made family."

Daisy winked. "What about me, Doc?"

Rising on tiptoe, Letty planted a kiss on the taller young woman's cheek. "You're my eldest, and you know it."

Daisy hugged the doctor. "If it hadn't been for you, I don't know what would have become of me. I might even be dead—"

"Hush, now," Letty said. "Let's just be thankful for the gifts the Father brings us."

Her words reminded Phoebe of her two newly arrived "gifts."

"I may be in need of your professional services," she said in a quiet voice.

Letty's brow furrowed. "Are you unwell, Phoebe dear?"

Phoebe shook her head. "Do you mind if we wait to speak about this until after the sewing session? I'd hate for everyone else here to make me the object of their curiosity. I don't think it would help the situation. It could, perhaps, even make it worse."

Daisy gestured toward the quilters. "Curiosity's their disease. But it's a pity you can't cure that malady with your pellets and tinctures, don't you think, Doc?"

Only then did Phoebe realize she'd made her request within Daisy's earshot—Daisy, the newspaper's typist who made no secret of her hankering after the chance to become a reporter like her fiancé.

"I truly need privacy in this matter," she told the girl. "I can't have this appear in the newspaper. At least, not right away."

Daisy's hazel eyes sparkled. "I know to keep my mouth—and my pen—quiet. But whenever you're ready for whatever it is that could go into the newspaper, you'll let *me* know, right? You won't go telling Ford first?"

Letty arched a brow. "Have the two of you had a tiff?"

"No, but he thinks my efforts to persuade Mr. Wagner to let me report news are pure foolishness."

"Hmm . . . . A courting couple debating what should and shouldn't go into the newspaper. Fancy that."

"You should know," Daisy countered with a chuckle. "Why, you and Mr. Wagner made the whole town stand up and listen, what with his editorials and your letters to the editor."

"Our courtship became too public. Don't let that happen to you." She turned to Phoebe. "Especially since in this town even secrets become public in a snap."

"Secrets?" Naomi Miller asked. "Did you say Phoebe's learned Mr. Gamble's secrets?"

The three friends turned and found all the others frozen on the spot, some with needles poised in midair, the rest with scissors at the ready. Rampant curiosity burned in every face.

"Oh, for goodness' sake," Daisy muttered again. "I can't stay here and listen to all their cackling about that poor man. I'm heading home."

She marched to the door, and when she opened it Mrs. Stone stepped inside. "Why, Daisy dear. Where are you going?"

"Back where you came from, Auntie Stone. I can't stomach these tittle-tattling cats." She let the door slam behind her as she left, presumably for the manse where she lived with the Stones and their other ward, Mim.

Naomi made a beeline for the coffeepot. "I don't see where *Miss* Daisy has room to judge. Why, not so long ago she was nothing but a strumpet straight from a cat house—"

"Naomi!" Mrs. Stone and Letty reproved in unison.

"What's wrong with calling a polecat a skunk?" Emmaline Whitehall asked. "We all know what she used to do."

Dahlia hissed to draw attention. "I surely did hear say she—"

Mrs. Stone's "ahem" and Letty's glare put an end to her words. Dahlia offered no apology.

Back at the frame, Emmaline leaned toward the mouse-drab Ruthie McMiniver. "I don't want to hear anything more about Daisy," she said. "I know all there is to know about her kind. I'm just interested in learning more about that smart-looking Mr. Gamble."

Ruthie nodded. "He does wear a suit mighty well, doesn't he?"

"A pricey suit," Naomi added. "I wonder how a man that handsome and rich has gone so long without being caught by an enterprising woman."

Dahlia gave a knowing smile. "And who says he has, sugar? Why, I'd be willing to wager he has a string of enterprising women who've caught him, one in every town where he's been. He's just the kind to leave broken hearts in his path. I reckon it's a case where not a one of them has known how to keep her catch interested long enough to march him right down that aisle to keep her heart in one piece."

A cat licking cream off his whiskers wouldn't have looked any more satisfied than she did.

Ruthie gulped and her eyes bulged. "And you're of a mind to do just that. But we know nothing about him, not who his folks are, not even where he hails from. How do you know he's not hiding something positively horrid with his silence?"

"What? Like a thieving and killing past? Pshaw! You're just plumb jealous you can't have him. Being married to that Percival of yours—" Dahlia gave a saucy look around the room—"it wouldn't surprise me none if you'd want a try for dear Adrian, too."

Phoebe's distaste for gossip grew into horror at its sinful nature. "I can't stay and listen to this," she said. "I have to go."

"Not before you tell all you know about our newcomer, you can't," argued Naomi.

Phoebe's eyes widened farther. She looked at Mrs. Stone, whose expression revealed shock equal to hers. She then glanced at Letty and took note of her friend's fierce frown. A measure of relief filled her, but it did nothing to persuade her to stay.

"This is wrong. I've nothing to say about others," she said on her way to the door, "and neither should anyone else."

She retrieved her cape, and before she'd done up the clasp at the throat, Letty and Mrs. Stone were at her side, also donning their outer garments.

The three women stepped outside. Phoebe welcomed the crisp night air and wished it could cleanse her. She felt dirtied by the mocking, ungodly exchange.

"I can't condone that kind of talk, and I certainly won't take part in it," Mrs. Stone said. "Even my warning failed to bring a pause to those sinful comments. I'd best go home and seek Mr. Stone's counsel in the matter."

"They've no idea the harm they can do," Letty added. Her eyes blazed, and she held her head high. With brisk, determined steps she marched from the church. "Daisy had it right, as do you, Phoebe. Leaving is the only thing to do when they won't listen to admonishment. Besides, you said you had something to discuss with me. I've my buggy over there, and I'll gladly drive you home."

Praying she was about to do the right thing, Phoebe followed Letty to the rig and told her about her newly arrived guests.

"So I left my claim when it was plain to see it had no gold to it," the owner of the Silver Belle told Adrian after nearly a half hour of his life story.

"I see," Adrian said out of politeness.

The grubstaker-cum-restaurateur rubbed the palms of his hands together. "Done pretty well for myself since, too. Never knew I had me a knack for cooking and feeding folks, but I'm mighty lucky I learnt it real quick. Now I have me a cook to do even that for me."

Adrian forked up the last bite of his less-than-tender steak and wished he'd been able to enjoy its dubious pleasure in peace. Seth Narramore was a good sort, even if he did have a tendency to drone. Adrian didn't have it in him to offend, so he indulged the man.

"So, Gamble," Seth started. He pulled out the chair opposite Adrian. "May I?"

Mouth full, Adrian nodded.

His new tablemate leaned forward in a conspiratorial way. "Tell me something just between the both of us, you know. Where'd you come up with all that cash to buy up the whole mine, store an' all?"

Adrian gulped at the intrusive question, and the chunk of leather lodged in his throat. He fisted his hand and pounded on his chest, tried to cough up the obstruction, tried to swallow hard, all to no avail. Seth, recognizing his customer's predicament, leapt up, rounded the table, and began to beat on Adrian's back with remarkable vigor, all the time howling fit to split sensitive eardrums.

The offending morsel shifted under the onslaught, Adrian gulped once more, and he realized he'd again cheated death—this time death by overcooked steer rather than by bullet or noose.

Overwhelmed by the restaurant's close call with murder, Seth spun in circles, flapping his arms. "Oh! Fetch the doctor," he asked no one in particular. "Hurry, hurry, hurry. This man's dying."

The two miners at the table nearest the door stopped shoveling victuals long enough to take a look around the room. When they found no future corpse in their midst, they resumed chewing and one of them yelled, "Quit'cher bellyaching, Narramore. A man's likely to wind up with a scorching case of dyspepsia, what with all your caterwauling. Ain't no one here's about to die."

After a soothing gulp of water, Adrian stood and placed a hand on Seth's well-padded shoulder. "Narramore, my man, I'm hardly at death's doorstep thanks to you. You're a hero, you know. You may have saved my life."

Seth paused. He studied Adrian. Finally a smile crept upward from beneath the well-waxed handlebar mustache. "By my Great-granddaddy Mortimer's top hat, I do believe I have."

Satisfied that he'd eased the man's distress, Adrian reached for his hat. Seth snatched it away.

"Oh, no," he said. "You can't go. Not right away. You couldn't possibly leave now. I—I have to make this up to you."

"No, no," Adrian said, longing for even the fussy furbelows of the Hart mansion. "I'm fine. Nothing untoward happened."

"I insist." Seth headed for the kitchen door. "Monty! Serve me up the biggest wedge of your finest apple pie."

Turning to Adrian, he said, "Take a seat. I'll fetch you a cup of good, fresh coffee, the best apple pie next to your mama's, and a chunk of fine cheddar to go with it all. Sit, sit."

Adrian sat. He ate the pie, which was good, but not as good as the ones he'd enjoyed at Whitelawn. He savored the cheese and sipped the scalding coffee, all the while dodging Seth's personal questions.

Suddenly, Seth stood. "Have I offended you, Mr. Gamble?"

"Of course not. Why would you think that?"

"You haven't said but a handful of words, and you sure as shooting straight haven't answered a single question. What's a body to think but that you're bearing a grudge or angry or gotten your drawers in a knot from something I said?"

Adrian felt himself blanch. He stood. "I'm sorry, Seth. I'm not one for talking and don't make for very good company. It's nothing to do with you."

Seth's black-marble eyes studied him. "You sure?"

Adrian forced a smile. "Sure as shooting straight. Just as you said."

"If you say so."

Adrian held out his hand, and Seth shook it. "I really must be on my way, but please know I'm grateful for your help with that minor matter earlier."

"Think nothing of it. What's a hand in a pinch between friends?"

Adrian made additional polite comments then crammed his hat on his head and left the dining room as fast as he could without breaking into a run. It seemed he would indeed have to learn to cook for himself. Being out and about brought him in contact with the most curious folks he'd ever met.

Was there nowhere he could go to find anonymity? Hadn't folks around here learned when they were tots that it's rude to pry?

He ambled down Main Street, pondering his situation. He knew those who were after him would never give up the hunt. He really wasn't ready to head for heaven just yet, and he needed a means to earn a living. He'd thought he'd find asylum in Hartville, but every other resident of the town seemed determined to get to know him more intimately than his own mother.

He was also tired of running.

"So," he muttered, "it's time to learn to cook and wash and do for yourself. And you can start by taking your pick of the foodstuff in your own store."

Adrian stepped up onto the boardwalk and strolled to the general store. As he approached, he noticed the black buggy at the hitching post in front. On its side, in blazing white paint, were the words LETITIA WAGNER, PHYSICIAN.

Phoebe!

He unlocked the store, flung open the door, and ran inside. The darkness didn't deter him.

He hurried to the back, burst into the hallway, and yanked open the door she'd identified as hers. Inside he blinked at the light, then came to a complete stop.

Of the three startled women, Phoebe recovered first. "Mr. Gamble. What are you doing here? And at this late hour?"

The minute lady doctor gave him a stern stare but didn't speak, obviously awaiting his response.

A Chinese woman on the bed in the far corner of the room stared at him, fear radiating from her every pore.

The haunting wail of an infant broke the silence.

"I . . . er . . . well, you see . . . I saw the doctor's rig outside on my way home from taking a late supper at the Silver Belle, and . . . well, I feared you might have been hurt or fallen ill."

Phoebe's cheeks colored. "As you can see, I'm quite fine, sir. The doctor's not here on my behalf."

"Might I ask why she is here?" He looked for the weeping baby but didn't see it. "Did you just deliver a child, Dr. Wagner?"

The two women standing exchanged a look, and then Phoebe turned to the patient. Her almond eyes, still filled with fear, flew to him, then darted back to Phoebe again.

"Well?" he asked.

Phoebe shrugged.

The stranger in the bed gave a brief nod.

"Perhaps it's just as well you're here," his storekeeper said. "This is Mei-Mei. She's come to Hartville to find her husband because she hasn't heard from him since the spring, shortly after he came back from a visit home."

"Where did she come from?" he asked. "And when did she arrive? Surely she didn't travel far this late in the season, did she?"

Phoebe stepped closer. "I'm afraid that's what she did. She borrowed enough for train fare from . . ." She glanced back at Mei-Mei. "She came from San Francisco, Adrian, and I'm awfully concerned. She's weak and admits she hadn't been sleeping well before starting her trip." She lowered her voice. "I'm afraid Li Fong is dead."

Adrian placed his hands on her shoulders, hoping to lend her a measure of calm. "Why would you think that?"

Phoebe cast another look at Mei-Mei and Letty, at the girl's side. She turned back to him. "Because she says he wrote and sent his wages home regularly. But the last she heard was back in May. The accident occurred the first week of June."

He remembered reading a vague description of the event on some documents Douglas had provided. "I know Hart died that day, and I've been told your husband did, too. How many miners also lost their lives?"

"Eighteen," she said as a tear rolled down her cheek.

"Wouldn't she have received some form of notification?"

"I would have thought so, but I can't know. Mr. Hart kept his business to himself, so there was no one to take over after he died. Who knows what kind of records he kept."

"Excellent ones when it came to dollars and cents," Adrian answered, unease in his gut. "I haven't yet read through all the books, but I don't recall a roster of foreign names."

Phoebe compressed her lips for a moment. "John went into the mine because he believed Mr. Hart forced the Chinamen to work in horrid conditions. My husband even told me one day that Mr. Hart didn't consider them truly human, just working bodies that did his bidding for lower wages than his regular miners."

"That's repulsive."

"That was John's opinion. I must confess that I didn't pay his concerns as much attention as perhaps I should have. If I had, I might now know what's become of Li Fong. Mei-Mei's so young, and all alone with that baby."

Adrian looked more closely at the new mother and saw that she really was little more than a girl. "Please don't fret," he said, "I'll go through every piece of information I have, and I'll find out what happened."

"But what if he did die—"

He placed his finger on her lips. "Don't go borrowing trouble. We'll deal with that when and if we need to."

The warmth of her mouth registered on his skin, and Adrian recognized the intimacy of their contact. Phoebe's mouth was soft and satiny, her eyes wide and fixed on him. A startled expression had replaced her concern, and he watched her pulse beat faster at her temple.

His sounded a matching beat in his chest.

"Mr. Gamble?" Letty said.

Adrian released his storekeeper as if she were a searing ember. He took a hasty step away.

"Yes, Dr. Wagner." The husky timbre of his voice dismayed him.

"I hope you will help us resolve this matter."

How was he going to accomplish that when he couldn't even control his heartbeat?

"I'll see what I can learn. Rest assured I'll do everything possible to help Miss . . . uh . . . May, was it?"

"Mei-Mei," the young woman said in a lilting voice.

Adrian had to leave before he got himself into more trouble. As he went for the door, the distance between him and Phoebe grew, a distance not measured by inches and feet. The dark, empty place in his heart now felt more fractured than a cracked mirror.

"Ladies, I must be on my way." He turned the doorknob and stepped into the hall. "I've a great deal of reading ahead of me if I'm to learn what happened that day. Please forgive my intrusion, even though it may have been for the best in a strange sort of way. I'll keep you informed as to what I learn."

He left before he further disgraced himself, but he knew his thoughts would remain in that room the whole night through. But not on the young Chinese mother, as perhaps they should. No, his thoughts and whatever dreams he was likely to have would be filled with the memory of Phoebe's warm lips.

6

"Mr. Gamble, Mr. Gamble. Wait up, there."

Adrian paused and held the door to the general store ajar. He hadn't slept the night before and was in no mood for feminine wiles today.

The breathless young blonde rushed up, hand clamping her hat to her head, cheeks red from the exertion, breath coming in great gulps. She straightened her skirt with one hand, while she clutched a small black book and pencil with the other.

"I've a favor to ask."

He frowned. What could this one's approach be?

"I work for the *Hartville Day*—"

His heart skipped a beat.

"—and yesterday I had an idea."

She paused, but he had nothing to say—*nothing*.

She squared her shoulders and went on. "It would seem beneficial if you were to give me an interview—"

He grew queasy.

"—since everyone, and I mean every single, solitary soul in Hartville, is dying to know more about you. Some of them are busy weaving the most outlandish yarns out of nothing more solid than their own hot breath. I think you'd do well to have me put something real in the paper. It might satisfy all that curiosity. As the owner of the Heart of Silver Mine, you're a most important man in town."

Before he could escape, Phoebe approached. "I think Daisy's idea is brilliant, as I've already told her. I have no patience with wagging tongues, and you should set everyone straight with a simple public statement. Then they'd have no cause for gossip."

"I'm a private man, and I don't care for this sort of nonsense."

Both women went to object, but he raised a hand to stall them. Phoebe's blue eyes were his undoing. He couldn't deny her anything.

"But perhaps you're right. What would you like to know, Miss Daisy?"

Daisy's mouth gaped, and she seemed more startled than even he was by his acceptance. Then she pulled herself together again. "You mean it? You really mean it?"

Fool that he was, he didn't take the last chance offered him. "Yes, I do."

Daisy drew up to her full height, flipped open the cover of her little book, and licked her pencil's lead. She then slanted a look at the rear of the store. "Could we start with a tour of your office?"

Phoebe had said the former owner of the mine had kept the area off limits to everyone. Adrian realized the girl wanted a scoop—far more than a mere interview with him. Seeing the broad scope of her interest, and hoping that by giving her volumes of information about the business he might divert her questions away from a more personal direction, he nodded. "If you're willing to climb a steep and narrow spiral staircase to get there."

"Pshaw! I've seen it when I've come to visit Phoebe. If fat old Mr. Hart could get up there, I certainly can."

He grinned. "Allow me to lead the way."

"I'll be right behind you."

As they entered the back hallway, Adrian heard Phoebe's musical laugh. It didn't even bother him that this time it'd come at his expense.

༖

When Daisy finished noting every last detail of the fairy yarn Adrian wove, he helped her descend the iron stairs and followed her into the store. He wanted another glimpse of Phoebe.

He also wanted to know how Mei-Mei and the baby had spent the night. Since Phoebe had given them her bed, he wondered if she'd managed to rest.

He asked as soon as she made change for her customer.

"I hope you don't object," she said, blushing, "but I took the liberty of using one of the cots we sell. I was tired and felt I shouldn't wear myself out. I would be of no use to Mei-Mei or to the store if I didn't get any sleep."

"You know our stock best, and I trust your judgment."

Her blush deepened.

He went on. "I don't want you to do without when I have more than I can ever use here in the store."

She averted her gaze. "We'll likely have to supply Mei-Mei with everything. She only brought a small carpetbag, and all it contains is a handful of things for the baby. Her clothes aren't warm enough even for today, and although I hear the snows have been unusually slow in putting in their appearance, she's going to need far more than she has once they do. She has nowhere else to go. Her father died this past summer, so there's nothing waiting for her back in California."

"I wouldn't dream of sending her back in her condition, much less at this time of year. Providing her with some essentials is the least we can do for her until I learn what's become of her husband."

"You're a good man, Adrian Gamble." Her smile warmed his heart. "That's all those busybodies out there need to know."

76

Her words made him feel a thousand feet tall and more powerful than a load of dynamite. "I hope Daisy's story gives them what they want to know. There really isn't much to tell. I'm just another man who came out west to find his fortune."

"Oh!" She ran to the counter. "The post came today, and you received a letter. Here it is."

When Adrian spotted the precise Spencerian script of his man back home, darkness enveloped him. The sudden fear grew so great that his knees weakened and his hands trembled. A rushing roared in his ears, and his temples pounded.

The letter could only mean trouble. They'd agreed to sever all contact. It was the only way to make sure no one would doubt reports of his death and avoid leaving a trail that followed him to his new home.

What had happened?

"Adrian?" Phoebe asked. "Are you unwell? Is there something I can do for you? A glass of water, perhaps?" She took his hand and pulled. "Come, take a seat by the stove. You're whiter than Shaker Sisters' linens fresh from their laundry room drying racks."

He might not have made it but for the soft hand holding his. He collapsed onto the chair and made himself draw deep, even breaths. He gripped the wooden arms, needing to grasp something solid.

Phoebe's footsteps indicated her departure. Then, after a brief silence, they heralded her return. A cool, moist compress against his forehead gave him something to feel besides fear.

"You're cold and clammy," she said. "Do you think you've come down with something? I hope it's not the influenza."

Adrian forced himself to concentrate, to say something to ease her concern, anything but the truth. "Perhaps it's the lumpy, half-cooked, half-burnt oatmeal I had for breakfast that's to blame."

"It wouldn't surprise me. The kitchen Sisters always said breakfast was of utmost importance. A body can't be expected to run properly if you don't feed it right."

She handed him a glass of water, and he took a sip, then a couple more. The cool fluid soothed his parched throat if not his fear.

Phoebe didn't seem to notice that his distress was far from physical. "Now don't go moving from that chair." She gave him the envelope. "Rest a spell and read your letter. I'll be back with something to set your innards to rights."

With hands that still shook, he unfolded the single sheet. He skimmed the message, every line another nail in his coffin. His man had received numerous inquiries about him, it read, even though they had destroyed all connection to his past. Those intent on finding him were proving relentless, as he'd feared. This would be the last communication, his man stated, but he'd felt it vital to send the warning. It hadn't only been those on the one side of the law seeking to uncover his whereabouts. Both sides were now keen to find him.

Why? He'd only transgressed against the one side.

Phoebe returned with a steaming cup in hand. "Here. This is what the Sisters rely on for the digestion. There's not much chamomile and mint tea won't help."

Although he would have rather stuck to plain water than the flower-scented brew, right then Adrian didn't have the strength or the will to object. He took the cup and drank, surprised by the pleasant, if unusual, taste.

The clanging cowbell announced a customer. Adrian straightened in the chair, unwilling to give cause for more comment by looking peaked.

Not just one but three Chinese men entered the store, their demeanor humble, their expressions serious.

Phoebe hastened to their side. "I'm pleased to see you again," she said. "What can I help you with today?"

"Need supply," one said. The other two nodded.

"Of course," she answered. "Please come with me to the counter, and we'll write down everything."

As she ushered them farther inside the store, the three came to a halt when they spotted Adrian. They balked and stared at him. Their intense scrutiny made him squirm.

He tried to rise, but his legs still shook from his momentary lapse, and he plopped back down onto the chair, making it squeak against the floor. The sound caught Phoebe's attention, and only then did she realize her customers hadn't followed her.

"Oh," she said. "Gentlemen, this is Mr. Gamble, the new owner of the Heart of Silver Mine. He's your new employer."

To Adrian's dismay, fear, visceral and nearly palpable, appeared in the faces of the miners. They exchanged glances; one darted a peek at the front door, while another shot Phoebe a questioning look. He'd never been the cause of so much distress, and he had no idea why he was just then.

"Phoebe . . . ?"

"I don't understand," she whispered. "I've never seen them this upset. They don't say much when they're here, and I haven't been able to learn their names, but they're always pleasant."

"Well, I certainly have to do something to set them at ease." Adrian struggled to his feet. He turned to his foreign miners. "I'm pleased to make your acquaintance. Please feel welcome to shop at your leisure. I have business awaiting me."

He left the room by the rear door but once in the back hallway didn't pull it all the way closed. He wanted to see if those poor fellows overcame their fright. If anyone could help them, it was Phoebe.

He watched the men hold a brief consultation among themselves, their conversation musical and reminiscent of the intonation he'd heard in Mei-Mei's voice. Could one of them be her husband, Li Fong?

Phoebe's gentle smile could have stopped the rain on a cloudy day, but it seemed to have scant effect on the men. They hurried through their business, helping her load a wooden box with a fair amount of supplies. Rice, tea, tinned vegetables, dried fish, vinegar, and a small bottle of oil went into the crate. Moments later they paid, bowed a farewell to the storekeeper, then left.

Adrian hastened to Phoebe's side. "Do you think—?"

"One of them might be Li Fong?"

"Yes."

"I wouldn't know. They were all in such a state that I didn't dare say anything that could make matters worse." She looked toward the door at the rear of the store. "But we do need to know—Mei-Mei needs to know. And someone will have to ask. There's no other way of knowing. Have you found anything in Mr. Hart's books?"

"I'm afraid not. So far I've only found one listing of employees. None of the names is Chinese. I've seen nothing about those men. I can't understand it."

Phoebe's brow creased. "I don't understand either, but I can tell you Mr. Hart was no kinder to the Chinamen than he was to the store regulars."

"But they all worked for him. Wouldn't he have been grateful for their efforts? He couldn't have built his tidy fortune had it not been for their contribution."

"I agree with you. I just don't think he saw matters that way. Perhaps he felt that finding the mine in the first place entitled him to everything that could be extracted from it, no matter who did the extracting for him. That would explain his lack of respect and gratitude."

"Perhaps. I don't know if we'll ever find out his reasons." The irritation and frustration hit him all at once. He returned to the chair by the stove and his neglected chamomile tea. Although the beverage had cooled considerably, it was still palatable, and his innards would likely benefit.

Two women entered the store and headed straight for the bolts of calico. Phoebe joined them, and all three discussed the merits of darker colors and their ability to disguise dirt, an attribute much valued in a mining town.

The customers soon left, but thoughts of Mei-Mei, the Chinese miners, and his own troubles remained with Adrian. Before too long the cowbell sounded again, and this time a girl of about thirteen or fourteen walked in.

"Hello, Aunt Phoebe," she called. "Mama sent me to see if you needed her this morning. I'm to go tell her if you do."

"Thank you, Caroline," Phoebe answered. She gave her messenger a warm hug. "Please let her know we're all fine so far today. If I do see a need for her care, assure her I'll send for her."

Adrian could find no resemblance to the doctor in Caroline, but she could be none other than Letty's daughter. And although she delivered her message and accepted Phoebe's response without any effort to learn more about their meaning, he saw curiosity in her eyes. It increased as she stepped around him.

"Good morning," he said. "You must be Dr. Wagner's daughter."

A radiant smile lit the girl's features. She tipped up her chin and stood taller. "Am now. I'm Caroline Patterson Wagner, Mister Gamble."

He arched a brow. "You already know who I am."

"You were to church last Sunday, and you're all the girls wanted to be chatting about."

They started them young around here. "I see. And what do they have to say?"

She clasped her hands at her waist and twisted her fingers until the knuckles whitened in obvious discomfort. "I'm not repeating the silly things they say. I ain't one to carry tales or gossip."

Adrian took another sip of the tea. "An admirable stance, but you wouldn't be gossiping if you let me know there's something I need to address."

Caroline wavered. She lowered her gaze and rubbed the toe of her high-buttoned shoe against the clean floorboard. "*I* didn't say so, but there's some that says you're the black-sheep son of the king of France."

The mouthful of tea spewed from Adrian's lips and sizzled and sputtered against the hot iron stove. "Why, that's preposterous. Wherever would they get that silly notion?"

"Same place as them who say Gypsies stole you from the cradle in your family's castle in Tra . . . Transyl-va-ni-a and them who say you were a pirate off the Barbary Coast."

Adrian stood. "Might I assure you that none of those notions has even the slightest shred of truth to it?"

"Never thought they did, Mister."

"Tell your mother she has a wise daughter. And thank you for your honesty."

"Welcome, Mister. I have to be going. Missus Sauder will be wondering where I've gotten to after class. She counts on me to help with baby Willy. Good-bye, Aunt Phoebe!"

"Good-bye, dear," Phoebe called from the dry goods side of the store.

Adrian hadn't realized how late it had grown. He'd spent the better part of the day with Daisy, who'd peppered him with more questions than he'd thought a person could contrive. Then he'd suffered the disturbing episode when Phoebe handed him the letter.

The cowbell clanged against the glass in the door. Jovial male voices told him the stove regulars had come to claim their spots. He rose and looked around for Phoebe, but found her by a rack loaded with different-sized and variously colored chamber pots, deep in consultation with a woman who wore a formidable frown.

His empty stomach growled. Perhaps he'd do well to rethink his decision of the night before. It might be unwise to avoid the Silver Belle. If his inedible oatmeal gave any indication as to his future cooking ability—and he feared it did—he'd soon starve while trying to save his hide by eschewing Seth Narramore's establishment.

"I'll be on my way, Mrs. Williams," he said.

"Good evening, Mr. Gamble," she responded, her smile as radiant as ever.

Maybe his woeful cooking skills and his reaction to Phoebe would render him unsuited to a hermit's life after all.

❦

When he entered the Silver Belle, Adrian noticed a group of men at two tables pulled together in the center of the room. He recognized Douglas Carlson, and he figured the barrel-chested man with the badge on his pocket must be the local arm of the law. At the head of the table, Amos Jimson, the livery owner, led the gathering's discussion. He remembered seeing the others around town, but he didn't know any of their names.

He hoped to keep it that way, especially since they had a sheriff in their midst.

Seth suggested the venison stew, and Adrian followed that advice. Still reeling from the news he'd received in the letter from home, he kept half an eye and ear on what the lawman might have to say. Regrettably, the men kept their voices low.

As he spooned up the last morsel of apple cobbler, someone cleared his throat at his side. He looked up into the sheriff's leathery face.

"Evening," the man said in a deep bass voice.

Adrian stood and took the fellow's extended hand, hoping his didn't shake so much as to arouse suspicion.

"Max Herman at your service."

"Adrian Gamble."

The sheriff gave a crooked grin. "No need for an introduction. You're the talk of the town. Now Eric tells me that little Daisy from his office has written something up about you for the paper."

"Seemed the best thing to do to put an end to all that talk."

The sheriff's mud-colored gaze snagged his, and it took all of Adrian's control not to flinch under the weight of that stare.

"Nothing wrong with folks wanting to know who you're rubbing elbows with," Herman said. "It's one way we keep things on the up-and-up around here. Little happens without half the town knowing about it before morning."

The venison took up arms in Adrian's gut. "I hear say that's a small town's reality."

"So you're a big city man, then."

He shrugged. "Haven't lived in one place too long."

"Long enough to come up with the dough to buy yourself a pretty pricey piece of country, a producing mine's operation, and a right successful store, I'd say."

"Can't blame a man for making good use of a windfall."

The gleam in those dirt-brown eyes made the cobbler join the venison's uprising. "Awful good luck you have there, Gamble. I'm sure there's many a man who wishes he'd come by a windfall like that."

Adrian tipped his head, conceding the point. "One never knows when fortune's going to give a helping hand." He donned his hat and tapped the brim in salutation. "I've a great deal of reading to do on the mine's books. I'll be heading on home now. You have a good evening, Sheriff Herman."

"Likewise, Mr. Gamble. Likewise."

He'd only taken two steps when another man called his name.

"A moment of your time, please," the tall man with dark blond hair and brown mustache said as he approached. The inevitable handshake followed.

"I'm Eric Wagner. As you likely already know, I own the town paper. My wife speaks well of you, and my typist just declared herself promoted to the position of reporter on the grounds of the interview you gave her. I figured I'd do well to make your acquaintance."

"It's my pleasure," Adrian said. "I've also met your daughter Caroline. She's a wise young woman and a credit to you and the doctor."

Eric smiled fondly. "She's only been our daughter for a few months. Letty and I adopted her and her four siblings not long after they were orphaned. Our five scamps are the greatest blessing a man could want."

They stepped out into the chill evening. "I wanted the opportunity to speak in private," Eric said once the door had closed behind them.

"Oh?"

Eric glanced around. There was no one in their immediate vicinity. "I'm sure you're more than aware of the speculation about you in town," he said. "I've read the piece Daisy wrote up, and while she did an excellent job, I find it woefully lacking in substance."

Adrian offered a prayer for help. "I'm a private man, Mr Wagner—"

"Call me Eric, please."

"And I'm Adrian. I'm also the kind of man who doesn't care to serve his personal matters for public consumption. I hope you can accept that."

"I can, but I've also found that's the way men feel when they have something to hide. Take this as a friendly warning. I'm not ashamed to own to loving my wife and children, and I don't want anything untoward to happen to them. Secrets have a way of exploding, Adrian, and that kind of explosion rarely results in a rich vein of ore."

Adrian stared at a far-off peak, unable to argue against Eric's sentiment. "I mean no harm."

"I'm not implying that you do. I'm just concerned that whatever's haunting you and that you're working so hard to hide might harm my town or the people in it."

"I'll grant you're tenacious—"

"A boon in my occupation."

Adrian shrugged. "Since I doubt you're likely to give up now that you've begun to nose into my business, I'll admit there's been trouble in my past. Nothing current, I assure you, but it's safest if I don't share details."

The sheriff exited the restaurant, followed by Douglas, Amos, and their other companions. The men exchanged a flurry of farewells, and Adrian was glad to see them go.

Eric, however, didn't budge.

He smoothed his mustache, and lines marked his brow. "I'm not finding anything that adds up here. On the one hand, you tell me your troubles aren't current. On the other, you tell me it's safest to keep quiet about it. Seems to me if your troubles were over, then there'd be no reason to hide. And something tells me you've come to Hartville to do just that."

Adrian studied the man at his side. Intelligence lay behind his direct stare, and no small measure of compassion as well. The urge to talk burned in his throat, but he couldn't deny the truth. Sharing his burden with Eric would put his new acquaintance in danger. Adrian couldn't do that to an innocent man. Not even to gain a measure of comfort in his self-imposed isolation.

He shook his head. "It's not that I lack trust in you or anyone else. My silence is for the best. The less others know of my circumstances the safer they'll be."

"I'll reserve my right to disagree. Sometimes secrets are more harmful than straight talk about the problem could ever be. If one at least knows what to look out for, one can prepare. In the case of silence, no one is forewarned."

Adrian had to get away. "Consider yourself forewarned. And I'll keep my troubles to myself. You're a decent sort, with a lovely wife and daughter—children, you said—and I could never live with myself if by speaking I put you or yours at risk."

He extended a hand and waited as Eric weighed his words.

Finally, Eric shrugged and took his hand. "We've only just met," he said, "but I want you to know you can trust me. If you need to talk, you know where to find me. My office is always open and, with a doctor for a wife, I'm used to folks knocking on our door at any hour of the night."

"I appreciate your offer. Should there come a time when I can do so, I'll take you up on it. I'd like you to know you can trust me, too. However, there are others I can't trust. Rest assured that they aren't in Hartville."

"Yet."

"Nor as long as I can help it."

They parted company, and Adrian returned to the Hart mansion, disgusted with himself. He'd hated the evasions he'd returned to Eric's offer of friendship. The newspaperman struck him as a fine man, one with wisdom and compassion, someone he'd like. And it didn't sit well with him to rebuff kindness, but what other choice did he have? He didn't think Eric would betray a confidence, but the fewer people who knew the truth, the safer he'd be—they'd be.

Once inside the overdone monstrosity of a house, he went straight to the well-appointed library. He did have a great deal of reading to do.

At the desk he picked up the sheaf of papers he'd dropped earlier that day and resumed his search for information.

Soon he conceded defeat. He couldn't concentrate. His troubles had been dredged up too many times that day. He couldn't set aside the feeling that everything he'd done so far had been for naught.

"Lord God, I'm so alone," he said. "Why is buying the mine and maintaining sufficient output to sustain those who depend on it not enough? Why do these strangers want to know so much about me? Why do they care?"

The inner turmoil continued, and the Lord didn't offer a ready reply. "Are you testing me, Father? Testing my determination to protect others where it's in me to do so?"

He reached for his well-worn Bible and remembered his late father's favorite verse, one he'd repeated many times while hale and vigorous. On his deathbed he'd whispered, "I have fought a good fight, I have finished my course, I have kept the faith."

Clasping the volume to his chest, Adrian closed his eyes. *Lord, I'm trying to fight that good fight. But I need your help. I can't do this alone. Give me your strength and your comfort. Running this race is a very lonely thing.*

He leaned back in the leather armchair then looked around the room. He'd begun to remove many of the excesses from the more obvious locations, and while the place no longer inspired horror, he knew he'd never be comfortable within its walls.

He wondered if he'd ever be comfortable within the skin of the person he'd had to become.

7

Early the next day Adrian sought out his mine foreman.

"I have a question for you. I've spent hours poring over company records and studying lists of miners' names, but I can't locate any reference to the Chinese workers."

Stan Fulton shrugged. "Don't reckon there is none. We just pay them for the days they work every week."

"Mr. Hart didn't have you record their wages?"

"I always handed him a paper with how many of them men worked for how many hours, and he gave me the money for them."

"So you've no accounting of how many Chinamen work in the mine and nothing about their pay?"

"'S what I said. But they don't cost the mine much. Mr. Hart always said they were his bargains. They ain't important enough for you to be wasting your time on. I handle them fine."

The image of Mei-Mei returned to Adrian's mind. "I'll judge where and how I spend my time. From now on we'll do business my way. We'll start with my need to account for all the mine's workers from the first of this year."

The large man rubbed his forehead with the back of his dirty leather glove. "Every worker for the whole year? That ain't gonna be easy. I can't rightly recollect every man what's worked here. Especially not them squinty-eyed ones."

The man's attitude soured Adrian's still uneasy stomach. He strove to control his expression. "I suggest you find someone to help you with that recollecting. I expect a full accounting of every worker and what he was paid. I will wait for it at my office. I need it by tomorrow at four o'clock."

Fulton's glare grew stormy, and he ground his teeth. "What's the hurry? We're running shifts, and I can't leave this place run itself. If I'm not here watching them every last minute, who knows how much silver will find its way into thieving pockets."

"You do as I say. I'll worry about theft."

Fulton's pugnacious jaw jutted, and he folded his arms over his brawny chest.

"A full accounting," Adrian repeated. "By tomorrow. Have I made myself clear?"

The man's coarse features reddened, and anger flashed in his eyes. Adrian wondered if that temper had ever made trouble. He hoped not. And he hoped it didn't become a problem while Fulton worked for him. He didn't want to call on the sheriff, but if one of his workers caused injury to another, then he'd overcome his reticence and bring down the law on the guilty party.

"Do you have any questions?" he asked when Fulton still hadn't answered or budged.

"No." The miner spun, then lumbered toward the mine entrance.

"One final thing, Mr. Fulton." The foreman stopped. "The men are Chinese or Orientals or even foreigners. Not the insult you leveled on them. I'm certain they even have given names you could use if you asked."

Fulton's face turned puce. Adrian decided on the spot that come spring he would find someone else to oversee the mine. This man was a keg of explosive with a too-short fuse—not something he wanted inside the already treacherous belly of a silver mine.

☙

Phoebe debated whether to attend the quilting society session that evening. Not only did she have two needy guests, but she also had no stomach for the gossip she'd endured during the most recent sessions.

But she couldn't use Mei-Mei as an excuse to stay home. Her guest insisted she go. The young woman was up and caring for her son, although she still looked pale and tired. Phoebe suspected her wan appearance reflected worry over her husband's fate.

"Go, Missus Phoebe," the girl said over and over again. "Mei-Mei and boy fine. We sit, we eat, we sleep. We fine."

Phoebe feared Mei-Mei found her needy state distasteful. Pride often showed in her posture or expression when she was forced to accept help. Phoebe understood that aversion to pity. She'd felt the same way after John's death. She thanked God each day, first for Mrs. Hart's willingness to hire her and then for Adrian's lack of interest in changing matters at the store.

She hated feeling beholden to anyone. The Shakers had taught her that God blessed hard work with abundance, and she'd seen enough of that teaching's truth to know she agreed. Besides, she liked to think she resembled the industrious ant in the Book of Proverbs.

In the end, she decided to go, and now, at the door to the fellowship hall, she paused for a moment of prayer.

"Father God," she whispered, "I know the talk that went on here the last time was offensive to you. Help me stand against it, even if doing so means going without something that has grown precious to me."

Phoebe entered the hall with no fanfare. The chatter abounded as usual, and when she scanned the faces around the quilting

91

frame, she saw Daisy, Randy, and Mrs. Stone. She didn't find Letty, but perhaps the doctor had run late as she often did, caring for her large family or seeing to a patient's need.

She took the empty chair at Randy's side. "Did you leave Emma at home?"

"No. She's sleeping in the manse. I asked Mim to watch her."

"Isn't it a lovely thing the pastor and Mrs. Stone have done for Daisy and Mim?"

"They're wonderful girls who only needed someone to love them. It's unbearable when folks think so little of children that they practically throw them away."

Phoebe nodded. "They leave them to their own devices and make them easy prey for the unscrupulous."

She thought about Mei-Mei, cast away, not by her elders, but by widowhood. Who knew what would become of her, all alone and with that sweet baby boy to feed?

Consumed by her thoughts, Phoebe didn't pay close attention to tonight's conversation. Until she heard Adrian's name. Once again Naomi had brought up the new mine owner.

"What about Mr. Gamble?" Emmaline said.

"You'd never believe what poor Stan Fulton told me today when he came to bring me this week's laundry."

"Who's Stan Fulton, sugar?" Dahlia asked. "Would I know him? Is he handsome? Married? Rich?"

Naomi gave the younger woman a disdainful look. "The mine foreman. No. Yes, if you like the strong, hardworking kind. No. And no."

"Oh." Dahlia turned back to her stitching.

"Don't pay her any mind, Naomi dear," Emmaline urged. "What happened to Stan Fulton? And what did Mr. Gamble have to do with it?"

Naomi preened and sat straighter in her chair. Everyone watched her, even Phoebe, who feared this would be the start of another gossip session. She stole a peek at Mrs. Stone and noted the older woman's frown. Daisy, at Mrs. Stone's left, wore a stony expression.

"I'm leaving if they start picking that man apart again," Randy threatened.

"I'll go with you," Phoebe said.

"We-ell." Naomi paused, drew out the suspense. "Mr. Gamble's taken some odd notion about the Chinamen at the mine. He wants poor Mr. Fulton to recollect all of them who've worked there and how much they've been paid."

"My lands! Why ever would that lovely man want to know that?" Dahlia asked.

"Why would he care?" Ruthie McMiniver chimed in.

Emmaline sniffed. "I've said it many a time, but no one wants to listen to wisdom. Those foreigners are nothing but trouble. I never understood why Mr. Hart would want to hire them in the first place. There's many a good American who can do the work. We ought to keep our mines and our work to ourselves."

"I'm sure I don't know the whys and wherefores," Naomi said. "They don't matter much, Mr. Fulton says, other than to do the work no one else wants. He told me it's not worth the danger for him to send his regular miners after the gleanings or to have them set off the dynamite. That's why they hire the Chinamen. I wouldn't want to risk one of *our* men that way either."

Ruthie tsk-tsked. "Poor Mr. Fulton. How's he going to figure who they all are? They all look alike, don't they? And they don't even speak a civilized tongue. Besides, didn't some of them get themselves killed in that accident? They likely didn't know any better and brought the whole shaft crashing down on their heads. Their own ignorance caused their deaths."

Phoebe's tears rolled down her cheeks as she shoved the chair away from the frame and ran for her cloak. Mrs. Stone's voice broke the silence behind her. "I'm appalled by what you're saying. I won't stand for one more minute of it. Please leave." Phoebe didn't have to be asked. Nothing would have made her stay in a room with such cruel, conscienceless creatures.

"Phoebe!" Randy cried. "Please wait."

She couldn't. She had to get away. The poor Chinese men hadn't been the only ones to perish. John had died in that mine, too. He hadn't gone into the shaft out of ignorance. He'd gone out of concern for the men who lived in what he'd called "deplorable" conditions. And while John hadn't known much about mines, Phoebe doubted he'd done anything to cause the collapse.

She didn't think the Chinese miners had either.

That accident had robbed her of her husband. It probably had robbed Mei-Mei of hers, too. And it appeared that a baby boy had lost his father before even being born. Although she'd never given much thought to the circumstances that had led to John's death, she now knew she'd been wrong to avoid the difficult matter.

She needed to know what had happened. She needed to know if John's concerns had been well founded. She needed to know if Li Fong had died and how it had all come about. And she had to make sure Adrian helped. He now owned the mine. If things weren't quite right, then he had to make them right. She'd make sure he did.

He had to start with Mei-Mei.

❦

Tong Sun was the name of the only Chinese miner willing to speak to Adrian the next day. "I help," he said, bowing.

"Thank you. I hope you know you can come directly to me. I've come to realize that my ways are different from Mr. Hart's."

At the mention of the mine's former owner, Tong Sun's jaw tightened. He said nothing further.

With a brief prayer for help, Adrian continued. "I need to familiarize myself with everything that happens here. I've been to the store, have moved into the mining company office and the house, and have come here to the site a number of times. I understand the company provides your housing, and I need to inspect it."

"Fine," Tong Sun said, but Adrian got the feeling that agreeing to his request was anything but fine for the quiet, dignified man. Without further comment Tong Sun turned and led him back to Main Street.

As Tong Sun walked before him, Adrian assessed his costume. He wore faded denim trousers with a well-mended tear near one knee. His coat also showed substantial wear but appeared to provide a measure of protection from the elements. Leather gloves covered his hands, and he'd tied his cowboy hat to his head in such a way that the length of wool he'd used also covered his ears.

At the far end of Main Street, Adrian spotted a cluster of small log houses. During their approach, he took note of the minuscule windows and narrow, short doors. A whisper of smoke drifted up from each of the short chimneys, and a handful of the dwellings had dirty mining tools propped against the outside walls.

"Come, Mister Gamble," Tong Sun said, opening the door to the second house.

Adrian entered and took a moment to adjust to the difference in light. What he finally saw appalled him. The room measured no more than fifteen by fifteen feet. Wooden bunks, three high, lined three of the walls. On these shelf-like bunks, each owner had fashioned his individual form of cushion, and only two boasted ticking with some kind of fill. He saw no pillows, and the blankets looked threadbare at best.

A barrel-shaped iron stove sat in the center of the room, a large pan of water simmering on its top. A large metal tub leaned up against the stove, and nine white bowls nested at its side, one on top of the next. The stovepipe rose straight to a ceiling that didn't inspire much confidence, since more patches spanned across it than did original logs.

What wall space he could see between the bunks also wore a wide variety of repairs, starting with some chunks of lumber, followed by what looked like empty food tins straightened and nailed to the logs. Large cracks appeared to have been filled with mud, and even newspapers were used to ward off the wind.

Packed dirt made for an uneven floor, and the men had only three chairs for the nine who called this shack home. Adrian saw no table in the place, and there was no space for one to hide. The room lacked any hint of comfort and, despite the men's efforts otherwise, the wind cut in through the leaky walls. Still, everything was clean—even the floor, with broom tracks visible on the small area between beds and stove.

"Eight men live here with you?" Adrian asked.

"Yes."

"Nine in each house?"

"No."

"What do you mean? Not all the houses are full?"

"No. Some house for three men."

"Are the houses all for your countrymen?"

Tong Sun averted his face. "No."

The man's brief responses gave Adrian a clear picture of the situation. Taking pity on his guide, he thanked him for his willingness to bring a stranger into his home.

"There is another matter where I'll need your help. Mr. Hart's books don't have complete lists of miners' names. I'll need you to prepare one for me of all the Chinese workers this past year. You've been here that long, right?"

"Tong Sun three year here."

"Excellent. Have the other fellows help you if you can't remember everyone, but please have the list to me as soon as possible. I prefer to keep accurate records, and lacking something as important as the names of my workers disturbs me."

"Tong Sun do list. Bring to store tomorrow."

"That soon?" After Stan Fulton's unwillingness to comply, not to mention his resistance to Adrian's sense of urgency, he'd thought the task might be a difficult one. "You don't need more time? Are the men who work here now mostly the ones who've been here all year?"

"No. I remember all. The men now, the men gone, the men dead. I remember all."

The stark words struck Adrian with their burden of pain. The house bore testimony to an untenable situation. Tragedy had occurred when the mine caved in. Yet he also knew that accident wasn't the only misfortune visited upon these men.

Hart's negligence showed everywhere, but he no longer owned the mine. Adrian refused to have the men who worked for him, who lived far from their loved ones, who daily risked their lives, suffer in such mean circumstances. His late father had taught him better than that. The Heart of Silver Mining Company was about to undergo a number of changes now that he called the shots.

He'd start by improving the quarters of these strangers in his land. He'd show them the respect and gratitude their work had earned.

And he'd do whatever it took to learn the fate of Mei-Mei's husband. It was the least he could do as the man's employer.

The next morning when Phoebe arrived at the store, the place was in shambles. Her neatly stocked shelves looked half empty, their contents jumbled with the items on the tables. Phoebe scanned the store and saw Adrian intent on his destructive assault.

"What are you doing, Mr. Gamble?" she asked, stunned by the mess.

"I need supplies for at least twenty-five miners."

"Supplies," she repeated. "For twenty-five men."

"That's right. I want blankets, pans, towels, a rug—no, two rugs—per cabin." He waved a sheet of paper. "I've a list, and it includes some of every kind of victuals we carry. Good leather gloves will also help, and we'll need winter-weight drawers as well. Do we have three good lanterns? And where would I get chairs this time of year?"

"We have plenty of lanterns, and Mr. Davis, just off Main Street on Pine Road, is a fine carpenter. I'm sure he has a chair or two for sale in his shop, and if you need more, he can make them. I doubt an order could be filled and delivered from St. Louis before the heavy snows start."

Phoebe kept her voice calm, hoping to soothe Adrian's urgency. She wondered what he had in mind, why he needed all those things, but she respected his privacy and didn't push for an explanation.

"I'm sorry," he said. "I'm sure you think I've gone mad."

She smiled. "I wouldn't put it quite like that, but I do find it remarkable that a man with a fully outfitted mansion would need this assortment of items, and for twenty-five men."

"It's not for me, as I'm sure you know." She nodded and smiled, and he handed her the list. "I visited the Chinese workers' quarters. I found the men living in terrible conditions. I can't let it continue."

"And so you're going to try and make up for Mr. Hart's deficiencies. All at one time."

"No. I'll just correct the problems I've seen. I can't change the past, but I can make the present and future better for those men. They've endured under those conditions long enough. I know I don't have to fix everything this morning, but anything I do to help will improve matters considerably."

His kindness touched her. "I told you once before, Adrian Gamble, and I'll say it again. You're a good man."

A crooked smile appeared on his lips. "I suspect that if you help me do this, the men will see Hartville's singing angel, not the new mine owner, coming to their aid. And that's as it should be. Your concern for Mei-Mei set me on the right path."

She waved his words aside. "That's not important. What matters is correcting the problem. I know their plight weighed heavily on John."

"I've seen where they live, and I can see why a man of God would be troubled. I only hope I prove equal to the task." He squared his shoulders. "But I suspect it's just the beginning. I'll have to go down into the mine itself. And I've sent for an expert from Ouray. We'll see what he has to say."

As she gathered the items from Adrian's list atop the counter, Phoebe felt an easing of the guilt that had overcome her the night before.

"John would have agreed with everything you've done and want to do yet. He hated meanness and unfairness, and his anger on this matter was great for a very even-tempered man."

"Did he tell you why he was going into the mine?"

"No. He never mentioned that he intended to. He did spend a great deal of time with Eric Wagner, Douglas Carlson, and Pastor Stone right before the accident. I watched them carry on very serious conversations. They took notes and then tore them up. You might want to talk to them."

Adrian averted his gaze. "I'd rather not impose. They strike me as busy men. I can start with the supplies, and then I'll wait for the expert."

"I'm sure they wouldn't think you were imposing. They already knew how John felt."

His jaw tightened and a muscle leaped under the taut skin. Phoebe dropped the matter.

"I'm sure that whatever you decide will be fine," she said.

"I just know that Mei-Mei's appearance here made me realize I should have asked John more about his concerns. My only thought at that time was to make us a home in our new town, and I closed myself off to what he believed God had led him to."

"He likely thought it a matter for men—"

"A woman can handle the same difficult matters a man can." Phoebe's years of hearing the Shakers speak to the equality of men and women didn't dispose her to accept that easy excuse. "I wasn't open to God's call then, but I won't make the same mistake again. I intend to help Mei-Mei."

"It occurred to me she might work here in the store. You can use the help—"

"Have I done something wrong?" Phoebe's innards lurched. "Are you dissatisfied with my work?"

"Not at all. I've no idea why you'd think that." He gave her an odd look and shook his head. "I'd feel better knowing you didn't have to bear all the responsibility for running the store. And I want to help Mei-Mei, too. She could offer you valuable help."

"I see." If Shaker experience was anything to go by, Phoebe did see merit in sharing the work. "It might work. Her little boy could sleep back here next to the counter."

"That would be perfect. And the next thing we'll need is a place for her to live. The three of you can't keep sharing that back room. It scarcely offers you adequate quarters."

"It's better than what the miners have, isn't it? We do well to remember our blessings."

As Phoebe stacked dried fish on a sheet of brown paper, wrapped it, and tied the bundle with a length of good hemp twine, she gave the matter of Mei-Mei's lodgings further consideration.

"The Harts had a housekeeper," she finally said, placing the fish inside the nearly full box. "Surely you can spare a room or two for them in your home."

"Of course! I can't believe it didn't occur to me in the first place." He shook his head. "Then again, I feel more like a temporary visitor there than its new owner. Even this store has become more of a home than that great monstrosity. There's too much . . . too many things there. It reminds me of the stores back east."

"Mrs. Hart did set great stock by her 'pretties.' Gemma, her Italian housekeeper, had a standing order for the vinegar and lemon oil she used for cleaning and polishing."

He gave her a crooked grin. "Can you see me fussing with dainty figurines and fancy tables and antimacassars strewn every which way?"

She laughed and shook her head. "Perhaps what you need is a housekeeper. You might want to ask Mei-Mei what kind of work she'd rather do."

"That's another excellent idea."

He turned on his heel and opened the back door. Phoebe continued packing supplies, thanksgiving in her heart and in the song she sang. God had answered yet another of her prayers. Mei-Mei and her baby would soon have a new home, and there would be work for the mother and food enough to nourish her and the child.

God's blessings abounded. Surely He'd sent Adrian Gamble to right many wrongs in town.

෧

"Did you hear?" Naomi asked Emmaline when the two crossed paths on the street outside the general store.

"I've heard plenty, but until you tell me what you've heard I can't know if I heard what you did."

Naomi hitched the basket of clean laundry she'd set out to deliver higher on her right hip. "That Adrian Gamble has brought himself one of those Orientals to keep house for him. A woman. And I hear say she has a babe with her."

Emmaline gaped. "You don't say."

101

"I do. I have it on sound assurance. Stan Fulton went to the store to deliver that list of workers Mr. Gamble had asked him to write, but Phoebe sent him to the mansion. When he got there, he found Mr. Gamble with this young Oriental hussy, showing her every treasure in that house."

"You don't think . . . No, it couldn't be."

"What?"

"Do you think she might be his paramour? I hear many men in San Francisco prefer her kind for that sort of thing."

Naomi drew in a sharp breath. "Oh my. If that's the case, then I wonder if the baby might be—"

"Hush, woman. Don't even say it." Emmaline shuddered. "I certainly no longer find him an attractive sort. Imagine. A man who could marry any good American woman doing . . . *that* with one of *them*."

"And siring a half-breed." Naomi pursed her lips. "Who would have thought? And him looking so fine and upright in his fine pressed suits and that air of princeliness."

"Just goes to show, my dear, there's no judging a man but by his actions. And Adrian Gamble's actions are reprehensible indeed."

Naomi switched her load to her other hip. "I do agree. Oh, look. There's that Dahlia Sutton. We'd best tell her what we've learned. It's our Christian duty to keep her from making a dreadful mistake and marrying that heathen-loving fool."

They hurried over and wasted no time in sharing their thoughts.

Dahlia fanned her flushed face. "I do declare, ladies. That is the most . . . most distasteful state." Then she shook herself and stood taller. "A lady can overlook a transgression or two," she drawled, a hint of steel beneath the treacly accent, "provided, that is, they aren't repeated once she weds the cad."

"What?" Emmaline and Naomi cried in unison.

Dahlia nodded decisively, a smile of triumph on her lips. "Of course, sugar lambs. I just have to make sure I march him right up that aisle sooner rather than later. Once I'm Mrs. Adrian Gamble, things will change. That little foreigner and her by-blow will be on the first train out of town right before the very moment he says 'I do.'"

8

"Absolutely not, Adrian Gamble," Phoebe said. "You will not persuade me to stay here at the store. I want to help those men as much as you do, so I will go with you. I might see needs only a woman would notice."

Her argument did nothing to soften the stubborn set of his jaw. "Miners' shacks are not proper places for a lady. I can't expose you to danger. Only men live there, and I don't know any of them well enough to trust them around you."

"You won't have to trust them. We'll trust the Lord."

Satisfaction filled her when his cheeks ruddied and he couldn't counter that truth. She gathered the basket she'd packed with old cloths, a sturdy brush, a bottle of vinegar, and a box of Arm & Hammer's Baking Soda. She knew she could clean just about anything with her trusty tools.

"I'm ready," she said. "Shall we go?"

The sky didn't boast a single cloud, and Phoebe could count all the stars in the heavens. The wind's usual feisty force had lessened somewhat, affording them a reasonably pleasant stroll. The temperature, however, still hovered near freezing.

They walked in companionable silence, Adrian carrying a large box of supplies, Phoebe's basket swinging from her arm.

"There really are holes in the walls?" she asked.

"I'm afraid so. You'll soon see for yourself."

Phoebe stole a glance at him and noticed the squared set of his jaw and the heightened color on his cheek bones.

"Those shacks aren't fit for animals," he said, his voice deep and rough, "much less men, and especially ones who work so hard. I'm ashamed to own the company that employs them and even to admit that those awful places belong to me."

He fell silent again.

Phoebe rejoiced in the opportunity to do something for the needy men. When she'd helped Mei-Mei move to the Hart mansion, the young woman's happiness had rubbed off on her. The new mother had insisted she could handle the housework and repeated her gratitude for the opportunity to prove her worth.

She'd also shown her appreciation for the warm wrap Phoebe had brought from the general store, as well as the two skirts, two shirtwaists, a dress, undergarments, and sturdy shoes. The two women had giggled at Mei-Mei's lack of familiarity with western-style clothes. In the end, Mei-Mei had looked lovely, and Phoebe rested easy knowing she'd prepared the girl for winter.

Deep in thought, Phoebe didn't notice much on the trip down Main Street to where it narrowed into little more than a dirt track. But soon they reached the shantytown, and she followed Adrian to the second house on the right side of the rough lane. She frowned at the small windows and insubstantial doors, but she also saw the sparkling glass panes and the well-swept front stoop.

In response to Adrian's knock, the door opened to reveal the Chinese gentleman she most often served at the store.

"Good evening, Tong Sun," Adrian said. "I've planned various improvements to the company-owned houses and an increase in the items supplied to my workers. Your group is first on my list. May we come in?"

Tong Sun studied them in silence, and Phoebe feared he'd deny them entrance. Someone inside spoke in their musical tongue. Tong Sun replied. Finally, with a small bow he stepped back and held the door to let them in.

While Adrian made small talk, Phoebe studied her surroundings, trying not to look as though that's what she was doing. She noted the hodgepodge of oddments someone had used to try to seal the holes in the walls and ceiling, but she could still feel little currents bite at her almost as sharply as the wind outdoors had.

A dented tin pan steamed atop the stove, and to one side, a substantial metal soaking tub filled with dirty water showed evidence of recent bathing activity. Three men occupied the three chairs in the room, while four others lay on the stark, plank-like bunks. The bunks reminded Phoebe of the sardine cans on the shelves at the store. Tong Sun remained on his feet.

No wonder Adrian wanted to help.

"I've arranged for the delivery of mattresses," he said, "one for every man who lives in a company house. Pillows, too."

Tong Sun's eyes widened, but he didn't speak.

"We've blankets with us tonight, as well as a cooking pot and a skillet, plates, cups, and canned goods."

He set the box down on the floor and sought his employee's gaze. Tong Sun nodded but again said nothing.

Phoebe gave Adrian a great deal of credit for his determination in the face of such unresponsiveness. Seemingly undaunted, he plowed ahead, pulling items from the box and displaying them to the miners.

"Each man will receive new gloves, long winter drawers, socks, boots, and a hat if he wants one. I've no desire to see anyone suffer from the cold, much less wind up with frostbite."

The oldest man in the log house reacted then. He pointed at the gloves with a hand lacking two fingers and spoke angrily in his language. Tong Sun said something in a placating tone, and the elder scrambled off his bunk to approach Adrian.

"Thank you, Mister Gamble." He bowed deeply, and Phoebe noted a liquid glint in his dark eyes. "Thank you much."

Tong Sun didn't express any gratitude but instead retained his cloak of wariness. He watched Adrian's every move. When Adrian finished emptying the box onto one of the unoccupied bunks, he asked, "How much?"

"Nothing," Adrian said. "Now that the company belongs to me, this is part of my miners' wages. You work for me, and I'm responsible for your well-being."

"Why?"

Adrian blinked, and Phoebe was also taken aback.

"Because it's the right thing to do," he replied. "Because God calls me to provide for those under my authority, to do for others what I'd want done for me at my time of need. I couldn't face myself in the morning if I failed to do so." He waved toward the ceiling and then at the floor. "These houses weren't built well in the first place. I've hired a man to do repairs to the walls, and especially to the chinking, as soon as possible. It's not good to have winds tear right through a house while you men sleep."

Again Tong Sun absorbed Adrian's words but didn't respond.

While Phoebe hadn't expected a repeat of Mei-Mei's warm acceptance, she hadn't expected this outright distrust either. When a hint of hurt crossed Adrian's face, she felt it in her heart as well. The strength of the sensation surprised her, as did the urge to reach out and touch his shoulder, to comfort him, to commend him for the genuine kindness that had brought him here.

As she took a step forward, the door to the shack burst open and two men dragged a third inside. The reluctant one screamed his objection, presumably to the others' treatment, but he seemed frail and ill, in a wasting condition. His eyes burned with a feverish glare, and sores crusted the corners of his mouth. His efforts to shake his captors failed.

Tong Sun made a curt remark, while two of the men in the bunks spat in disdain. Phoebe turned to Adrian, bewildered by the scene.

He shrugged as he came to her side, close enough that her shoulder felt the solid warmth of his arm. A sense of safety swelled in Phoebe, and she whispered, "Thank you."

"I asked you not to come," he reminded her in an equally quiet voice. "I don't know what this is about, but I'm not comfortable having you here."

She blushed, now regretting arguing so vehemently about coming with him. "I needed to see this," she said. "And I feel perfectly protected with you at my side."

Her words seemed to surprise and please him. A small smile formed on his lips. "Thank you for the compliment. But I doubt I can provide adequate protection against this many."

"It doesn't look as though their fight is with us. It must be with the three who just arrived."

Adrian again studied the men embroiled in the squabble. "I don't think the trouble is between all three and the others. I suspect it's the one the two dragged in who's at fault."

"But he looks ill. Why would they quarrel with a sick man?"

He shrugged. "I don't speak their language. But I do think enough is enough." He approached the melee and called out, "Tong Sun!"

The man turned. "Mister Gamble. You go. *Go.* Take Missus Phoebe with. Tong Sun fix here."

"What exactly will you fix?"

The Chinese miner turned to his skirmishing countrymen, uttered a series of sharp phrases, and brought silence to the shack. As if to underscore what he'd just said, he graced the group with yet another glare and then turned to Adrian. "See? Tong Sun fix. Is fine."

Phoebe scanned the faces of the others and took note that, excepting the one who'd been dragged inside, purposely neutral expressions seemed the order of the moment. The reluctant arrival displayed a strange kind of urgency—perhaps desperation better described his mien. Nothing looked fixed to her.

When it appeared that the men were not about to explain, she sighed. As clean and tidy as they kept the shabby interior of the shack, bringing her basket of supplies had been a wasted effort. Aside from witnessing what had so troubled John and now Adrian, perhaps her presence here was equally futile.

"Very well," Adrian said, although his tone of voice told her he didn't find any of this at all well. "We'll be on our way. Do tell your colleagues that supplies will arrive for them in the next day or two and that I'll let the residents of each house know when its repairs will begin."

"Tong Sun will do." With a last warning look at his men, he went to the door and held it open. "Good-night."

"Well," Adrian said under his breath as he and Phoebe went to the door. "He's certainly let us know our presence isn't welcome."

Once outside, Phoebe placed a hand on his forearm. "It must be some private matter that led to the argument, and then to our abrupt dismissal. I'm sure that even though they didn't show any emotion to that effect, your concern will be recognized."

He gave her a crooked smile and started walking back toward town. "I didn't do it for recognition."

"I know. You did it because you recognized a need. I know they'll appreciate what you're providing for them." Phoebe shuddered. "I'm appalled by their lack of . . . of everything. John was right. Their conditions are deplorable."

"Were. They will no longer be deplorable. At least not as long as I can help it."

"I'll say so again, Adrian Gamble. You're a good man indeed."

He stopped. "Thank you, Phoebe. Your opinion matters a great deal."

She met his gaze, and despite the chill night, she felt a new warmth build inside her. His gaze said things she couldn't quite read, but she knew she wanted to; she knew they would please her, and what she saw in his eyes meant a great deal to her, too.

His expression changed from one of mere appreciation to one more intense, more personal. A smile curved his mouth, and the creases on either side of it deepened. A lock of dark hair fell across his forehead. She reached up and smoothed it back.

He caught her fingers, held them for a moment, then removed her glove. Still holding her gaze, he brought the captured hand to his lips and placed a tender kiss in the sensitive palm. Sparks flew up her arm, burst somewhere near her heart, and shot straight up to her head. A sparkling sensation fizzled in her middle. She marveled at the delicious feelings.

With the same gentle care he'd used to open her hand, he curled her fingers back over his kiss. Still holding on, he used his other hand to run a finger down her cheek. Phoebe leaned into his touch, a smile on her lips.

"You're a lovely woman, Phoebe Williams," he whispered. "A veritable treasure indeed."

The knot in her throat kept her from voicing a response. Right then she felt treasured, even cherished, and she felt foolish for thinking that. They were practically strangers, and her response was intense and unusual.

Phoebe knew she should pull away, but she found herself unable—unwilling—to do so. To her relief, he slipped her gloves into her basket, tucked her hand into the crook of his elbow, covered her bare fingers with his, and set them back on their way once again.

What a precious moment the Lord had just given her. She stole a glance at Adrian's face and admired the smile still on his lips. What else might the Lord be giving her?

Did He perhaps have a second chance at love in mind for her?

❦

Adrian came to his senses the moment Phoebe closed the door to her apartment. If she'd dumped a bucket of icy water on his head, it would have had no different effect.

He had no business romancing a woman, not one like Phoebe Williams. She wasn't the type to let a man take liberties if she didn't care for him.

First, he'd covered her lips with his finger the other day to stop her objections. He should have realized then that he had to stay as far from her as possible. She hadn't rebuffed him. And he hadn't used the common sense God had given him.

Now he'd made matters much worse. He'd revealed how much she appealed to him, and he'd allowed himself the pleasure of touching her soft, warm cheek. Her skin was as satiny as he'd thought, only firmer and even more enticing.

The worst thing he'd done, however, was to elicit her response. He'd felt the delicate shimmer run through her when he'd kissed her hand. He'd seen the wonder in her blue eyes. He'd read the pleasure his attentions had brought her in the return of her glorious smile.

He'd given life to a certain expectation. One he couldn't fulfill. He had no expectations—he couldn't have any. At any given time, his past could catch up with him, and when it did, he doubted he'd survive.

He couldn't expose a woman to that. He certainly couldn't let Phoebe come to care for him any more than she already did.

Adrian knew they had to return to their earlier businesslike relationship. He had to back away from the most magnificent woman he'd ever met.

Phoebe deserved better than a second widowhood.

"Phoebe Williams," she chided the next morning when she caught herself staring into the small square mirror, wondering if Adrian might find her plain hairstyle too . . . well, plain. "You really must stop this foolishness."

But try as she might, her heart refused to obey. She expected him to arrive early, as he'd taken to doing recently. He'd stop and chat with her, helping her straighten either the items on the shelves or the ready-made garments on the tables.

She enjoyed their conversation, even though it always revolved around store matters. Pausing to consider that, she realized it wasn't the conversation itself she so enjoyed, it was the person with whom she conversed that she appreciated.

And he was due to arrive any minute now.

She hurried to the store and went straight to the counter, tied her apron, and took up her broom. She preferred to be done with this chore before he came. That left her more time to spend with him.

When she heard his steps on the boardwalk, her heart picked up its beat and her stomach fluttered. She caught her breath, telling herself to stop acting like a young girl. She was, after all, a widow.

But her heart didn't listen. The clanging of the bell coincided with the clatter of the broom against the floor. She picked it up and propped the tool in its right spot.

"Good morning." Oh dear. Had she sounded as breathless as she felt?

Adrian's steps sped, and he spared her a glance. "Morning."

Without a pause, he went straight to the back door, entered the hallway, and disappeared, leaving Phoebe blushing and mortified.

She stood, frozen in her tracks. Had she misread his actions of the night before? Worse, had she imagined it all?

She'd heard tell of widows who often did such foolish things, throwing themselves at eligible men. Had she behaved as poorly as Naomi and Dahlia and even Emmaline?

Dear Lord Jesus, I hope not. Please show me, Father, if I've gone wrong, if I saw something where there was nothing more than Adrian's abounding kindness. And please, God, keep me from unseemly behavior. I want my life and my ways to reflect You, only You.

The cowbell jangled, and she spun to wipe the tears on the hem of her apron. Fortunately, her customer didn't come straight to the counter but strolled over to the display of tonics and liniments.

Phoebe gathered her dignity, squared her shoulders, and resumed her daily work. Through the morning she managed to serve her customers with her normal efficiency, if perhaps with less conversation than usual and with fewer smiles. To her relief, no one seemed to notice, or else they had the good manners not to comment.

Then Wynema strode into the establishment, her sensible shoes clunking against the wood floor, her tripod knocking into everything in her path. She'd devised a neck strap for her camera from an old leather belt, and the contraption bounced against her belly.

"Hello, Phoebe," she called. "Has my order of supplies arrived?"

Before Phoebe had an opportunity to respond, Wynema released her tripod, leaned against the counter, and peered at her. "What's wrong? Have you been peeling onions this early? What are you cooking for supper?"

Phoebe didn't know whether to laugh or to cry. Wynema could always be counted on to be direct. "I haven't touched an onion since day before yesterday. And supper? Why, dear, I haven't given it a thought."

At her friend's crestfallen expression, Phoebe hastened to add, "But why don't you give me a suggestion, and we can plan to share the meal."

Wynema beamed. "I figure just about anything you cook is fine. All your Shaker food tastes better than even Mama's French cook's cuisine did back in Philadelphia."

Somehow, Phoebe couldn't quite imagine this girl in the life she'd known before her widowed father's prospecting brought her to Colorado.

"I appreciate the compliment, and now I'll have to think of something special to live up to such praise."

"No, no, no. Any old thing will do. I just enjoy the company and the conversation."

"And you hate your own halfhearted efforts at feeding yourself."

Wynema nodded. "So. Have my chemicals come?"

"Oh. I'm sorry. I've been woolgathering all day." *More like dreading the moment when Adrian descends those stairs to go back home.* "They're here. This great big crate is yours."

"My goodness, that is a large box. I'm afraid I won't be able to get it home on my own. I'll have to think of someone who might stop by and load it into their wagon . . . or their rig . . . something."

The cowbell clanged again, and the two friends looked up. Ruthie McMiniver turned the corner at the table of denim trousers and went straight to the bolts of wool.

"Go help her," Wynema said. "I'm going to try to lift this thing to see how much help I really need. Maybe I'll measure it, too. Or I could always unpack it and carry the chemicals home one at a time . . ."

Phoebe left her friend muttering to herself and went to assist Ruthie. At the moment, the middle-aged woman faced the enormous task of choosing between the navy wool and the moss green for a new dress. Phoebe drew on all her patience as Ruthie weighed the merits of both, spread out lengths from each bolt, decided first on one, then just when Phoebe had stowed away the unchosen one, she'd reverse her decision.

Wynema continued to fuss over her supplies, as Phoebe's glances attested. She'd rather listen to Wynema worry her dilemma to bits than juggle heavy bolts of fabric.

"That's it," Ruthie finally said. "I'm going to take the gray."

Phoebe's jaw sagged. The woman had never even looked at the bolt of gray material. Fed up with the entire endeavor, she yanked out that bolt, measured out the yards Ruthie requested, folded up the length, and hurried back to the counter.

She wrote the charge in her ledger for monthly paying customers and wrapped up the fabric in brown paper. She tied the bundle with twine, paying no attention to Ruthie's odes to gray wool.

When the difficult woman picked up her parcel and headed for the door, Wynema burst out laughing. "Good riddance!"

"Oh hush," Phoebe urged but still smiled.

The cowbell sounded one more time, and Phoebe glanced that way in automatic response. She'd thought Ruthie had opened the door to leave, but she realized now that Emmaline had just walked in. She and Ruthie greeted each other like long-lost sisters and chattered about the frock Ruthie was planning.

Wynema shook her head. "Perfect partners," she muttered and went back to her conundrum. "I think I'll just take the Eastman film with me right now. It's the lightest of the lot. I'll come back for the chemicals . . . or perhaps I'll send someone to fetch them for me . . . or maybe I'll take some with me after supper . . ."

Phoebe smiled and returned to her ledger. As she tallied up the McMinivers' account, Emmaline's voice caught her attention.

"That man's behavior is absolutely reprehensible. Can you imagine? And utterly brazen. He but arrives in town and then brings in his private harlot, as if Hartville needed any more of their ilk."

"Just goes to show what a man's baser instincts can make him do," Ruthie said. "And it doesn't do to mingle with one whose family you don't know. A mistress . . ."

Phoebe's heart began to break. No wonder Adrian had gone past her this morning with nothing more than that "Morning" of his. Last night had meant nothing to him. The pain was sharp, sharper than she would have thought possible. A fresh batch of tears welled up in her eyes.

Emmaline harrumphed. "Now we know why he's so fond of Orientals. He shares his nights with one."

"Well," Ruthie said, "from what you've said, he's sharing a great deal more than his bed with her. Why they even share a child."

A Chinese woman? A child?

Phoebe stared at the two gossips and in a flash made the correct connection.

She stepped toward them. "Ladies, I would much rather you refrain from gossip in the store, certainly about its owner. Especially since you have your facts all wrong. Gossip is usually false, you know."

The two women turned on her. "How would you know anything? You never listen, nor do you share," Emmaline said.

"I do indeed choose not to carry tales about others, and I also prefer not to listen to any who do."

Ruthie lifted her nose high in the air.

Emmaline compressed her thin lips to where they almost disappeared from view. Her nostrils flared and her beady eyes glared.

"Aren't you the righteous one?"

Phoebe stood her ground. "The young woman you've described is Mr. Gamble's new housekeeper—"

"So they all say," Ruthie said.

"In this case," Phoebe continued, "she is. What's more, she's married to a miner, but we fear he might be one of the men who died with John and Mr. Hart last June."

Ruthie's face showed signs of wavering. Emmaline retained her mulish mien.

Phoebe felt driven to set the record straight about two people she liked and respected. "The young woman, Mei-Mei is her name, waited until their child was born in California, then she came here to see why she hadn't heard from her husband, Li Fong, in many months. Mr. Gamble needed someone to keep house in that large mansion, and Mei-Mei needed a means to support herself and her baby. He solved both their problems and is now looking into Li Fong's fate."

Tears rolled down Ruthie's round face. "How tragic," she wailed. "How sad. Did you hear that, Emmaline dear? Why, it sounds just like something right out of a dime novel."

For the briefest span of a second, Emmaline's eyes betrayed a softening. Then she gave one of her sniffs. "A likely story, I tell you. Just goes to show how far a debauched man will go to continue to wallow in his sin. Come, Ruthie, we really should find somewhere else to talk."

Phoebe was aghast. "But—"

"She," Emmaline continued, staring pointedly at Phoebe, "will of course defend her employer. She knows who butters her bread."

The two women stormed out of the store, leaving Phoebe to fight tears for a third time that day.

Wynema wrapped an arm around Phoebe's shoulders. "They're despicable. Don't let them bother you. They have a lot of answering to do before God."

Phoebe tried to speak but found the knot in her throat too large and too tight. She waved her hands, gesturing without sound, then dropped them to her sides.

The cowbell rang yet again, and at the same time, the door to the back hallway opened. Phoebe turned and hurried back to her stool by the cash drawer, her head lowered. She couldn't explain herself to Adrian, not when the subject matter was so ugly.

Wynema waved farewell and strode off.

"Mr. Gamble," Phoebe heard Pastor Stone say as she knelt behind the counter to wipe her eyes. "Might I have a moment of your time?"

"A moment, yes," Adrian said. "I've a man to meet down by the company workers' houses."

"This won't take long," the pastor said. "But it's a confidential matter. Should we go to your office?"

"It looks as though the ladies just left. And I doubt you'd like Hart's treacherous stairs any more than I do."

Phoebe stood. "Excuse me, gentlemen. I couldn't help overhearing your desire for privacy. I'll just step outside a moment."

The pastor caught her by the arm. "At first I didn't think

you should know of this, but the more I've prayed about it, the more certain I've grown that you should. It was John who first suspected the problem."

She found herself unable to keep from looking at Adrian. "John?"

With a sigh, the pastor removed his black wool hat and ran a hand over his thinning gray hair. "I should have listened more closely to him. Perhaps we could have done something sooner."

"What?" Adrian asked in an anxious voice. "What's the matter?"

"I'm afraid, son, we have a problem here with what your Chinese miners call the demon mud. It looks like someone is selling opium to them and making himself rich from their addiction."

"But—"

"That's not all," Pastor Stone added. "I've begun to wonder if it didn't have something to do with the accident last June."

9

Phoebe felt faint. "Opium? Here?"

Adrian said nothing, but the tension in his stance and the narrowing of his eyes broadcast his anger across the counter to where she stood.

With a visible measure of control, he finally said, "What do you know? Tell me everything. I need to know exactly what I've bought besides shafts in the ground and a general store."

The pastor reached for one of the chairs by the stove. "May I?"

Phoebe took a bracing breath. "How can something like that happen in Hartville? It's not that large a town, and everyone knows everybody else's business. How could we not know? How could I not know, running the store and all?"

"It's not something anyone would discuss here," Pastor Stone replied. "The store's too public, and something as foul as an addiction is best suited to secrecy and hidden places."

Adrian swung a leg around the horseshoe keg and sat down. "How's the stuff getting here? And who'd do something like that?"

Phoebe took the empty chair. "Is it only the Chinamen who are involved?"

The pastor shrugged. "I don't know. John was certain some were using the drug, but I don't know how he learned about it. I've suspected all along that one of the men, one who objected to the sale and use of opium, confided in John, hoping he'd help put an end to the destructive trade."

"You've no idea how deeply I regret not paying closer attention to John's concerns," Phoebe said. "I should have been a better helpmate. If I had, I might know something of value."

"Or perhaps," the pastor said, "you'd also be dead."

Phoebe gasped at the harsh words.

"What makes you think that?" Adrian asked.

"Because shortly after John told me and a few of the other men in town what he suspected, the mine collapsed and he died with a large number of Chinese miners."

He took out his handkerchief and wiped his forehead. With great care he refolded it and tucked it back into his coat pocket. He leaned back in the chair and clasped his hands on the brim of the bowler on his knee. He kept his gaze downcast.

"It strikes me as an extraordinary coincidence that since the cave-in not another clue has surfaced to suggest drug use. But I've never put much stock in coincidence. You can account it to the whims of an old man, but I feel it in my heart. The two matters are connected."

"Although I knew John's capacity for compassion," Phoebe said, "I wondered if there wasn't more to his interest in the miners than just their awful conditions. The only time I tried to learn more about his efforts, he said he was taking care of the problems. I took him at his word." A sob hitched in her throat. "I should have made him tell me more."

"What do you think you might have done that he didn't?" Adrian asked. "I'm afraid I agree with the pastor. If this is indeed happening in Hartville—among the Heart of Silver miners—then you'd most likely have been killed, too."

"Surrender your guilt, child," the pastor said. He stood and went to Phoebe's side and placed a hand on her shoulder. "It's not of God. John didn't want you involved. He made a point of telling us to keep you removed from it all."

"A wise decision," Adrian said.

Phoebe stood. "Well said by the man who tried to keep me away from the miners' cabin last night."

Adrian stepped in front of her. "And now, if this matter of opium is really a problem here, you're right in the middle of it, aren't you?"

She raised her chin. "Indeed. I have been from the moment Mei-Mei walked into the store looking for—Oh!" She grabbed Adrian's crossed forearms. "Mei-Mei came to Hartville to look for John. She said Li Fong had mentioned him in his letters to her. Do you think she knows about the opium?"

The two men exchanged looks.

"I didn't know the man," Pastor Stone said, "but I have to wonder if that's something he would have told his wife."

Adrian shook his head. "I wouldn't have if I had one to tell." Phoebe began to object, but he stared her down. "And John didn't tell his."

Her chin rose a bit more. "But neither of you know. Not for absolutely certain. And I believe it can't hurt to ask. That's just what I'm going to do."

Adrian grabbed her arm as she turned toward the counter.

"Don't," she said. "I need to know if an accident took my husband's life or if he was killed because of what he knew. I must ask Mei-Mei what she knows."

"And then what? Get yourself killed in the bargain?"

"I don't intend to do anything that foolish. I'll take the matter straight to the authorities. Sheriff Herman will want to know about it, and I'm certain he'll know how best to handle matters from there."

"No."

Phoebe turned to the pastor. "Why not?"

"Because John insisted that we shouldn't do that. At least not until we knew who was behind the trade. What if . . . ?"

Adrian released her. "Yes, what if the sheriff himself is involved? It wouldn't be the first time a lawman has gone bad."

She thought quickly for a potential plan. "I'll go to Silverton or Ouray or even Denver. Colorado has jails and courts and even nooses enough to handle such crime." She squared her shoulders and untied the apron strings. "Mr. Gamble. You have a store to mind for a spell. I'll return as soon as possible, and I invite you to become better acquainted with the stove regulars. They're an education unlike any you received back east."

She left the room, crossed the hallway, and slipped into her apartment. There she grabbed her cape, slipped the hood over her head, and clasped it closed at her throat. Without wasting another minute, she stepped out into the gray afternoon and hurried to the Hart mansion.

Mei-Mei opened the door at her first knock. "Come, Missus Phoebe, come see boy."

Her new friend's pride in her son made it impossible for Phoebe to question her right away. She followed Mei-Mei to her rooms behind the kitchen and took true pleasure in the baby's marked improvement. She preferred the innocent discussion of a baby's reality to the grim misery of opium and possible murder.

"He's grown," she noted, holding the little one in the crook of her arm. "And his hair . . . look at all that."

Phoebe crooned and swayed gently as Mei-Mei hung her cape on an ornate brass hall tree. The piece looked more like something Mrs. Hart would have used in her vast entry hall than in the housekeeper's quarters, and she wondered if Adrian had consigned the overdone thing to this part of the house.

"Do you like your rooms?" she asked.

"Very much. Mister Gamble bring things for Mei-Mei and boy."

That explained the hall tree.

"Is the work too much for you? I'd hate to see you worn out."

Phoebe held the infant up and rubbed her lips against his downy head. "This little angel needs you in good health."

"Work good. Mei-Mei work hard. Mister Gamble say good dinner, too."

"I'm glad, very glad, you're satisfied."

And she was. She knew all too well the anguish of widowhood, of not knowing what to do, where to go, or how to sustain yourself. And as a new mother, Mei-Mei bore an even greater responsibility than she ever had.

"Have you chosen a name for him?"

"Yes. Boy is Lee, American name Lee." She came to Phoebe's side and ran a slender finger down her son's cheek. "He American boy, born San Francisco. Missus Phoebe want tea?"

Since she couldn't postpone the purpose of her visit, and because it was bound to turn difficult, Phoebe accepted Mei-Mei's hospitality with a sigh. "Yea, dear, a cup would be lovely."

As the young woman left the room, Phoebe placed little Lee in the cradle Adrian had found in one of the rooms upstairs. He slept, his tiny hands fisted, his ivory skin tinted with the softest glow of rose on his cheeks. He was precious, and Phoebe thanked the Lord for protecting mother and child during what must have been a taxing trip.

Mei-Mei reappeared, bearing a tray laden with cups, a teapot, a sugar bowl, and a collection of what looked like sweets. She set the lot on the table by the window and invited Phoebe to take the chair across from hers. Then she poured the fragrant brew. "Here."

Phoebe wrapped both hands around the warm cup and breathed in the spicy scent of the tea. She took a fortifying sip.

The girl folded her hands on her lap, ignoring her own cup. "Missus Phoebe come talk, no?"

"Yea, I did. And I'm afraid it's not about a pleasant subject."

Mei-Mei drew in a sharp breath. "Li Fong?"

"Nay, I haven't learned anything about your husband yet."

Phoebe placed her cup on the table and met her friend's questioning gaze. "I came to ask you what Li Fong wrote about my husband, about John."

"Oh." The young woman averted her eyes. "Li Fong say John good, he help."

"What kind of help did John offer Li Fong?"

Mei-Mei clasped her hands and pressed her lips together. Then she pressed her hands on the table, palms down, and carefully extended each finger. As she studied her own actions, she began. "Li Fong see men smoke . . ."

"Opium," Phoebe inserted.

The girl nodded but offered nothing further. Her fingers whitened from the pressure against the table.

"Did Li Fong smoke it, too?"

Hot color flooded Mei-Mei's porcelain skin and horror filled her eyes. "No. No, no, no. Li Fong want men stop. He ask John Williams help stop."

Pastor Stone's story had been true. "When did Li Fong come to Hartville?"

"April."

"Right about the same time we did."

Mei-Mei nodded. "Li Fong say John Williams new, too."

"Was this the first time Li Fong worked in Hartville?"

"No. He work before. He come San Francisco. Li Fong father have laundry, want Li Fong help." Her hand fluttered as she chuckled. "Li Fong no like laundry. But Li Fong like Mei-Mei. We marry."

"And in the spring, he returned to the mine."

"Yes."

"Why did he leave you in San Francisco?"

"No nice house here. But Mei-Mei no want house. Mei-Mei want Li Fong."

The anguish in the girl's eyes brought pain back to Phoebe's heart and a lump to her throat.

"And now you're living in the nicest house in town . . ."

"But no Li Fong." A single tear rolled down Mei-Mei's smooth cheek. "No Li Fong. No John Williams."

Phoebe couldn't bear the grief in that single drop of misery. Practically a newlywed, Phoebe had lost all dreams of forever with John. Mei-Mei had lost her dreams of a future for her family, of a father for her son. She reached out to her new friend, who in turn took her hand. Culture and language separated the two women. Loss united them.

After a brief silence, determination prodded Phoebe to her feet.

"I promise you I'll learn what happened to Li Fong. And I'll learn everything I can about the accident that killed John."

"Li Fong letter say John Williams help with demon mud."

Phoebe slipped her cape over her shoulders and pulled up the hood. She prayed for courage and God's immeasurable protection.

"Even though John is no longer with us, I'm still here, Mei-Mei, and Mr. Gamble is a good man. We will help with the opium . . . the demon mud. We'll find out who's bringing it here, and we'll make sure they stop. We'll also help those who are suffering from its effects. I promise you. Mr. Gamble and I will finish what John and Li Fong began."

In the cavernous, silent store, Adrian sought his Lord in prayer.

What did I buy here? I thought the mining company would provide me with the means to support myself, and the out-of-the-way town would offer a place to hide from those who want me dead.

He propped his elbows on the counter and leaned his forehead against his palms.

But, Father, it sickens me to think that because I once did what I had to do—the only thing an honorable man could do—my life has become a downward spiral of running to escape death with new dangers at every turn.

Adrian didn't know what to do, where to go, or even when to stop running. As he'd worked his way through the mining company records, a slight discrepancy had grown, and today he'd had to face the truth. Since Mr. Hart's death, someone had charged the store more for the items it stocked, yet nothing indicated that the various suppliers had instituted the increases. He didn't think Phoebe had anything to do with the matter, even though she placed the orders and received the bills.

Evidently, Mrs. Hart had turned the accounts to Douglas Carlson, and he'd written the checks for the merchandise. No one had suspected a need to compare the current accounts with the records from before Mr. Hart's death.

Even so, Lord, I liked it better when I thought this petty thievery was my most serious problem here. Now, in comparison to the opium problem, it seems silly to worry about someone skimming profit off the top.

He prayed for wisdom, for guidance, for the words to persuade Phoebe to stay far, far away from the filth of the opium trade. He'd already killed one human, and in the doing he'd destroyed his life. He didn't think he'd be able to live with himself if something happened to Phoebe because of her association with him or his store.

The cowbell's clatter startled him, and he rubbed the spot on each temple where the throbbing refused to retreat.

"Are you unwell?" Phoebe asked.

"Aside from the pounding in my head that gets worse every time I think of someone profiting from the sale of poison to my miners, I'm quite fine."

She folded her charcoal cape and draped it over the stool he'd just vacated. "I don't know whether what I've learned will help or hurt." She reached for a slender tin on the shelf to her left and handed it to him. "But first let me offer you some willow bark tablets. They always help my headaches."

He pocketed the green container. "I'll take some as soon as you tell me what Mei-Mei had to say."

"She confirmed what Pastor Stone had already told us. Li Fong learned of the opium and told John about it. John assured Li Fong he would help uncover the source and rid the town of the problem. I'm certain Li Fong is no longer alive."

"I haven't learned anything about him, but I suspect you're right. They must have come too close for the guilty party's comfort. I'd like to know how they achieved the supposed accident."

"Explosives are used to break the rock and reach the ore."

"Was there an explosion?"

"Some of the miners say so. Others insist otherwise."

Adrian groaned and brought his thumbs back to his temples. "And someone is celebrating the disagreements and confusion." He reached a decision. "I've uncovered another matter that needs attention. When I compared the records in Mr. Hart's office to those Douglas Carlson kept for Mrs. Hart, I noticed that someone is overcharging the store for the merchandise we stock."

"Surely you don't mean to suggest that I've—"

"No, I don't." More tired than he remembered ever feeling, Adrian crammed his hat on his head. "If there's one thing I know for certain, Phoebe Williams, it's that you're as honest as the days are cold on this Colorado mountain."

He turned to leave, then glanced over his shoulder. The peach blush in her cheeks still enhanced the satin smoothness of her skin, and he wished . . .

He forced his wishes aside. "Someone has been taking advantage of the Widow Hart, of Douglas Carlson, of me, and of you. And I intend to put a stop to that, too."

"I hope you don't expect to try to keep me from doing everything I can to stop that kind of thievery. It reflects poorly on me and the job I do, sir, so I won't be put aside like some useless miss who hasn't an ounce of sense in her head."

Adrian chuckled. "Believe me, Phoebe, that's the last thing anyone would ever think of you." He shrugged. "If you want to try to find the thief, I won't stop you from helping. I don't think I could even if I tried."

Her sudden smile lit the entire store and brought him a surge of strength. "I'm so glad you now know me that well. It's always best to know one's partners, Adrian. Wouldn't you agree?"

"Partners?"

She nodded and a soft blond tendril slipped from the hairpin that had held it in the bun at her crown. It grazed the corner of her mouth, and she blew it away.

"Partners, Adrian. You and me. Together we'll get to the bottom of all the troubles plaguing the Heart of Silver Mining Company. Please remember that wherever two or more gather in His name, our God is there. With Him on our side, no evil will prevail."

Once again Phoebe's faith and wisdom rendered him speechless.

§

That steely determination of hers was going to get him in trouble sooner or later. Adrian slanted another look at the woman sitting beside him. The train ride into Rockton would take no more than an hour, but fighting the temptation of that tantalizing closeness wouldn't be the most challenging part of the trip. It would be even more difficult to learn something helpful about his troubles while at the same time ensuring that Phoebe didn't wind up as another casualty in his life.

Unlike any woman he'd known before, she didn't seem to need a steady stream of chatter. Although eloquent when she spoke, Phoebe appeared comfortable with herself, and she wore an air of serenity that Adrian envied. Had he ever known that kind of comfort? Of peace?

No. He'd never known a time when he'd been capable of that sort of extended silent contemplation. He wondered what she was thinking, but the soft curve of her lips and the smooth line of her brow didn't invite interference. Just to admire her was enough.

Adrian knew his feelings for Phoebe were dangerous. He cared about her. As complex and intriguing as she was, he suspected it would be all too easy to fall in love with her.

He couldn't. No matter how much he wished he could. No matter how much it hurt to ignore the joy in her face, as it had when he'd arrived at the store the day before. It would be wrong to let her care more deeply for him. It would be unconscionable to encourage her.

He couldn't entertain even the slightest shred of hope for them.

Once in Rockton, as they went about the business of tracking down the middlemen in the chain that brought supplies to Hartville, Adrian found himself more and more charmed by the woman at his side. Her conversation was clear and concise, and everyone they dealt with responded to her with respect and what appeared to be total honesty.

Phoebe inspired sincerity, and evidently, he was the only person who didn't respond in that vein. He hadn't lied to her, he just hadn't told her everything . . . he'd hardly told her anything that mattered.

And yet, she continued to smile, to treat him with her sweet kindness, her gentle determination. And he shamelessly enjoyed every moment in her delightful company.

"Tell me," he said, at the end of their dinner at the Excelsior Hotel's dining room. "How did you come to live with the Shakers?"

"My father fought for the Union during the War between the States. He died shortly before the end. My mother tried for eight long years to make ends meet. When influenza spread through town, she was too weak from too much work for her body to fight off the disease. She died after a brief bout, and a neighbor figured the Shakers would do well by me."

"It appears they did. You've turned out quite well."

The color rose in her cheeks. "Thank you for the compliment, although I'll point out that at times you've found me more contrary than you'd like."

"Your determination is impressive." He grinned. "But that doesn't really detract. It's just difficult to accept when you're fighting me."

A twinkle brightened her gaze. "When one is right, one must not be swayed. Even when one stands against the tide of the majority."

"I can see the Shakers had a great effect on you."

"If by that you mean that they taught me that a woman has as much right to her opinion as a man . . . well, then they did."

"I suppose they didn't mention that sometimes strong opinions can land a person in trouble."

"Only when they're the wrong ones."

"And you're saying mine are wrong?"

"Only when they go against mine."

He arched a brow. "Do you always get your way, Phoebe Williams?"

Sadness wiped the humor off her face. "Not at all. I wanted my mother to get well, and I prayed with everything I had in me. But I didn't get my way. And I wanted a family, a nice church to help John pastor, children, a little house . . . I didn't get that either."

I can give you those things—minus the pastorate.

The thought caught him off guard, as did the strength of his desire to give her the life she wanted. He wished he was like any other man, that he could tell her he was on the brink of falling in love with her, that he thought that little house and a handful of children sounded like heaven on earth. He wished he could put his arms around her and kiss the sadness away.

But he couldn't.

The best he could do was find out who was taking advantage of his mine's prosperity and his vulnerable Chinese workers and then ensure the future of the company that let her earn a living.

She spoke of the time she'd spent tending the exceptional Shaker gardens. Adrian's imagination drew a picture of her working on a smaller plot, a little boy with dirt on his cheek at her side.

When she recited the lyrics to a favorite Shaker hymn, he envisioned her in a rocking chair with an infant at her breast.

And as she described the brotherly love shared by the celibate members of the Shaker community, he knew that he wanted far more from her than that. He wanted her friendship, her company, her tenderness, and yes, he also wanted the passion he knew lived within her. A woman with such fire in her gaze would give a man everything he could ever want.

Adrian wanted everything she had to give.

He sighed and shook his head.

Phoebe continued her explanation of the enormous ovens with turning racks that baked the vast quantity of bread needed by a community as large as the one at North Union. Adrian sipped the last of his coffee and took a look outside the window. It was late, and they'd have to head for the train station before long.

Although they'd resolved nothing, it had been a day he'd never forget. He smiled at her, and just then a strange sensation overtook him. The skin on the back of his neck prickled, and an odd form of buzzing sounded in his ears.

He had the distinct impression of someone staring at him . . . at them.

Adrian could have cursed himself for ten thousand kinds of fool. But it would have served for nothing. Without a look behind, he caught Phoebe's hand as she sketched in the air the peculiar ovens the Shakers had invented.

"Our train will be leaving soon. If you're done with your tea, then I suggest we head for the station."

She smiled. "I drink more tea than I should. If you're ready, then I am, too. I'd like to be home again. I know Randy is quite capable, but I prefer to be right where I belong—behind the counter at the general store."

You belong in my arms.

The crazy thought hit Adrian so fast that he feared he'd spoken it aloud. But when Phoebe gathered her reticule and stood, he realized his secret was still safe. He stood, held his hand out to help her up, then offered her his arm.

Again that strange current crawled up the back of his neck. This time he allowed himself an expansive look around the room. In a voice meant to carry just far enough, he said, "Excellent establishment, don't you think?"

He hoped that whoever was watching—if someone really was—would read his perusal as that of a satisfied customer of the restaurant. Out of the corner of his eye, he caught a hint of quick movement, but when he slowly turned to smile in that direction, he saw nothing untoward, no one he recognized.

Still, the best plan of action was to leave. Hartville's location high in the mountains and its smaller number of residents offered greater protection than a town like Rockton or even a large city with a great deal of traffic.

Without alerting Phoebe to his anxiety, he made their return to the station a quick one.

"I do miss the Sisters," she finally said as they boarded their car. "And the children. Little ones are such a joy. Tell me, have you had the pleasure of their company?"

"No, I can't say that I have."

"Oh, then you must have been an only child."

"No, I—" He caught himself before revealing any more. How had she managed to slip within his carefully guarded boundaries? What was it about Phoebe that made him lose all sense of self-preservation in her presence?

"I don't have happy memories," he said. It was true enough. His most recent memories were of death and fear. "I prefer not to revisit the past."

She lowered her gaze. "I'm sorry, Adrian. I didn't mean to pry."

"I know you didn't. You're a very open person, and you have those lovely experiences with the Shakers to share. To someone like you, it would seem quite normal to invite a similar retelling. I . . . I just don't have much that merits telling."

"I see."

They fell silent. His refusal to talk about himself hung between them. That distance grew with every mile closer to town.

By the time they arrived at the general store, Adrian was desperate to leave her side. He'd hurt her, unintentionally, but he'd done it nonetheless. And his heart urged him to do what he'd wanted to since the moment they'd met. But he couldn't hold her, couldn't apologize or ask her forgiveness for his reluctance to let her any closer than she'd already come.

He couldn't even give her a gentle good-night kiss.

As they approached, they noticed a figure leaning against the door. The window revealed only darkness inside, and something about the way the man stood made Adrian uneasy.

"Is that you, Gamble?" Herman asked.

"Yes, it is. Is there a problem at the store?"

"No, not here." The lawman stepped onto the road and met them there. "But I do have bad news."

Adrian felt a chill to the marrow of his being. At his side Phoebe stiffened. "Let me have it then."

"It's about that Chinese woman you had working up to your house."

Phoebe moaned.

"Mei-Mei?" he asked.

133

"If that's her name."

At Adrian's nod, the sheriff took a last draw off the cigarette in his hand, then threw the burning butt into the middle of the road. "Pastor Stone stopped by your house somewheres about two hours ago. He found her dead."

A cry tore from Phoebe's throat, and she stumbled. Adrian reached for her and wrapped his arm around her waist, pulled her close to his side.

"The baby . . . ," she whispered.

"He's at the manse," Herman said. "He'll be fine with Mrs. Stone until we figure out what we're gonna do with him. First, though, you two'll have to come with me to my office. I've a mess of questions for you."

Adrian's knees threatened to give, but because Phoebe needed him, he made himself lock them tight. He hoped she could still count on him by the end of the night.

He also hoped the sheriff didn't ask the questions that would force him to lie.

10

As Phoebe followed the sheriff, the ground dropped out from under her. Blackness surrounded her, and pain constricted her chest. She couldn't see, couldn't draw breath, couldn't stand.

She fell into an endless abyss and spun dizzily through the murky vastness, a deafening roar in her ears. At long lengths, her body caught on something solid. Her disorientation continued, yet she somehow knew the chaos was better than regaining her balance. During her descent through emptiness, she heard . . . something, perhaps voices, but she didn't recognize a word they said. Or even who spoke.

Finally, after what seemed longer than a lifetime, her senses returned, and she drew shaky breaths. The pain in her chest eased enough for her to consider opening her eyes, and when she tried, she caught a glimpse of lamplight.

The voices grew clearer, and they now sounded familiar, even though she still couldn't make out the words. She concentrated on her eyes and with great effort pried them open.

Adrian's dear face came into focus only a whisper away from hers. She tried to say his name, but her throat remained constricted, her mouth dry. Bands around her tightened, and she saw that Adrian held her in his embrace.

"Don't," he whispered. "Don't try to talk. You fainted, and you need time to recover."

So that was what fainting felt like. She'd never given it much thought, but now that she'd experienced it, she didn't want to do it ever again. She blinked and shook her head but found that the dizziness returned when she did so. She tried to swallow hard to ease the tightness. That worked a bit better.

"Water . . . please."

A cup touched her lips. The cool liquid eased into her parched mouth, slowly, drop by drop. She swallowed, glad that this time it didn't require as much effort.

As she drank she felt herself regain a measure of control. Her head stopped spinning, her breathing deepened and became natural again, and she realized she lay sprawled across Adrian's lap.

She struggled to rise from the embarrassing position, but he held on tight.

"We'll get you to bed," Letty said. "You shouldn't try to sit up yet. You've had a severe shock and might faint again."

Everything came rushing back. The pain again gripped her chest, but this time she held her own. She whispered, "Mei-Mei."

"I'm so sorry," Letty said. "I know how you'd come to like her. It's a dreadful tragedy for such a young, lovely girl to die that way."

"How did she die?"

"Not now," Adrian murmured at her temple. "Right now you need to lie down and rest."

"Nay. I need to know what happened to her." With her last ounce of strength, Phoebe sat up and made herself ignore the scandalous nature of her seating. "I must know now."

"She was killed," Herman said. "Someone stabbed her to death."

Again Phoebe's senses reeled, but this time she exerted uncommon control over them. Adrian's arm offered a brace at her back, his chest supported her side. She would not give in to the pain and grief. Deep in her heart she now knew that John had been killed, not by an accidental mine cave-in, but rather by a killer who had just struck again. She also knew she had to learn who was to blame. She couldn't surrender to the natural grief that threatened to steal her resolve. Not now. Perhaps later, after she uncovered everything that had transpired in June as well as today.

"Where was she?" she asked.

"At home," the sheriff said. "In the kitchen, cleaning by the looks of it."

Adrian drew in a deep breath. "You may as well tell us everything. She's not likely to rest until she extracts the last detail of the tragedy from you."

She knew how hard that had been for him. Adrian's kind nature always sought to protect and comfort. Nothing the lawman could tell her would do either.

"Thank you," she said.

The wry twist of Adrian's smile and the warmth in his eyes spoke volumes. "I did it because I want you to rest, and this is the quickest way to get you to do so."

She placed a hand on his chest. "You are coming to know me, aren't you?"

"Oh yes," he said. "I know you quite well by now."

His widening smile did more to restore her strength than days of sleep ever could.

"Go ahead," he urged the sheriff.

The man slapped his hat against his thigh and grimaced. "Well, it's like this. Girl was stabbed in the back, somewheres about seven or eight times. I don't think she even knew she wasn't alone no more." He shook his head. "Awful thing to do to a pretty little thing like that. And that baby boy . . ."

"Where's Lee?" Phoebe asked.

Letty looked at her. "Lee?"

"Mei-Mei's baby."

"Oh, so she did name him."

Phoebe nodded.

"He's with Adele Stone. She'll take good care of him. You needn't worry about—"

"I have to go to him," Phoebe said, and this time when she pushed against Adrian, he let her go. She gave him a look filled with all her gratitude, but his glare said he'd acquiesced only because he recognized the futility of further argument. He'd still rather she took to her bed.

Phoebe wrapped herself in dignity. "I may have fainted momentarily, but I'm no wilting lily. I have a promise to keep to Mei-Mei, and a wave of lightheadedness is not about to prevent me from doing so."

Adrian sighed. "Neither am I. Just don't fight me. I'm coming with you."

"Certainly." She drew her cape tighter around her. "I'll be glad for your company."

"Wait!" Herman called. "I've a passel of questions for you."

"Nay, sir," Phoebe said. "You'll have to wait. The baby comes first. I'll be glad to meet with you at your office in the morning once I've kept my word to my dead friend."

To her surprise, the lawman stepped back as she walked past him, and his slow-to-bloom smile and polite nod revealed a grudging admiration. Satisfaction filled her. Despite the horrid circumstances, she'd gained from the two men a very precious gift tonight. Respect was a hard-won treasure, one she guarded with care.

Adrian took hold of her elbow, and she smiled her thanks for his support.

"It appears," he said, "as though the Widow Williams has again found reason to state her position and hold her ground in Shaker fashion."

"Nay, Adrian, my resolve has nothing to do with my Shaker

upbringing. That young girl is no longer. The woman who has taken her place has a mission, one that means a great deal."

His pace slowed and he came to a stop. Phoebe did likewise and felt the warmth of his sustained scrutiny. She wondered what kind of thoughts had brought that longing into his eyes.

Adrian's gaze stayed fixed on Phoebe, her words an echo of thoughts he had entertained a million times. He wondered, for the shortest fragment of time, if perhaps she might understand his plight.

But the events of the night gave him no opportunity to consider the thought.

An hour later, they were on their way back to the store, the baby in Phoebe's arms swaddled against the icy wind that had blown in. Myriad thoughts swarmed in Adrian's head, making it impossible to sustain a coherent conversation. Fortunately, it was Phoebe at his side. Despite the tragic news, she retained her cloak of serenity. It seemed to him as visible as the dark woolen cloak she wore.

Little Lee was a fortunate child. Phoebe had left the Stones no alternative but to let her take the boy. She'd promised Mei-Mei she'd care for the two of them, and now with the mother gone, she insisted that no power on earth would persuade her to betray her word. As Mei-Mei's employer, Adrian supposed he had as good a call as anyone to decide the fate of the orphan. But one look at Phoebe's big, beseeching eyes had robbed him of the will to say no.

He was, no doubt, a fool for going along with her insistence, but he'd come to accept that sometimes life's choices were all of the bad kind. It was doing his best once he'd made a choice that let him live with his conscience.

"I'll enter Lee's name in the company ledger and add Mei-Mei's wages to yours." When she opened her mouth to object, he cut her off. "This time, I won't let your beautiful eyes or your sweet smile sway me. This is the right thing to do. Mei-Mei was killed in my house while in my employ, and I have certain responsibilities toward her child."

Her rueful smile touched something deep inside him.

"I don't know whether to thank you for those compliments or argue against your charitable donation. But in view of baby Lee's prospects, I'll go against my better judgment and not comment one way or the other."

Adrian chuckled. "You're a strong woman, Mrs. Williams."

"And you're a true gentleman, Mr. Gamble."

They finished their walk in silence, and once outside the store, they faced one another. Adrian suspected Phoebe had something to say, but oddly enough, she held her tongue. He, too, had things to say, many deep, private thoughts he wanted to share. But he couldn't, he didn't dare. Instead, he removed his glove and permitted himself another touch of her satiny skin.

Beneath the chill coolness imparted by the cold night, Phoebe's cheek was warm, soft, and firm. As he stared into her blue eyes, he recognized the depth of her capacity to care, that exceptional warmth in her nature that pulled at him. Her gentle soul offered the kind of comfort a man craved for those difficult moments in life, and he longed to avail himself of that soothing care. Yet one could also measure her inner strength during a brief conversation, by a glimpse into her thoughts, by how she lived her life.

Phoebe Williams was a woman of conviction, and her Christian faith supported her action.

With every moment that passed, Adrian came closer to a precipice. He feared he was no longer falling in love with her. He suspected he'd toppled over shortly after they'd met. All that remained was to admit the fact to himself—the point of no return.

"Will you two be all right?" he asked.

"Of course."

"If you need anything, please let me know."

"I will."

Need. Now there was a word. He smoothed the tip of his finger across the line of her jaw, along the curve of her chin, into the well beneath her lips. He remembered the time when he'd covered her rosy mouth with that same finger. He did so again, only this time he didn't have to halt her words. This time, he caressed the smile that blossomed under his touch.

Her warmth and sweetness seeped into him. *Dear God, are you showing me all I threw away when I acted on impulse? I never chose to kill. I only stepped forward to prevent another wrong.*

In the silence after his prayer, Adrian felt bereft . . . until he again noted the tender softness of Phoebe's lips.

Before he could stop himself, he curved his finger and captured her chin and tilted it just so. He brought his mouth to hers and kissed her, wanting to drown in the sweetness of her caress. He wondered if a lifetime of Phoebe's kisses could fill the emptiness inside.

As the kiss grew more passionate, he fought for control. He couldn't cross that boundary, so he released her lips. He pulled away, and despite the darkness of the night, he saw wonder and joy in her eyes. What had he done?

He'd kissed the woman he loved, that's what he'd done. And to his regret, it was the most cruel thing he could have done. He had to leave her side, not just for the night, but forever. He had no right to expose her to the danger he faced. Especially not now, not after recognizing how deep his feelings for her ran. Not now that he knew he'd always love the Widow Williams.

He'd love her to the day he died.

Through the window in the store, Phoebe watched Adrian walk away. The night's shadows seemed to shift and weave, but his stride carried him forward with purpose.

As he'd kissed her, he became the single concrete thing in her universe. Her world tilted in those moments and threw her off kilter, not unlike when she fainted. But instead of the oblivion she experienced when she felt unwell, Adrian's kiss had made her feel more alive than ever before. He'd kissed her gently at first, with a tenderness that brought tears of joy to her eyes.

Then the kiss had changed. It had sparked with a new, unfamiliar passion. It didn't surprise her to recognize the richness of her feelings for Adrian. After all, he was as unique and distinct an individual as she'd ever met. But the heated desire that had struck her left her stunned and even a bit afraid.

As Adrian walked out of her sight, she turned and went to her apartment. She pulled out the bureau drawer that baby Lee used for a bed during the days he and Mei-Mei spent with her. With one hand she made a nest of toweling in it. She kissed his smooth ivory cheek and laid him down. A surge of fierce protectiveness rose inside her.

"I won't let anything happen to you," she whispered. "I promised your mother that, and I'll keep my promise." She prayed the Lord would help her keep that promise in this flawed and sinful world.

Phoebe lit the lamp and picked up her Bible. She went to the Shaker rocker Eldress Clymena had given her just before she left North Union and opened God's Word.

She'd loved John with her whole heart, and she'd grieved his loss. But she'd never known the urgent desire Adrian had awakened tonight.

Was it wrong? They weren't married, and they'd only shared a kiss.

Memories of Shaker teachings barraged her. Mother Ann's followers believed that sensual pleasure in the Garden of Eden had caused man's original sin, and it lay at the root of all evil. Since Jesus remained unwed during His earthly ministry, and since a Christian was to emulate Him in everything, then it followed that the celibate life was essential to purity and holiness, in their view. Scripture did call those who received the gospel of

142

salvation to take up the cross and deny their flesh in every way, and Mother Ann included marriage in that denial. Only then could believers take their place in the kingdom of God.

But Phoebe had never believed that God called everyone to such abstinence. In the book of Genesis, God Himself told His children to go forth and multiply. How else was His creation to continue? Where would the children the Shakers took in to augment their number come from if no one conceived? And the New Testament offered guidance for a good marriage.

But now, in the face of the strength of her desire, Phoebe wondered if there wasn't some truth in Shaker teaching. Yea, she'd known she had feelings for Adrian from almost the first time they met. And tonight when respect and admiration had filled his gaze, she'd known she was falling in love with him. The desire, however, had nearly stolen her sense of propriety. How could that possibly be right? Hadn't she been married and experienced physical love between man and wife?

Father, grant me wisdom. She chuckled. *I've been asking for that gift quite a bit of late, haven't I? Well, Lord, I can't say I feel one whit wiser than the first time I asked. Keep me from stumbling. Help me to be the woman You want me to be. I want to honor You in everything I do, and I couldn't bear the thought of bringing shame to either John's memory or to You. Help me to know Your ways more intimately each day.*

Somewhat comforted after praying, Phoebe found the chapter where she'd left off the night before and continued her trip through the Scriptures before turning in for the night.

"Dearest girl," Emmaline called out the next day. "You'll never believe what I saw last night."

Naomi's smug smile matched Emmaline's superior expression. "Well, Emmaline, *you'll* never believe what *I* saw last night."

Ruthie approached the others at the corner of Main Street and

Willow Lane, just outside the Silver Creek Church. "What have you two been up to that you've been seeing so much?"

"You first, Emmaline," Naomi suggested.

"I wouldn't dream of it. You go first."

Naomi needed no further urging. "I went yesterday to post a letter to my brother Eldon in Kansas City, and I ran late. I hurried to the train station, hoping to get it into the mail bag for the last train, and you'll never believe who I saw getting off!"

"Who?"

"Who?"

Naomi licked her lips while her two friends nearly tripped over themselves with curiosity. "Mrs. Perfect Pastor's Wife Phoebe Williams was clinging to our debauched mine owner's arm, the two of them looking cozy as could be."

Ruthie gasped. "You don't say? Why, I thought he'd brought his Chinese mistress and their child here to live in sin with him."

"Well," Naomi said, "you know some men aren't satisfied with just one."

Emmaline turned a putrid shade of puce. "That's disgusting."

Ruthie echoed, "Disgusting."

Naomi then asked, "And what do you have to share?"

Emmaline jerked her head toward the west end of town. "That just proves what I saw with my very own two eyes."

"What?"

"What did you see?"

"I saw the two of them engaging in physical improprieties right on the boardwalk outside the store."

Naomi's eyes glittered. "You don't say!"

"On the boardwalk?" Ruthie asked. "Wouldn't that be frightfully public?"

Emmaline nodded. "Indeed it was. Glued to each other like leather to the cover of a book, I tell you."

"So . . . ," Ruthie said. "It was the storekeeper and not the housekeeper, then?"

"No, no, no, silly," Naomi chided. "Surely it's both."

"Indeed," Emmaline concurred.

Naomi squared her shoulders. "I say we go see about the blond Jezebel straight away. I've never known that kind of woman before."

"And her playing at prim and proper." Emmaline snorted. "A preacher's widow and all, if you'll remember. That poor Pastor John must be spinning in his grave."

The three women made their way down Main Street.

"I wonder what she'd say if someone demanded she confess," Emmaline mused.

Naomi gasped. "Surely you wouldn't ask her straight out, now, would you?"

Emmaline gave the question due consideration. "It would depend on the circumstances."

"Just make sure I'm there when you do it," Ruthie pleaded.

Naomi concurred.

"Oh, don't fret, dears," Emmaline said. "I wouldn't dream of seeking a confession in secret. When a person in the church transgresses, she does so against the whole congregation. It's only fitting for the membership to witness the confession."

Ruthie's eyes glittered. "Oh . . . that should be . . . interesting."

Across the street from the general store, Naomi fixed her gaze on its half-glass door. "Shall we go see what that loose woman is doing this time of day?"

Phoebe counted out Mr. Wharton's change. The elderly postmaster fancied licorice candies, and he shopped for them every Wednesday morning, just before the first train was due to arrive in town.

She handed him the parcel of sweets. "There you are, sir."

He switched his bowler from his right to his left hand so he could take the small bundle. "Much obliged, Mrs. Williams. I'm mighty fond of my goodies."

"A treat now and then never hurt anyone," she said, smiling.

"That's the idea." He tapped his bowler against his forehead and went outside.

Since the store had no other customers at the moment, Phoebe took the time to lift Lee from his bureau-drawer bed. The little one was awake. She swayed side to side and rubbed his downy head. The knot again formed at her throat, but she swallowed hard. She wouldn't cry. She couldn't.

She had a child to raise, a store to run, questions to answer, a killer to find. Tears wouldn't serve any purpose. She needed to find that core of peace she'd learned came only from trusting God for everything.

He would see her through.

A new diaper was in order, and she hurried to her apartment, leaving the hall door open so she could hear if anyone entered the store. She chatted at Lee, and her heart swelled with love when he focused on her face. He then drank from the bottle Mrs. Stone had given her and fell asleep again as soon as he finished.

Phoebe returned to the store and tucked him back into his bed. A little later the cowbell announced the arrival of customers.

A small flock of ladies entered the store and gathered around the display of linen handkerchiefs. Although Phoebe hated to intrude in their discussion, as the storekeeper, she felt bound to at least offer to help.

"Do you ladies have questions about the hankies? The linen and lace come from Ireland. Very pretty, don't you think?"

The three women started, gave her odd looks, then exchanged glances among themselves.

"They're fine," Bettie Fitch said, then lowered her gaze.

Phoebe studied her customers for another minute, shrugged, and returned to her stool behind the counter. They'd decide on their own. Purchases were often made regardless of her efforts.

She peeked at Lee and took note of the satisfied slumber of a healthy child. She resumed her perusal of the dry goods catalog she'd been studying before Mr. Wharton's arrival.

The cowbell jangled again. Emmaline, Naomi, and Ruthie walked in. Phoebe called out a polite greeting.

Ruthie gaped.

Emmaline blinked.

Naomi looked at one and then the other of her companions, then replied with a weak "hello."

"May I help you find something?" she asked.

Emmaline's snort gave her all the answer she needed.

"Let me know if I can be of service," she said, then returned to her catalog.

Soon Phoebe heard footsteps, and she reckoned the women would help themselves to whatever they'd come to buy.

Shortly, however, the bell rang yet again. This time Dahlia made her entrance, a vision in emerald trimmed in black velvet ribbon.

Bettie Fitch called Dahlia's name before Phoebe could offer assistance. Then she heard the hum of quiet chatter and the occasional beat of heels against the floorboards.

Eventually, she realized that an unusual length of time had transpired and no one had come to the counter to purchase a single thing. She looked up and, to her surprise, found all the women in a cluster, heads close together.

What could they be discussing so avidly?

Phoebe decided the time had come to see if she could help or perhaps hasten their departure. Their strange behavior had begun to bother her. With a glance, she saw that Lee continued to sleep.

Since the women were close to the large rolls of grosgrain ribbon, she approached and said, "Would you like me to cut sample pieces of a selection of our best ribbons? That way you can take them home with you and match them to your costumes."

Dahlia Sutton pulled away. She gave Phoebe a look rife with contempt. "I do declare, Widow Williams, I wouldn't buy a thing you'd touched if it was the last bite of food on earth and I was plumb starving to death."

With a toss of her luxuriant curls, she marched straight down the aisle of the store, the rest of the women close behind. Emmaline brought up the rear. As she held the door open for her friends, she shot Phoebe a censorious glare.

"Disgusting," she declared and then left with the others.

Although she told herself their comments shouldn't matter, Phoebe couldn't deny the hurt they caused. What had she done? Had she offended one of them?

Baby Lee chose that moment to wake up. Phoebe gathered him close to her breast and blinked away the tears. She lived a quiet, private life. She rarely had contact with folks outside of the store or church. How could they find enough to hate about her to make them spit so much venom?

11

When the opening door made the cowbell sound about an hour later, Phoebe froze. She wondered if she'd ever again hear the bell without dread overcoming her. To her relief, Randy marched into the store in search of a new kitchen pan. Her warm embrace soothed Phoebe's feelings somewhat.

After a bit of pleasant chatter, Phoebe scrambled up her trusty ladder and held out the best saucepan the store carried.

"It's a solid one," she said on her way back down. "I doubt you'll ever need a tinker or the smithy to repair it."

"I'm sure you're right." Randy tested the heft of the pan. "You are indeed an excellent saleswoman, knowing as much as you do about everything you stock. This pan is perfect. I can always trust your judgment."

Phoebe tore off a length of sturdy brown paper and wrapped the pan. With a wry smile, she commented, "Not all my customers feel the same."

"Well, then they're fools."

Phoebe laughed. With Randy, there was little equivocation. "Oh, I don't know about that. Customers can sometimes be . . . oh, I don't know . . . *vexing*, is perhaps the word."

"Considering some of the 'fine' folks we have in town, I'm

not surprised you've come across some of the odder ones here and there."

Phoebe hated bearing tales, but she felt she had no other choice. "I don't know that I feel quite right about bringing this up, and if you think I'm indulging in gossip, please let me know. I'll keep any such further thoughts to myself."

"You're the least likely person to waste time on tittle-tattle. If you've something on your mind, then I suspect it's legitimate."

"We'll see." Phoebe took a deep breath. "Dahlia, Emmaline, Naomi, and a few others were in the store earlier today. They looked at the hankies and then at spools of ribbons, but after at least a half hour of nattering to each other, none of them had bought a thing. I even offered them samples of ribbon so they could match them at home, but all I got in return was the rudest response I've ever heard from Dahlia."

Randy planted her fists on her hips, the pan jutting out behind her. "And now you're fretting about the feather-brained blither that girl spouted?"

At Phoebe's nod, she went on.

"Why, Phoebe Williams, I thought you were far more sensible than that."

"So did I, Randy. It's just that she said . . ." Phoebe thought, trying to remember Dahlia's exact words. "She said she wouldn't buy a thing I'd touched if it was the last food on earth and she was famished."

"See?" Randy jabbed the pan in the air. "I told you not to pay any mind to what she had to say. That's the most absurd thing I've heard from her, and that's saying a great deal."

"She wasn't alone, you know. They all looked at me as though . . . I don't know, as though I were tainted with some foul disease." She closed her eyes to better recall the women's faces. "Oh, yea. How could I forget? Before she walked out, Emmaline called me disgusting."

"Why, those mean-spirited biddies! I've no idea why they

treated you that way, and I don't truly care. They're the ones who disgust me, what with all their hissing and gossip and nasty ways. Don't you waste another minute fretting over them. You have a lot of friends here in town, Phoebe, and you'd best not forget that."

"Thank you for your kindness," Phoebe said, clasping the redhead's hand. "I'll try to remember your words the next time their insults come to mind."

"You do that, and you'll be right as rain." With a tug to the front of her forest-green wool wrap, Randy added, "I must be on my way now. I left Emma Letitia at the manse with Mim while I ran this errand, but I suspect the dear girl has better things to do than to watch my daughter fuss over her sore gums."

Randy marched off, her anger still evident in the set of her shoulders, the carriage of her head, and the pan-punctuated mutters that wafted back to Phoebe. After the door banged shut, the store remained quiet for a while. Phoebe chose to spend the time cuddling little Lee. After she changed his diaper, he spent a spell batting his tiny fists in the air.

Phoebe held him tight to her heart, breathing that soft, sweet scent unique to infants, succumbing to the rich emotions he brought forth in her. During the few hours she'd spent with him, she'd come to recognize him as the tiniest thief of hearts. As helpless as he was, he still watched her with those dark, dark eyes full of trust and found comfort in her arms.

She'd wept for endless days after John's death, grieving his loss, grieving the death of her dreams of motherhood. Her heart had broken, and the pain had left her helpless for weeks. But then her common sense had taken up the reins again. She lived, even though her husband and their dreams didn't. Still, she'd feared she'd go mad each time someone said she was young, that she could remarry, that she should look beyond the immediacy of her loss.

Having someone tell her to look toward the future had done

nothing to hasten her recovery. Little by little, in her own way, she'd come back, the heartbreak taking its time to ebb. She'd had to wait out the lifetime of her most acute pain with patience. Through the devastating process, God had upheld her, and then He'd led her into His precious peace once again.

Now the Lord had taken yet another roundabout way to answer her prayer. He seemed to have provided her with a child. If Li Fong had died, as she and Adrian grew more certain was the case each day, she would see Douglas Carlson and make this little angel hers in the eyes of the law. Love had already done so in her eyes.

Shortly after Lee fell asleep again, Mrs. Stone came in search of a large box of washing soda and some bars of Fels-Naptha soap. Phoebe marshalled her gumption and asked the pastor's wife if she knew of any occasion when she might have transgressed against any of the other women. Like Randy, Mrs. Stone had no idea what might have caused the wretched exchange.

"I can't think of a body who holds you in anything but high esteem, respect, and a great deal of fondness," she said. She bent down to stroke Lee's cheek with her plump finger. "Why, look. In spite of all you've been through, you've even taken on the care of this poor little mite."

Phoebe blushed. "I don't think one thing has anything to do with the other."

"But of course it does," the pastor's wife said, straightening. "You've the kindest heart and the gentlest soul of anyone I know. What happened earlier today must have been yet another of Dahlia's tantrums. The girl is given to such fits, and I find that a most unfortunate trait in a woman."

Somewhat comforted, Phoebe waved farewell as Mrs. Stone left the store. She then returned to her catalog but found she could no longer concentrate. Love hummed in her heart, and she watched the even rise and fall of Lee's chest. Mei-Mei's death had dealt her another hard blow. Friendship had begun to bloom between the two widows.

She'd loved to watch the young woman with Lee. Mei-Mei had been so proud of her little boy, and now she'd never see him grow into a good, strong man. The tears began to flow, and she did nothing to stop them.

Phoebe had known a mother's love only during her first ten years. Then she knew abandonment. The Shakers took good and gentle care of her for the following ten years, but their efforts never fully erased the fear Phoebe had felt the day she watched the neighbor who brought her to North Union leave her behind.

Despite the Sisters' efforts to persuade her that the love of the Brothers and Sisters in the North Union family was far better, more blessed, than the worldly love of man and wife, of even parent and child, Phoebe had yearned for someone of her very own. She'd found that someone in John Williams, and he in turn gave her hope for a family of her own.

Then the mine accident took him away, leaving her more alone and bereft than even the day of her arrival at the Shaker dwelling house. God had given her friends in town, but that secret corner of her heart yearned once again. And now, because of the vicious act of a God-forsaking sinner, she'd become a mother. Bittersweet feelings tugged on her heart at the thought.

Her tears flowed, tears for John, for Mei-Mei, for Lee, and for the lonely child she'd been. Phoebe knew she'd have to pull herself to rights soon enough. She had hours before she could close the store, and then she was to meet Sheriff Herman at his office and submit to his questions. Even more difficult, she figured, would be her trip to the Hart mansion. She had to retrieve Lee's meager belongings and whatever of Mei-Mei's she could put away for when he grew up. Despite the pain she knew awaited her, she wanted to see to this matter herself. It was the last thing she could do for her late friend.

That, and to ensure that Lee never lacked a mother's love.

Later, after she'd dried her tears and tended to Lee, Phoebe welcomed the stove regulars at their usual five minutes past four.

Right behind them Letty bustled in, a frown on her otherwise smooth forehead.

"I have to speak with you," she said. "But it must be in private."

Apprehension knotted Phoebe's middle. She scooped up the baby and led Letty through the back door and into the hallway. "What is it?"

Letty wrung her hands. "I don't know how else to say this. I guess I'll have to just spit it out . . . Perfectly horrid rumors are blazing through town about you." She closed her eyes and moved her lips in obvious prayer.

Phoebe also sent up a hasty plea for courage and strength. No matter how dreadful it might be, at least she'd know why Dahlia and Emmaline had made those awful remarks.

"What are they saying, Letty? Please, it's best I know."

Her friend squared her shoulders and tipped her head in that birdlike way she had.

"They say that you and Adrian were seen in a . . . compromising position last night. The gossips have run wild with the tales."

Before Letty spoke again, Phoebe knew just what she was about to say.

"Oh, Phoebe, it's horrid. They insist baby Lee is Adrian's son by Mei-Mei. They say he's been alternating between your bed and hers."

Dear Lord Jesus, help! It was far worse than she'd thought.

"That's not true. None of it."

"Of course it's not. I didn't consider it for a second. But as bad as that is, it isn't all they're saying."

"Isn't that more than plenty? Have they really concocted more wild tales?"

"I'm afraid so," Letty said. "It's much, much worse. They're saying that Adrian had tired of Mei-Mei, and to make things simpler with you . . . he . . ." Letty seemed to struggle for words, then, in a mad rush, they tumbled right out. "They say he killed her, Phoebe, and then took the train out of town to keep a tryst with you."

☙

For the first time since she'd gone to work for the Heart of Silver Mining Company, Phoebe shooed the stove regulars out well before her normal closing time.

"It won't hurt them the least bit to go home and have an early supper for a change," Letty said. "We must speak with Pastor and Mrs. Stone. The spreading blight of gossip has greatly distressed them, and at a time like this you need the company of folks who wouldn't dream of questioning your integrity."

"But Adrian hasn't . . ." She knew in her heart he hadn't killed Mei-Mei. "That's a serious accusation—much worse than just idle gossip. I'm sure it will have a dreadful effect. They're accusing him of murder, Letty. And he had nothing to do with Mei-Mei's death."

"I don't know the man well, but I tend to agree with you."

Holding Lee tighter under her cape, Phoebe locked the store, then smiled at her friend.

"Thank you for your trust. It means a great deal to me. Especially right now."

"Oh, I've fought my bouts with Hartville's gossipmongers myself." Letty shook her head. "They're nothing if not vicious."

Both women fell silent as they hurried to the manse in the chill of the afternoon winds. Once there, Letty didn't bother to knock but went right inside. The small vestibule was vacant, but voices echoed from deep inside the house.

As they headed for the kitchen, they heard Emmaline's nasal gripe. "You simply must do something about this scandalous situation. You can't turn a blind eye to her loose behavior with that . . . that lascivious killer."

Phoebe cringed. Letty held out her hand, indicating they

should stay silent. Silent? She wanted to run, return to the store, maybe even leave town.

"You have nothing more than gossip to support your opinion, Miss Whitehall," Pastor Stone said.

"I most certainly have more. I saw them groping and writhing on the boardwalk outside the store."

Phoebe gasped. How could anyone distort something so beautiful, so tender? Hot tears scalded her cheeks.

"Now, Emmaline," Mrs. Stone said, "I doubt you're portraying what you saw in a truthful way. Why would you misrepresent a simple embrace?"

"Simple?" Emmaline said at a piercing pitch. "I'll have you know, Mrs. Stone, there is nothing simple about a man who keeps two women at one time."

A chair scraped against the floor. "As your pastor, Emmaline Whitehall, I must admonish you against your attempt to sully the reputation of not one, nor even two, but three people who aren't present and can't defend themselves."

"All you'll get if you ask them is a passel of lies. You don't need to do that, you can trust what I saw with my own eyes."

"What you *think* you saw," Mrs. Stone corrected.

"If you don't believe me, ask Noami Miller. She saw them get off the last train from Rockton just a short while before they . . . before I saw them . . . I saw them—oh, *you* know."

"No, Emmaline," the pastor said, "I don't know. And neither do you. If you want a true picture of what happened last night, you need to speak with either Mrs. Williams or Mr. Gamble. Have you done that yet?"

"Why would I bother to associate with the likes of them?"

"Very well," Pastor Stone said. "I'll take note of all the pertinent details you've given me, and meet with the two in question to verify what you saw. You wouldn't want to speak falsehoods, now would you?"

"Oh. Well, surely you don't want to go to all that trouble.

All you need to do is bring that floozy before the elders. They'll bring her to account, I'm sure. You don't want someone with a cloud over her head leading our worship from the front row of the choir."

Letty took a step forward, but Phoebe held her back.

"That'll be quite enough, Emmaline," Mrs. Stone said. "I'd rather you leave my home before I say something I might regret. Until the day Mrs. Williams arrives at the decision to leave the choir on her own, she remains right where she is. I'm its director, if you'll remember."

"Do pray about your attitude," the pastor urged. "God doesn't look kindly upon those who bear false witness."

Emmaline's sharp footsteps signaled her advance toward the front of the house. "You'll see I'm not telling falsehoods at all." She stopped. "Why, I'm sure our sheriff is on the verge of arresting that debauched man for the murder of one of his two concubines."

Her footsteps resumed, nearly drowning the Stones' horrified protests. Neither Phoebe nor Letty moved.

"You'll see," she repeated. "You'll soon have to bring . . . *Mrs. Williams* before the congregation on account of her sins. Besides, just look at how she's taken her rival's child—even though he's one of that kind. Who knows? Maybe she even helped her lover do in the other woman to keep the man and child herself."

Bitter tears drenched Phoebe's cheeks. How could anyone invent such foul lies? "Lord Jesus," she cried. "What have I done to bring this kind of shame on myself?"

Letty grasped her by the shoulders. "Don't entertain the thought. You haven't done a thing. That woman has a serious problem, and if nothing else, a trainload of sins to confess. Why, she can start by seeking forgiveness for her gossip and finish up with an apology for her slander."

Emmaline chose that moment to stalk into the parlor. She whirled and glared at the Stones. "Well. No wonder you defend this Jezebel. You're harboring her here in the manse. And you call yourself a man of the cloth. We'll see what the elders have to say about this."

Emmaline slammed the door. Silence filled the room. Phoebe exhaled hard to try to break the knot in her chest.

"I'm so very sorry I've caused you such awful trouble," she said. "And please accept my resignation from the choir. I can't—"

"No."

"You mustn't let my troubles harm the church—"

"My dear, the church is your home," Pastor Stone said. "You mustn't let a woman so deluded by her own imaginings run you out. Especially since I can't give her tales the slightest validity."

"Exactly," Letty added. "If you turn tail and run, she and her friends will insist you're guilty of their absurd accusations."

Mrs. Stone laid a comforting arm around Phoebe's shoulders. "Come, dear. Let's go into the kitchen. We can discuss all of this over a cup of tea."

Phoebe continued to weep, her arms cradling Lee. "I can't do this to you, to the church, or even to this poor little boy."

"Bosh!" Mrs. Stone shook her head and led Phoebe to a chair. "Listen to me, dear. If you whimper away, those women will think they can do this with impunity. They'll do it again and again any time they take a notion to entertain themselves with gossip and falsehoods."

Phoebe sobbed. "But John . . . I've tarnished his memory."

"Of course you haven't." Letty took the baby from her arms. "Hold your head up, Phoebe. You haven't hurt anyone, and you've just taken in a motherless child. I seem to recall the Good Book calling us to care for widows and orphans. What kind of care are they offering you? And Lee?"

Her thoughts spun, and Phoebe no longer felt sure of anything. "I . . . I guess I have to think all of this through. And pray. I need to spend a great deal of time on my knees. I'd best go—"

"Are you sure you should be alone?" Letty asked.

Phoebe stood, her decision made. "I'll be fine. I'll trust the Lord to see me through even this. I don't know how, but I know He will." She held out her arms. "Here. I'll take Lee home. I'm sure he'll be hungry soon."

Letty planted a soft kiss on the baby's forehead and gave him to Phoebe. "I'll stop by in the morning."

"There's no need. I'll be fine."

Letty folded her arms over her chest. "Let your doctor be the judge of that."

Cheered by Letty's determination, Phoebe left and hurried back to the store. A familiar figure paced the boardwalk outside the store, and Phoebe's mortification grew with every step closer. For a moment, she hovered between running away and running around to the rear.

"There you are," Adrian said.

She couldn't avoid him now.

Did he know? Had he heard?

"Ye-es," she said.

He dragged his hat off and ran his gloved fingers through his dark hair. "I couldn't stay in that house another minute. All I could think about was someone killing that poor girl right there."

Phoebe kept her gaze on the floor as she crossed to the door and went inside. "I understand."

"Besides," he continued, evidently oblivious to her distress, "I couldn't rest a moment knowing you and the little one were here, unprotected."

She walked to the door to the back hallway, her back to him all the time. "That's very kind, but we're fine."

"No, you don't understand. I'm convinced Mei-Mei's presence here in Hartville scared someone. They must have felt they had to . . . to kill her."

In the hallway she turned right and stepped to the apartment door. "Here, hold Lee. I need to light the lamp."

She hurried to the table where she ate her meals, struck a match, and touched it to the wick. A golden glow filled the room.

"He most likely needs a fresh diaper," she murmured. To avoid Adrian's blue gaze, she retrieved the infant and crossed to her bed.

He drew a rough breath and, as she folded the fresh diaper, he continued. "Please listen to me. Don't try to turn to some other, simpler subject. Mei-Mei came to find her husband, the man who asked your John to help him stop the sale of opium to the miners."

"That's so. But it has nothing to do with the baby and me."

"Of course it does," he said. "You took her in. Now you have her child. If they're so worried that they . . . they . . . well, you know, I'm afraid they won't bother to see what you do know. Mei-Mei certainly didn't know anything and now she's dead."

Phoebe's heart leaped into her throat. She turned to face him. "Are you saying that they'll want me next?"

He grasped her shoulders, the baby between them. "I can't bear the thought of any harm coming to you. And whoever's behind this wants to keep his business going."

Phoebe's knees weakened. She stumbled back into a chair. "I can't argue against your logic. I'm convinced that Li Fong died in that cave-in."

"As am I."

"Have you asked Tong Sun about him?"

"Not yet. Remember, he hardly spoke when we went to the cabin."

Phoebe stood again and took the baby to her bed. She placed him on the mattress, between the wall and her plump pillow. As she thought back over all that had happened that day, she removed her cape and hung it on a peg near the door. Her instincts told her to burrow into her quiet little home, to focus on loving this tiny angel, yet her mind said that she had to act for John and Mei-Mei's sake.

Stiffening her spine, she opened her back door and found the fresh bottle of milk where Scottie Tompkins, the adolescent son of the couple who provided the store with fresh dairy products, always left it. She took care to close the door, then went to the stove to prepare Lee's bottle. Casting a glance over her shoulder, she noted that Adrian seemed to stare through the wall.

Memories assailed her, of John . . . of Mei-Mei. Rapid-fire thoughts tumbled through her mind, firming her resolve. She set aside all vestige of the embarrassment she'd suffered at Emmaline's hands. "We must speak with Tong Sun tomorrow."

Adrian faced her again. "I just finished saying you're at risk of becoming the next victim, and your answer is to fly in the face of that danger?"

She poured hot water from the kettle on the stove's back into a saucepan, then filled a bottle with milk.

"Well?"

She put the bottle in the pan. "Well, I've a few matters to see through, for John and for Mei-Mei." She looked down at the child in her arms. "And for Lee, too."

"What good will you do him if you get yourself killed?"

"What good will I do him if I can't ever tell him what happened to his mother and father?"

"You'll be alive. You'll be there to raise him."

"But will I be able to face him?" She shook her head. "I have to do this. I have to know."

He strode to the oak table, his shoulders taut with tension, his breathing rough. He stood there and stared at the child.

"Adrian?"

He smacked his hat on the tabletop, then faced her slowly, deliberately. The smile he fought to give her was so tender and sad that it hurt to see it. She thought she read regret in his gaze.

"I've never known a woman like you, Phoebe Williams. You're quiet and sweet, and yet you're also tough as leather and fierce as a bear."

161

His blue eyes glowed with an intensity she longed to plumb. "I wish . . . ."

She waited, her heart beating wildly at the emotions that ran across his face. But he didn't go on.

"What, Adrian? What do you wish?"

He hesitated, studied her with such fervor that Phoebe wondered if he could see straight into her heart. Then he reached behind him for his hat. His grip on the brim tightened, and his knuckles whitened.

Then something broke. He gave the headpiece an aimless wave and crossed the room to the door.

"I wish too much. Too much, and much too late."

12

The day after Letty came home with the sad tale of a new case of gossipmongering in town, Eric received an unexpected visit from Sheriff Herman.

"Good morning, there, Eric."

He smoothed his mustache. "Is it? You rarely come here with good news."

The barrel-chested sheriff seemed to deflate. He muttered an oath, removed his hat, and slapped it against his thigh.

"Well, I ain't coming to place an announcement for a Sunday picnic."

The man's reluctance led Eric to keep silent to give him time to reveal his business.

"Tell me," Herman said. "You've met the mine's new owner. What d'ya think of the man?"

"Can't say I know him well. He's only been in town a couple of weeks."

"I know. But that ain't what I want to know. I'm asking what your gut tells you."

Eric's gut wasn't saying anything he wanted to repeat. "Aside from him being a private man and not given to chatting, he seems a decent sort."

The sheriff jabbed his hat at Eric. "That's just what I mean.

He's cagey, and we ain't got any idea who we got here in town. Why, he could have a nasty history stretching longer'n those arms of yours."

"This wouldn't be about the to-do Emmaline Whitehall has caused, would it?"

Red ran up the sheriff's neck, over his face, and to his ears. "Well, she did trot herself to my office right early this morning and filed a complaint against him. Says she's good and sure he killed that Chinese woman he called his housekeeper."

"Do you have anything to go by other than her accusation? You know Miss Whitehall can get carried away with her imagination."

The lawman began ticking fingers. "First, there's the business with the child, and the Oriental woman was living with him. Besides, Miss Whitehall says Gamble's been carrying on with the junior pastor's widow. Could be some crime of passion we got us here."

Eric smiled. "Last night Letty came home in a lather about that very matter. She knows Mrs. Williams well, and she rejects Miss Whitehall's accusations." He slanted a look at his visitor. "I don't know about you, but I've learned to listen to our good Dr. Wagner."

The sheriff blushed. Eric imagined he recalled the scandal Emmaline and a few of the town's "upstanding" citizens had heaped on Letty last spring.

"You do have you a point there," Herman conceded. "But I can't say as I feel easy with leaving matters to lay on nothing much more'n your wife's faith in a friend—begging your pardon and no offense meant, you know."

"None taken, but you'd best not repeat that within her earshot."

"Can't say as I fancy having a strip torn off my hide anytime soon."

"You might want to mind your words around Randy Carlson, too, while you're at it," Eric added with a laugh.

"Yes, well, I do reckon I can do some investigating on my own. Quiet-like, and all. That's mainly the whyfore I came. I'd be much obliged if you'd let me use the photo that crazy Wynema Howard took of Gamble."

"You mean the one Daisy used for her article?"

"The very one."

"I don't have it, Daisy does. I hope you're not thinking she'll be any easier to persuade than Letty or Randy. My wife has taught Daisy well in the short time they've known each other, and Daisy's another good friend to Phoebe. The girl's as loyal as they come."

The sheriff's jaw took on a pugnacious prominence. "I ain't playin' no Sunday school games, here. This is a matter of the law. I need me that picture, and I aim to get it."

Eric laughed again. "I wish you the best of luck. But don't say I didn't warn you."

Cramming his hat on his head, the sheriff turned, muttered a farewell, and stomped out in search of Eric's typist-cum-reporter.

In the silence of the office, however, the episode soon lost its humor. The sheriff had only voiced Eric's unspoken concerns. He hoped whatever Herman learned would exonerate Adrian Gamble. He hated to think they'd welcomed an outlaw into their midst.

For the first time in her life, Phoebe wanted to stay abed in the morning. Had it not been for Lee's whimpers, she would have pulled the covers over her head and spent an hour or five in communion with her Lord.

But there was nothing like an infant's immediate need to get a body going. She changed her little boy's diaper, put his bottle to warm, and when it was ready, made herself comfortable in her Shaker rocking chair. She gave the chair a firm push with her toe, then used her body to maintain the rhythm, keeping her feet on the flat wooden footrest between the runners.

Just as Lee latched onto the nipple, someone knocked at her back door. "Coming," she called.

"Good morning, dear," Mrs. Stone said when Phoebe let her in. "I wanted to be here this morning to help you face what'll likely be a difficult day."

Appreciation filled Phoebe's heart. "You really didn't need to come, but I must admit I do appreciate it."

Mrs. Stone removed her wrap and hung it on one of the efficient Shaker pegboards Phoebe had installed on each of the room's four walls. Then the pastor's wife smoothed her cocoa-brown skirt and said, "Don't forget that burdens can be halved by accepting help and comfort."

A knot formed in Phoebe's throat, and she responded with only a nod. She kept her gaze on the hungry baby in her arms on her return to the rocker.

"You can't let a mean-spirited woman keep you from living in peace," the pastor's wife added.

Before Phoebe could speak, there was another knock at the door. Mrs. Stone took steps to answer, but Randy bustled in. Cheeks red, perhaps more from her anger than the cold, she said, "You'll never believe what those clucking, pea-brained hens are saying."

She stumbled to a halt when she realized Phoebe wasn't alone. She nodded a greeting to Mrs. Stone. "You've also heard, I gather."

Mrs. Stone nodded but didn't speak.

Randy met Phoebe's gaze and groaned. She ran and knelt by the chair. "Dear heart, you obviously know."

Misery held Phoebe's tongue.

With a glance over her shoulder, Randy addressed the pastor's wife. "Your husband must do something about this. He can't let them get away with such a dreadful attack."

Mrs. Stone nodded and sat on the edge of Phoebe's bed. "We don't intend to let them gossip and fabricate ludicrous fictions without bringing them to account." She lifted her hands in a gesture of helplessness. "But ultimately, they must choose for themselves. Either they'll acknowledge and confess their sin, repent, and stop their lies, or they'll reject our Lord's way."

The outside door again opened, this time with a bang to the counter at its right. The enameled pitcher and basin on the counter flew off and clattered to the floor. Wynema, decked out with tripod and camera, thumped in, her bowler tilted over one brow, her hair half-held by the pins on her crown.

"I've never seen less Christian behavior than in the women of this town," she declared. "Oh, hello, Randy, Mrs. Stone." She closed the door with a backward kick and continued with hardly a pause for breath. "I'm ashamed of womanhood. Maybe men have it right, and I'm stuck being the other."

Phoebe gave the young woman a watery smile.

"Goodness, Wynema," Randy said. "You needn't go that far. I'm a woman, too, and I'd much rather tie my tongue in knots than speak like that about anyone."

Wynema swept off the bowler. In the process she cast a pin-straight hank of hair down over her eyes. She then leaned her tripod against the counter, but the stand slid ever so slowly down, hit the basin on the floor, caught the lip of the pitcher, and sent everything skittering across the floor.

Letty entered the apartment at that moment and took an agile stride over the bouncing basin. "Hello."

Wynema scrambled to right the items, and in her efforts kicked the pitcher a few feet farther away. In a voice muffled by her inverted posture, she continued her argument. "Hello, Doc. I'm sure you'll agree that revolting comments slide from Hartville's gossips' lips like . . . well, like this pitcher slid across the floor."

Letty chuckled. "You're quite right. And I'm here to encourage Phoebe to stand strong against their wrongheaded talk."

Bent at the waist, Wynema shot Phoebe an upside-down look. "You're not thinking to hide and let them do this when you know they're wrong, are you?"

"You . . . believe me?"

Mrs. Stone placed a hand on her shoulder, and with the other, cupped her chin with a maternal touch. "Why would I not? I've never heard anything but truthful words from you."

"But I did . . . well, we . . ." Phoebe blushed. "Mr. Gamble and I did . . . embrace night before last."

"And did you sin against anyone by doing so?" the pastor's wife asked.

The Shaker insistence on total celibacy, even a repudiation of the most unintended touch, rushed to Phoebe's head. "I . . . perhaps against God . . . I don't know."

Wynema plunked the basin on the counter, clanged the pitcher into the basin, then turned and smacked her fists on her boyish hips.

"Just how many commandments did you break?"

Phoebe tried to reconcile that truth to the years of Shaker teaching. "Well . . ."

Randy raised her arms and waved her hands. "So you kissed the man. Is that it?"

The heat in Phoebe's cheeks grew unbearable. She couldn't speak, so she gave a tiny nod.

Letty glanced toward Randy, then met Phoebe's gaze. "Did the sky fall down?"

Phoebe gave a small hitching laugh. "No, but—"

"Oh, for goodness' sake," Wynema muttered. "They're jealous, Phoebe, can't you tell? They've all been sniffing after Mr. Gamble since the moment he landed a foot in town."

"Jealous?"

Mrs. Stone took the empty bottle from Phoebe, put it on

the table, and cradled Lee in her experienced arms. "I'd have to agree. There are few eligible bachelors around. This one doesn't seem interested in giving them the time of day."

"But I've done nothing to hoard his attentions."

Letty approached the rocker, took hold of Phoebe's icy hands, and knelt beside her. "Of course you haven't. You're just you, sweet and gentle and kind, and they aren't. Mr. Gamble obviously prefers your assets to their liabilities."

Phoebe tugged on her friend's hands, and the two women stood.

"I'm not after wedding again," she began.

She wondered, not for the first time since this disaster befell her, if she shouldn't have signed the Covenant and become a Shaker. If she'd chosen to live the celibate Shaker life, she would have avoided the pain of widowhood, and she wouldn't be in this position now.

"Now that I have Lee," she added, "I must focus on him."

She tried to ignore the pang that pierced her heart. It reminded her all too vividly that her feelings for Adrian had become rich and compelling, something far different from the comfortable, warm, deep affection she and John had shared. Were the new feelings good and right, as her friends said they were? As her friends evidently experienced in their marriages?

"Indeed . . . My little one . . ." Who was she trying to persuade? Her friends or the woman who'd responded to Adrian's touch with unfamiliar longings?

Were these longings what lay at the root of man's fallen nature since that fateful moment in the Garden of Eden, as Mother Ann Lee had taught?

"I'm really not," she insisted. "After wedding again, that is."

"That doesn't mean," Letty ventured, "that God's plans might not differ from yours. I, for one, came to Hartville convinced that marriage and children were not my lot in life because of my career." She shrugged and winked. "Little did I realize that God had more than I could ever envision waiting for me here."

"Nay, I don't think that's the case for me. I'm happy with the Lord and with Lee."

She stiffened her spine and her resolve, then took her watch from her shirtwaist's pocket.

"Oh dear. Just look at the time. I must open the store or I certainly won't be happy with my slacking."

"Will you be all right?" asked Letty.

"Of course." A knot formed in her middle.

"I'm staying long enough to make sure she is," Wynema said.

Randy's green eyes glowed. "That's why I came."

"As did I." Mrs. Stone moved Lee from the crook of her arm and settled him in at her shoulder. She patted his back and walked toward the door to the store's back hallway. "Shall we, ladies?"

"I don't know that I've ever heard of a store run by a throng," Phoebe said.

Wynema twisted the knob and held the door open for the others to pass by. "There's no time like the present for a first."

Buoyed by their cheerful support, Phoebe opened the store as usual, and soon fell into her routine. Although no customers showed up, she felt far better than she had upon waking. One by one her friends left as she regained the confidence she needed to handle whatever came her way.

She also decided she wouldn't stop until she learned who'd committed those horrid crimes, and indeed continued to commit them, as Mei-Mei's death proved. She would trust God to keep her safe and to reveal the truth, even to those who questioned her behavior.

She would strive to keep her actions beyond reproach. She owed that to John's memory, to her newly adopted son, and to the Lord she served.

Shortly after midday Adrian entered the store. Phoebe whirled around behind the counter to hide her burning cheeks.

"Good afternoon," he said, his voice serious.

"Hello."

"I came to fetch you, since you said you wanted to gather Mei-Mei's and Lee's belongings."

"The store—"

"Will be closed for a part of this afternoon. I consider this more important, don't you?"

Phoebe nodded, then knelt and gathered the baby close. She rounded the counter and stepped toward the back door.

"Wait," he said. "I stopped by the manse to see if Mim might watch the little one. I doubt you'll accomplish much with him in your arms."

Phoebe noticed the girl at the corner of the counter. She forced a smile for the Stones' ward. "Are you done with your lessons, dear?"

"Yes, ma'am. Auntie Stone said you needed help. I'm to bring the baby home with me, and you can stop by for him once you're done."

With a hug for Mim and a kiss for Lee, she placed the warm little bundle in the girl's outstretched arms.

"I'll fetch you his diapers and bottle."

Moments later, Mim went one way down Main Street and Phoebe and Adrian went the other. They walked in silence. Had he heard the rumors yet? If so, why didn't he say something? If not, how had he managed to avoid the gossip?

The awkwardness between them grew with every step, and Phoebe didn't draw a comfortable breath until they reached the Hart mansion.

"I'll let you know once I'm done."

Adrian unlocked the kitchen door. "I'm going nowhere but to help you. It won't be easy, you know."

Phoebe bit her bottom lip. "I know, but surely you're too busy with the mine to bother with something like this."

"Mei-Mei worked for me, and she lived in my home. Someone

killed her while she was under my authority. I take responsibility for my workers seriously."

"I'm sorry." She followed him across the gleaming room. Someone had cleaned up what must have been a gruesome sight. "I didn't mean to offend."

"No offense taken. I just wanted you to understand."

Phoebe suspected he'd been the one to undertake the difficult chore. She swallowed hard as he opened the door to Mei-Mei's rooms. "I can't imagine there's much here."

"She only had the one carpetbag when she moved in. Besides that, you know better than I do what you brought from the store."

A soft plum dress, two skirts, and two shirtwaists—all new —hung in the wardrobe together with the loose, faded-blue Asian-style blouse and pants Mei-Mei wore when she first arrived in Hartville. The sight of those empty, worn garments affected Phoebe as nothing else had.

Dear Lord, why? Tears rolled down her cheeks, and her hands shook.

She stood before the piece of furniture as long as her legs supported her. Then she crumpled, sobbing out her grief. She wept for the young mother and her child, for John, for the dead miners, for herself . . . for Adrian as well. All of them had been so full of hope once, and someone in Hartville had put an end to that hope, to those dreams. So many were dead, and now Emmaline was saying the vilest things about Mei-Mei's death.

Phoebe had lost a husband and a new friend. She'd never done anything to bring this on herself. She'd loved John and followed him where God had led him. Then she'd befriended a scared, lonely girl. She didn't rightly know why Adrian had bought the mine, but in her heart of hearts, she knew he hadn't hurt Mei-Mei. Still, they both had lost their good names.

Now she had to go on, her faith in Christ the only reason to live day after day. Well, and Lee, too. Was this the Lord's plan for her life? To raise Lee despite the knowledge that this fallen world would rob him of joy, hope, and dreams?

She'd lost everything, even her reputation, something she'd guarded as a treasure that once lost could never be regained. Now John's memory was tainted with the scandal surrounding his widow, at least it was in the eyes of many of those to whom he'd ministered.

"Phoebe . . ."

Through her misery, she heard Adrian, but she couldn't face him. At no time today had he shown her even the slightest sign of . . . of whatever had led to that kiss the other night.

"Don't cry . . ."

Don't cry? He asked her not to weep? How could he, when he'd been the one to put the distance between them? She felt such grief and pain and sadness. Did he even care about her? If so, then why didn't he comfort her? If not, then why had he kissed her?

"Please . . . you'll make yourself ill . . ."

With more strength than she ever thought she had, Phoebe closed her eyes hard and swallowed the ache in her heart. The tears continued to seep through her lashes, though not as many as before. The pain remained as sharp, but she'd learned to live with pain when her mother had died. She wiped her eyes with the hankie in her skirt pocket.

She gathered her dignity and stood. "I'll be fine."

Adrian responded with a noise that sounded like a snort. Had she been stuck with a pin, she wouldn't have reacted any more decisively to his doubting retort. She reached into the wardrobe and pulled out garment after garment, draping them over one arm, ignoring the tremors that still ran through her. Once it was empty, she closed the doors and placed the garments on the bed.

"I don't think we need to keep any of these for Lee," she said, relieved at the firmness in her voice. "They'll do more good in Mrs. Stone's missionary box."

"Of course."

She crossed to the bureau by the window and there collected Mei-Mei's undergarments. The awkwardness between them returned, but since Mr. Responsible Adrian Gamble had insisted on being present, she wasn't about to let him make a shrinking violet of her.

She pushed an assortment of plain unmentionables at him. "Here. You can dispose of them right away."

The red on his cheeks brought her the first bit of satisfaction she'd felt since . . . well, since the morning after their kiss. And that was another thing. Perhaps it hadn't meant a thing to him. Perhaps Mother Ann had been right in proclaiming all fleshly and sensual attachments the root of all evil in mankind, the reason for the fall.

During her years with the Shakers, she'd been taught that one could overcome such longings. By putting her hands to work and keeping in her heart only love for God, she would, too.

The Lord would gather her tears.

With a prayer for an extra measure of His peace, she opened the last bureau drawer and found the tattered carpetbag inside. Gently she withdrew it, then opened the corroded clasp. At first glance she saw nothing, but when she ran a hand inside, she felt something cool in the very corner. Phoebe wrapped her fingers around the circular object and brought it out, curious to see what she'd found.

It was a lovely carving of soft green stone, jade more than likely, an Asian character within a smooth tubular frame.

"Look," she said as Adrian walked back into the room. "I found it in the bag."

He took the piece from her and laid it on his palm, the red silk cord that looped through a small hole at the top hanging between his fingers. "It's lovely, and the jade is of high quality.

174

Since Mei-Mei didn't sell it when she found herself in dire straits, she must have treasured it."

"That's what I think. I'm going to keep it for Lee."

For a moment their gazes met, and Phoebe thought she saw a hint of the warmth she'd seen there right before their lips had met. But it soon vanished, so quickly that she wondered if she'd imagined it.

"Good," he said and thrust the pendant back at her. He turned and strode to the door. "Are you done here?"

At his dry question, more pain jabbed her heart. She fought down the imminent sob and slipped the jade into the pocket of her skirt. "As soon as I fold the clothes I'll head for the manse to fetch Lee."

Adrian waved at the clothes. "Leave them. I'll have one of my men take them to Mrs. Stone. I'm headed out to find Tong Sun. Would you care to come along?"

Phoebe blinked. "Did I just hear you ask if I'd like to come with you to meet Tong Sun?"

"That's what I said."

"Last time you were dead set against my going."

"I'm unhappy at the prospect, but will my feelings stop you from speaking with him?"

"Nay."

"Well, then it's best if you come with me rather than go alone."

Adrian was nothing like her predictable husband had been. With a shake of her head, Phoebe walked before him into the passage to the kitchen. He was the most incomprehensible, mystifying, and intriguing man she'd ever met.

And as she stepped too close and her arm brushed against his hand, the current that seared through her told her that Mother Ann Lee might not have fully understood the implacable pull of passion between a man and a woman. It was all Phoebe could do to keep from leaning into him and again seeking the heat and hunger in his embrace.

☙

Calling himself every kind of fool, Adrian tried to shake off the electric thrum the simple brush of Phoebe's arm against his hand had set off. Why he'd ever surrendered to the lure of her beautiful smile the other night, he'd never know.

But once he'd kissed her, he'd known he would continue to crave her caresses for the rest of his life.

However long—or short—that happened to be.

As he silently trod at her side, he acknowledged his lack of defenses when it came to his feelings for her. He'd never considered himself weak willed, but here he was taking Phoebe with him as he went to confront Tong Sun, just because he couldn't deny her anything—even against his better judgment.

It had taken every ounce of strength he had to keep from going to her when she'd crumpled at the sight of Mei-Mei's meager belongings. Her tear-filled eyes and grief-stricken face had etched an image in his mind that would last at least as long as any rendered in oil paints or photographic tints. He'd longed for the right to hold her, to comfort her, to share his strength with her, however feeble it might be in the face of the cruelty of violent men.

But he was still a hunted man, and the kind of closeness he wanted would endanger Phoebe's life, something he couldn't risk. So he'd kept his distance, fighting himself endless second after second after second. And he would continue to do so, no matter the cost to him.

The sight of the Heart of Silver Mine brought him uncommon relief—anything to distract him from his troubling thoughts would have. He spotted the foreman. "Fulton!"

His miner stopped in the black maw of the wooden structure built over the mineshaft. "Yeah?"

"I need to speak with Tong Sun," Adrian said. "Would you please fetch him or send someone for him?"

Anger flared across Fulton's coarse features, but he kept his control. "Which one is he? They all look alike."

At Adrian's side, Phoebe bristled. He reached out and placed a hand on her forearm.

"He's the one Chinese miner who speaks the most English. At any rate, he's the one I've most heard speak."

"Don't know which one that would be; but I'll send someone after him." He lumbered into the building and bellowed, "Jedediah! Go find me one of them squinties—the one named Tong Sun."

Phoebe pulled from his grasp and took two steps. "How dare you—"

"Stop." Adrian caught her shoulders. "It won't do any good. I've decided to replace him as soon as spring arrives."

"It won't come any too soon."

"I agree."

Fulton didn't return, and Jedediah took his own sweet time in coming. Adrian pulled out his pocket watch and counted a half hour's passage. Phoebe contented herself with pacing across the front of the mine building, every so often fixing him with her gaze.

"Are you sure it's wise to keep Fulton on until spring?"

"I can't replace a foreman this close to winter—"

"Do you realize how many more times he'll insult those poor men before the snows fall, never mind melt?"

"Yes, but I can't—Look. There's Tong Sun."

"Will you ask him about . . . discuss the matter with him here?"

"I plan to speak with him as we walk toward the company houses. I'm afraid we might be overheard anywhere else we go." He slanted her a glance. "You will let me speak, won't you?"

"Why, of course. Why do you ask?"

"I need to be the one to ask the questions. I'm his employer."

A faint line appeared between her brows. "I'm Shaker raised, Adrian Gamble," she said in a quiet tone, "and have been taught to recognize the equality of the sexes. If I find you've failed to bring up any important detail, why, I'll certainly do so myself."

"I was afraid of that."

Although he knew she'd heard, she didn't acknowledge his response. Instead, she straightened to her full height and drew dignity and assurance around her like a mantle. Phoebe Williams was indeed a magnificent woman.

Tearing his gaze from her, he beckoned the Chinese miner with a wave. "I—"

Phoebe's throat clearing cut into his words.

He sighed, closed his eyes, and shook his head. "*We* need to speak with you about a matter of grave importance. Please come walk with us."

For a moment, Adrian read dread in the man's expression. Just as quickly as it appeared, Tong Sun masked it. Without a word he nodded and fell into step with them.

When Adrian felt certain no one at the mine could overhear, and a fair distance still separated them from the cluster of company houses, he stopped.

"I'm sure you know what this is about."

The man's expression revealed none of his thoughts. After a few moments, he gave a nod.

Adrian met Phoebe's gaze. She sent him an encouraging smile. He drew a deep breath. "I need to know for absolute certain if any of my miners smoke opium—demon mud."

Whereas before Tong Sun had maintained control of his expression, now myriad emotions chased each other across his face. As Adrian observed the miner's struggle, he prayed for God's help.

The minutes dragged by. Adrian glanced at Phoebe and noted

the compassion in her gaze. Tong Sun's battle was not an easy one. Adrian sympathized with the man. But still, he had to know the truth.

Finally, with rage blazing in his dark eyes, Tong Sun faced him squarely and said, "Yes."

13

Her heart chilled, Phoebe walked silently at Adrian's side. Tong Sun's words reverberated in her thoughts, the anger in his features as clear as if he still stood before her.

"Well?" she finally asked her companion.

"I knew he'd confirm our fears, but I didn't know how much worse it would be to know than to suspect."

"I understand."

Silence accompanied them for another few steps. Then Phoebe couldn't stifle her most burning question any longer. "Do you believe him when he says he doesn't know who sells the opium to the men?"

"I can't see what he would gain by lying."

"I can't either." If she closed her eyes, she could still see the miner's every gesture, hear his every word. "He appeared as angry about the situation as I feel."

"As do I." Adrian increased his pace toward the manse. "Then again, he could lie to gain something for himself or his friends. Anything's possible."

The concern in Adrian's voice and the worry in his eyes touched Phoebe. He cared about the men's condition, not just about the mine and its profits, as she now believed Mr. Hart had.

She longed to reach out and comfort him and to seek comfort in his strength. But seeing how things stood between them, she knew that would never—should never—happen. That knowledge left her even lonelier than before.

She forced her emotions aside. "Tong Sun said all the miners were afraid. I can only imagine how frightened they truly must be."

"Frightened enough that they might hesitate at the wrong moment and make a tragic mistake in their work. A man worried about his fate at the hands of someone with that much power could be at the root of the accident last spring."

Phoebe stopped. "So you no longer think it was deliberate?"

Adrian rubbed his temple with a gloved hand. "I don't know, but I'd much rather consider the incident an accident. There's something about . . ." He averted his face, stared at the sheer mountain rock face that sheltered Hartville. Anguish contorted his features. "Murder is—"

"I understand." This time, she couldn't keep from reaching out, and she placed her hand on his forearm. "One who murders puts himself in God's place, deciding whether his victim should live or die. Then there's also the Lord's commandment to love one another. There's no explanation or excuse for a killing."

He swallowed hard. The light in his eyes seemed to go out, and everything about him sagged. He looked like a man facing the coffin of a loved one, devastated, bereft. Under her hand, a rough tremor shook him. Then he forced his face into a bland expression.

"Indeed," he said, his voice hollow, and he stepped toward the center of town.

Phoebe felt the rejection in the deepest part of her heart. Never in her life had anyone so coldly refused her comfort. And it was Adrian who'd just refused her, the man who'd brought to life the richest sensations she'd ever felt. The man who'd awakened in her the need to be near him, to share his troubles, to help him in every way.

To love him.

What a fool she was. She'd decided only hours earlier to set aside the silly emotions that kept her thinking of him and to focus only on God. She swallowed the knot in her throat and pushed down the heartache. As she squared her shoulders, she called up a mental image of the baby awaiting her.

She put foot before foot, held her head high, and said a prayer in her heart. She reminded herself of her renewed commitment to the idea of hands to work and heart to God. Not everything Shaker was flawed.

A block away from the church, Adrian again stopped. "What troubles me most is Tong Sun's insistence that the men who've died have, for the most part, been the ones who tried to do something to stop the drug trade. The deaths don't sound as though they happened because of a frightened man's fear."

It took Phoebe a moment to tear her thoughts away from praising her heavenly Father and back to the evil they'd uncovered. "That's the heart of the problem, isn't it?"

Since Adrian didn't respond, she tamped down her horror and added, "It seems awfully convenient for John and Li Fong to be victims of that particular 'accident.' They both wanted to stop the opium problem."

"But we have no way to prove whether that cave-in was an accident or someone set it up to look like one."

"In the end it doesn't really matter," Phoebe said. "The men are dead, and we can do nothing about that. But we must still find out who's behind the drug trade to keep others from meeting that same fate. Once we learn the truth, perhaps we'll know if John and Li Fong were . . ." She hesitated before the vile word. "If they were murdered, as Mei-Mei was."

Adrian's lips flattened and his eyes narrowed. "We have more questions now than we did before. I'd hoped we could make progress after we spoke with Tong Sun."

"But we know more now. That's why we have so many more

questions," she said. "Tong Sun confirmed that Li Fong died with John. And we also know that whoever is profiting from the poor Chinese miners' weakness for opium is still carrying on his trade."

"But we don't know who it could be." He waved a hand and headed for the manse. "Come on, you should get little Lee. He needs you . . ."

His words drifted into the early evening, leaving Phoebe to ponder the odd note in his voice. If he hadn't rejected her kindness such a short while ago, she'd think it was longing she'd heard. Nay, it couldn't be. A man who longed for a woman wouldn't repeatedly push her away.

In addition to the confirmation of her worst fears, she'd learned one additional fact. Adrian hadn't heard the gossip. If he had, he would have confronted it as squarely as he confronted the problems at the mine.

He should have left her at the manse with Pastor and Mrs. Stone. Why he'd insisted on accompanying Phoebe back to her apartment, he'd never know.

That wasn't quite true. He knew full well why he couldn't stay away from her. What he didn't know was why he couldn't exert his will on himself and overcome his intense desire for her company. What was it about those clear blue eyes of hers that managed to melt his determination more easily than spring melted winter snow?

So now he stood with her on the boardwalk outside the store, feeling more awkward than any adolescent male ever had. While every bit of him wanted more than anything to wrap his arms around her and the baby, Adrian clasped his hands behind his back to keep from doing so.

Phoebe thrust the blanket-wrapped bundle at him. "Here."

Adrian's eyes widened, and he clutched the child. His heart pounded, and he feared he'd drop Lee. "Wait!"

"I'm sorry," she said, "but I have things to do and would appreciate help with the baby. It's only for a moment."

She fumbled in her small black purse, withdrew a key, and turned it in the lock. Without waiting for him, she headed to the counter at the rear of the store to light the lamp. Then as he approached with the baby clasped securely to his chest, she marched to the hallway door and disappeared, the lamp held before her.

"Wait!" he called again.

"Please, do come in. I need to prepare a bottle for Lee."

As quickly as he dared, Adrian crossed to the doorway, entered the hall, and followed the golden lamplight into her home. The sparsely furnished apartment was neat and tidy, made warm by the wise use of appealing color. Phoebe didn't espouse Mrs. Hart's concept of decor.

She opened the back door and brought a quart of milk inside. She filled a bottle with the milk, placed it in a tin pan, and then set both on the massive wood stove in the far corner of the room. She hadn't even taken the time to remove her cloak.

Adrian shifted his weight from foot to foot, still gripping the baby as though it would leap from his arms and onto the floor. "Uh . . ."

Phoebe opened the clasp at the neck of her charcoal-colored cloak and slipped it off. She went to the wall and reached for a peg in the board that ran all the way around the room at about a five-foot height. The cloak joined a simple blue apron that exactly matched the color of her eyes. She obviously hadn't heard his stammer.

He tried again. "Er . . ."

She opened the door to the small icebox by the stove. "I hope you don't mind a simple supper. I can cook eggs and fry some bacon . . ."

As she rummaged inside the contraption, Adrian wondered how one of the rare conveniences had wound up all the way out here in the Colorado mountains.

She glanced over her shoulder. "Do you care for apple butter? I have some from the Richardses' apples. It's especially nice with fresh bread."

At the mention of food, his empty stomach gave a cheer. "It sounds wonderful, but what about—"

"Good."

Moments later she'd donned the blue apron, grabbed a yellow bowl, set it on the table, and broken a good number of brown eggs into it. She whisked them with a fork, and when satisfied with the condition of the eggs, she stepped to the shelves above the counter and brought down a large iron skillet. She then cut a hunk of golden butter. She thudded the skillet onto the stove and plopped the butter right into its center. Another few steps, and she returned to the table and her bowl of eggs.

At no time did she pay him the slightest attention.

Adrian approached panic.

Lee let out a shriek.

"Phoebe . . ."

He looked from the parcel of infant and flannel in his arms to the woman once again at the door of the icebox. She'd better come and retrieve her child before he did something dreadful like drop him on his head.

"Oh dear," she said, then pointed with the white-paper-wrapped package toward the area near her bed. "My hands are messy from the eggs. Would you please take a clean diaper from the basket next to the bureau and change him while I slice the meat?"

"But—"

"Oh, and I keep a sugar shaker full of cornstarch there to sprinkle on him before I do up the fresh diaper."

Adrian's shock was so great that he couldn't find words to express it. He just stood and stared at her, his jaw agape, the infant in his arms bellowing. Did Phoebe really expect him to change Lee's diaper?

Until recently, he'd never held a baby in his arms, much less given a thought to its . . . well, to diapers. Surely Shaker men didn't do that sort of thing. They farmed and made chairs and odd machines. Didn't they?

"His bottle will be ready any moment," she added.

She really did expect him to diaper the child. Should he be offended because she'd assumed he knew how to perform women's work or feel complimented because she thought him fully capable? Adrian took tentative steps toward the bed.

Lee began to squirm inside his cocoon of cloth. When Adrian set him down on the bed, the noise level threatened his hearing.

"Does he always cry like this?"

"Only when he's hungry or his diaper's wet, and I'm sure he's unhappy on both accounts right now."

The tantalizing aroma of the sizzling bacon reached his nose. Ravenous enough for his navel to tickle his spine, Adrian fumbled as he removed Lee's blanket. His heart nearly broke at the sight of the misery in the baby's little red face.

"Oh, hey. We'll get through this," he said.

He didn't know just how they'd get through it, but the poor mite was stuck with him. After he peeled off various layers of clothing, including unwieldy rubber pants, Adrian reached the damp diaper. A nasty-looking pin held together the soggy cotton on Lee's bottom. What if in his awkwardness he stuck the little fellow?

His stomach lurched. That couldn't happen. The baby was already miserable enough, and Adrian refused to do anything to make him feel worse.

The pin opened readily and he removed it without trouble. He paid careful attention to how the thing had gone together and removed the final layer, then shot a wild look around for the basket she'd mentioned.

With one hand on Lee's warm little tummy, Adrian scooped

a white cotton square from the willow basket at the side of the bureau. His fingers hit something cold and metallic, and he grabbed that too—the sugar shaker Phoebe had mentioned.

The intensity of the baby's wails increased.

"Hey, I'm no happier than you are about this," Adrian said. "I'd rather she handled the stinky, wet mess, too. But you only get to choose between me and the mess, so we're going to do it. Together."

He slipped the diaper under the baby and gathered the excess into folds resembling those he'd opened. He'd begun to feel somewhat competent, when a warm, wet stream hit his chest.

"Hey!"

Lee howled.

"Adrian!" Phoebe bustled to his side. "What's wrong with Lee?"

"Lee? There's nothing wrong with him. He . . . he . . ."

Adrian let his words die off. There was no polite way to say it. He pointed to the affronted spot on his coat.

The spectacular smile blossomed on Phoebe's face. Once again it came at his expense. He no longer cared.

She chuckled. "With experience, you get good at dodging the squirts." She swept away the now-wet diaper he'd just put under the child and replaced it with another clean one. "I'll take care of him now. I'm sure you want to clean up."

The dark drip down his camel coat made him grimace. "Clean up? This river runs all the way through. The coat needs a wash—as do I."

Her chuckles turned to laughter. She kissed the freshly blanketed Lee and handed him to Adrian again. "Tell you what. You feed him while I see what I can do for your coat."

He found himself holding the squalling baby again. With her help, he removed his coat, then took the warm bottle of milk she'd tested on the back of her hand.

He'd never done this either.

187

"Oh dear." She went to an enamel pitcher and basin, coat in hand. "This is lovely wool. I hope I can remove the stain."

Who cared about a stain? Adrian had to get the milk in the bottle into Lee to feed the child and to save his hearing. Awkwardly he brought the rubber nipple to the little boy's mouth, and blessed silence descended on the room.

In the sudden peace, a strange sense of accomplishment filled him. He glanced at Phoebe, and their gazes met. She smiled again. The solid earth shifted under him. His life would never be the same again. This woman . . . this child . . .

The moment itself was more perfect than any other he remembered living. Emotion swelled within him. He broke the visual connection, more moved than he could accept.

He returned his gaze to Lee and watched the boy drink with gusto, his dark eyes fixed on him, a little fist waving and patting his chest. A knot formed in his throat and a burn prickled his eyes. He was no longer the man who'd entered the room a brief time earlier. Not only had Phoebe captured his heart, but this tiny scrap of humanity had also burrowed inside.

A sense of awe swept through him. Only a magnificent Creator could produce a treasure like the one he held in his arms. Only a perfect God could give His children the ability to feel such rich emotions.

Love, real and true.

He wanted the moment to last forever.

He wanted Phoebe waiting for him every day after he'd wrestled the ins and outs of the mine, a delightful dinner on the stove, her smile sweetening every minute of his evening. He wanted to hold Lee for as long as the growing child would let him. He wanted to make sure the boy had enough to eat, and he even wanted to change another diaper or two in exchange for this priceless sense of rightness, of belonging.

But how? He couldn't see any way to claim what he longed for. He was still a hunted man. His stomach churned with a fear unlike any he'd ever felt before. He couldn't let anything happen to Phoebe and Lee, certainly not as a result of his love for them or his presence in their lives.

A futile rage threatened to overtake him, but he fought it and instead found himself overwhelmed with bitterness. Why? Why couldn't he have what other men took for granted?

A woman, a child, a family.

A future.

Those intense, beautiful feelings had the power to destroy him—if he let them. He knew what he had to do. He'd done it to protect his family back home, and somehow he would do it here once again.

Father God, give me the strength to stay away from them.

Lee's pink lips released the nipple, and he gave a soft, satisfied sigh. The little fist batted Adrian's chest right where his heart ached. Knowing he'd have to relinquish a future with the child brought dampness to his eyes.

"Adrian?" Phoebe said at his side. "Is something wrong?"

Wrong? Everything was wrong. Everything had gone wrong when he'd acted to avert a wrong. No matter how long or how short Adrian's life lasted, he'd never forget the blast of that one gun, its kick against his gut, the thick redness of the other man's blood as life drained from him.

And now, because of that one moment, Adrian had no right to the woman he loved and the child God had brought into their lives.

He shuddered. "I'm fine. Here. Take Lee. He drank every drop."

He turned so she wouldn't see the misery on his face, then strode to the table where she'd laid his coat. "I'd best be going."

"Nay. You can't. At least, not before you have something to eat."

Eat? A doomed man didn't feel the need to eat. "I'm not hungry."

She hoisted Lee onto her shoulder and patted his back, a crease between her brows. "Of course you are. A body can't be expected to work well—"

"Without it being fed decent food," he finished for her, his memory of the time she'd introduced him to that homey bit of wisdom quite fresh. Still, he regretted causing the concern in her gaze, in her frown. "If you insist, I'll have a bite or two."

Relief brightened her blue eyes. "Good."

With sure steps she crossed to the bureau and pulled out the bottom drawer. She placed the baby on the nest of padding inside and then set the makeshift cradle on the floor by her bed, and Adrian marveled at her efficient use of the apartment's scant furnishings.

She returned to the table and scooped fluffy eggs and crisp bacon onto a sturdy white plate. "Please take a seat."

Against his better judgment, he did as she asked. In silence he bowed his head and asked a blessing on his humble fare. After his amen, he tucked in. Had it been one of Mother's fanciest French dinners back east, it surely wouldn't have tasted any better. Moments later Phoebe sat across from him, bowed her head, and joined him in his meal.

"Tong Sun said he'd finished work and left the mine shaft only an hour before the accident," she said, startling him. His thoughts had been turned so deeply inward that he'd forgotten the problems at the mine and with his miners.

"Yes, I remember."

She waved her fork at him. "Surely he would have noticed a dangerous situation had one existed, don't you think?"

He nodded, his mouth full of savory bacon.

"Or the men might have received faulty instructions for the day's work."

Adrian swallowed. "Maybe."

"Who gives the men their orders?"

He saw where her thoughts were leading. "Fulton."

"I don't care for him."

"Do you want me to believe Fulton caused the cave-in because of his dislike of the Chinamen?"

"He could have."

"I think you're just expressing your dislike for the man." She shook her head and chewed, unable to object. He thought back to their conversation with Tong Sun. "There's one thing to remember."

"Oh?"

"Tong Sun said that the miners who tried to do something about the opium situation have turned up dead. Li Fong and your husband were trying to uncover the culprit."

"If it was a coincidence, then it appears like an awfully convenient one. But I still don't care for Mr. Fulton's behavior."

"Understood."

Moments later, Adrian stood, his plate scraped clean of every last morsel. The intimacy of the moment threatened to weaken his resolve once again. He didn't want to leave, but he had to go. He had to get away before he did something they might both regret. "Will you give me permission to go home now that you've plied me with food?"

"What silliness!"

"Ah . . . but it made you smile."

She pushed away from the table and reached for his coat. Their hands met. Without conscious thought, he captured her fingers and drew her close. He saw the beat of her pulse at her temple, the heightened color in her cheeks, the slight parting of her lips.

It would have taken a stronger man than he to keep from kissing her.

He poured all his impossible emotions into the caress, all his pent-up love, his tenderness, and his passion. Although at first she held herself rigid, as the kiss went on she melted into his embrace and wrapped her arms around him.

He trembled at the warmth of those slender arms and the

softness of her lips. Pure joy filled him at having Phoebe so close. This was where he wanted to stay forever . . . even longer than that. This was where he—they—belonged. The passion he'd held back burst forth, and he deepened the caress.

She kissed him right back.

As his senses spun, he heard a foreign sound. He tried to ignore it and drank in the wonder of kissing Phoebe, but the noise grew louder, sharper, more piercing.

"Lee," he breathed against Phoebe's lips. With great reluctance, but with full awareness of how badly he'd erred, he stepped away from her.

He took his coat from the table and shoved his arms through the sleeves. He jerked his head in the baby's direction. "I'd best go and let you take care of him."

He felt like the greatest kind of coward, when he sneaked a glance at her. Phoebe looked dazed, moonstruck, just as he felt. But he knew what she didn't. He had to keep his head and get away before he blurted out his love for her. Then he'd never be able to leave her. He'd never be able to protect her from the curse that followed him wherever he went.

"Let me know when the rest of the supplies for the miners' houses arrive," he said. "I'm anxious to make life better for those poor men."

She nodded as he opened the door. "Yea," she said in a breathy voice, "I'll let you know."

As though the very hounds of hell had been unleashed upon him—and surely they had in the persons of two vengeful killers—Adrian ran from everything he held dear.

The following week, the store saw little activity, the cowbell clanged infrequently. Each rare time she heard the loud sound, Phoebe glanced up, then struggled to mask her disappointment when it wasn't Adrian.

She hadn't seen him since she'd felt the need in his embrace and tasted the passion in his kiss. Was he avoiding her? Had he heard the gossip? Was that why he hadn't been to the store or even to his office?

"Here's your tea and flour and lard," she said to Elsa Richards.

The blond woman nodded and smiled. "*Ja, sehr gut.* I little have at home. Thank you."

Her customer walked away. Phoebe remained behind, only her thoughts for company. Adrian had kissed her again, and again he'd withdrawn.

Why?

Did he just kiss women and then traipse away without a thought? A leaden sensation settled in her stomach. Surely not. She didn't think he was that kind of man. At least, she hoped he wasn't.

"Morning," Wynema sang out. "I heard the train brought a load of supplies last night. Do you have my shipment?"

Phoebe reached for a box on the shelf to the right of the counter. "Yea, dear, here they are. And a good morning to you, too."

The young photographer plopped her bowler on the counter and propped her forearms on either side of the hat. She leaned closer to Phoebe, "Tell me. Are those nasty cats still bothering you?"

"Nay, but business has slowed considerably. I haven't seen Emmaline, Naomi, or Ruthie for days now."

Two red circles burst on Wynema's cheeks. "Why, those silly hens. Just you wait until they run out of their favorite things. They'll be back."

With a shrug, Phoebe glanced down at Lee as he slept in his drawer bed. "I should resign and look for other work. I must think about Lee, and it's not fair to—to Mr. Gamble."

Wynema smacked the hat back on her head. "Mr. Gamble seems bright enough to me. Has he complained or fired you?"

Phoebe turned away so her friend wouldn't see the distress on her face. "He hasn't been here in days either."

The bell jangled again.

"Well, you won't be saying that anymore," Wynema said.

Phoebe whirled, and her gaze flew to the front of the store. Sure enough, Adrian strode down the aisle, a grim look on his face.

She prayed the Lord would slow down her galloping heartbeat. "Good morning."

"Can't say that it is."

"What do you mean?"

"Yes, Mr. Gamble," Wynema said, "what's wrong?"

He gave the young photographer a caustic look. He turned to Phoebe, and the rage in his gaze sent dread to her middle.

"There's been another death."

She caught her breath. Their gazes met. "Who?"

"Remember the man who was brought to Tong Sun's house . . . indisposed?"

She nodded, horrid certainty in her heart. "How could I forget?"

"Or I," he said. "Fulton gave me the news a few minutes ago. I sent him to fetch Dr. Wagner, and I thought you'd want to know. I'm on my way to the mine to see what I can learn. I must speak with Tong Sun as soon as possible."

Resolve stiffened Phoebe's spine. "Wynema, I need you to stay here and mind the store and the baby. As you heard, we have an urgent matter on our hands."

Mulish stubbornness squared Wynema's jaw, and she smacked her fists on her hips. "Are you mistaking me for a governess? I'm the one the sheriff fetches whenever something like this happens. If you're going, I'm going, too."

"You can go, Miss Wynema," Caroline Patterson Wagner said. Only at the sound of her voice did Phoebe notice the girl. "Mama sent me to watch Lee, Aunt Phoebe."

Adrian looked around the store. "Sorry, folks," he called out to the two older ladies by the purses on the farthest table. "I'm afraid I must close the store for a spell."

They scowled but did leave. Phoebe ran back to her apartment, a prayer on her lips, and donned her cloak. "I'm ready," she said when she stood by the counter once again.

"Are you really?" Adrian asked.

"As I'll ever be."

"As am I!" Wynema chimed in.

All three headed for the door. When Phoebe drew it open, she heard a clatter behind her. She glanced over her shoulder, and not even the gravity of the situation could erase her smile. Wynema had, as was so often the case, dropped her tripod. In the process, she'd knocked over a stack of enamel pails from the bench where Phoebe kept them. The photographer bent to retrieve her equipment and lost her hat.

"Oh, go ahead," the young woman muttered from her inverted position. "I'll have to catch up with you."

"Yea," Phoebe murmured, with a look at Adrian, who'd come to her side. "We have to hurry before another man—"

"Before another minute goes by." Adrian gave her a small shake of his head.

She nodded. It was best to keep their suspicions to themselves. It wouldn't do to expose Wynema to the danger they faced. Phoebe now knew all too well why the miner had been uncontrollable that other night. Too many people had already died because of it.

Opium, the Chinamen's demon mud.

14

When Phoebe and Adrian arrived at the dead miner's shabby house, they found that Letty had already gone inside to examine the corpse. The look Adrian gave Phoebe told her it would be wise not to buck him right then. She stayed outside and braced against the bitter wind, certain she didn't want to come face-to-face with the kind of death the man had met.

While she waited, she turned to the Lord. She prayed for all the miners and the risks they faced. She prayed for Adrian; he needed all the strength the Lord could supply. She prayed for herself, that she might be the helpmate Adrian needed at this time. She even prayed for the culprit. It was only too obvious that he needed God's presence in his life. Anyone who knew God's grace, His goodness, His love, wouldn't seek to enslave others with a drug, much less kill anyone who stumbled upon his wrongdoings.

After a while Letty came out, pale and subdued. She shook her head. "No one should have to die like that."

Phoebe wrapped her arm around her friend. "I marvel at you, Letty. How do you do this part of doctoring? It can't be an easy thing."

"I try everything in my arsenal to keep my patients from coming to this kind of end. The Lord's call on my heart is to heal, not to try and determine why someone died in a hideous fashion. Even in these matters, He's merciful and lets me face few horrors."

With a squeeze, Phoebe released her friend. "And do you know why this man died?"

Fire flashed in Letty's normally tender, kind eyes. "He wasted away from his addiction to opium. And *wasted* is the appropriate word. His death began when he took up one of those pipes. No life should be thrown away in exchange for a filthy habit."

Phoebe closed her eyes. "Lord Jesus, help us."

"You don't sound or look surprised," Letty commented.

"I've suspected trouble since Mei-Mei came to town to look for her husband. Then Adrian and I learned that John believed opium had come to the Heart of Silver Mine. It seems that Li Fong, Mei-Mei's husband, had spoken to him about the drug, and the two of them were trying to uncover the truth."

She drew a shuddery breath. "They died before they could do anything about it. I'm convinced John went into the mine to learn more about the opium problem and not just to examine the abysmal working conditions Mr. Hart forced on his men."

"Now you and Adrian want to succeed where John and Li Fong failed."

"Yea. I owe at least that much to John."

"You don't owe your late husband anything," Letty countered. "He died doing what he must have seen as right in God's eyes."

"I know that. But what you don't know is that I practically ignored his concern for the miners. I should have been a better wife than that. I should have helped him, or gone with him, or—"

"Should you have died in the cave with him, too?" Adrian asked from the doorway of the house. "Would that have helped John? The miners? You? Would it have furthered the cause of Christ?"

"Perhaps . . . Nay . . . Oh, I don't know."

She closed her eyes to shut out the terror of the day and the circumstances that had led to it, but she couldn't. It all was ingrained in her mind, in her soul.

"I just know that I have to do everything possible to find out who killed Lee's parents and John. I know it's not wrong in the Lord's eyes."

She grasped Adrian's hand and gave Letty a pleading look. "You do understand, don't you?"

"Oh, I do indeed understand that burning need to know and to right a wrong," Letty said. "But my experience insists I warn you. It could cost you more than you might imagine. And don't try to do it alone."

Phoebe relaxed her hold on Adrian, but to her surprise, he held tight.

Letty turned to him, glared, and wagged a finger. "You'd best go speak with Sheriff Herman—if you haven't already shared your suspicions with him."

At Adrian's blush, Letty crossed her arms across her chest and tipped her chin up toward the slate-hued sky. "I suspected as much. This is a crime, Mr. Gamble. Someone sold your miner enough opium to kill him over time. True, the man took it, but you know that once those habits start, they steal a man's will and his sense. As far as I'm concerned, whoever sold him the drug is a killer just as if he'd shot him square in the gut."

Adrian blanched, but not a word escaped his lips.

What kept him silent? And why hadn't he spoken to the sheriff? Phoebe hadn't said a word, fearing the lawman would label her a meddlesome female with more imagination than sense. But now that they knew opium posed a problem, especially after this miner's death, things were different.

"Letty is right," she told Adrian. "We need to tell the sheriff all we know and everything we suspect. This is much bigger than just the petty thievery you first uncovered at the mine."

With a rough twist, Adrian pushed her hand away and fisted his at his side. His rejection tore a hole in Phoebe's heart.

His jaw tightened, a muscle twitched in his lean cheek, and Phoebe took note of the visible pulse-beat at his throat.

"Murder," he said. "We couldn't possibly let it go unpunished, now could we?"

Phoebe gasped at the raw quality of his voice. What was wrong with him? What made him so bitter, so harsh?

She longed to wrap her arms around him, as she'd done that other night, to watch him hold Lee awkwardly yet tenderly, to again witness the kindness he'd shown even the spoiled Dahlia, the predatory Naomi, the critical and slanderous Emmaline. But she couldn't, so she did what she could, what her heart led her to do.

A hand on his rock hard arm, she said, "Mr. Gamble, what's wrong—"

"We've no time for pretty words." He shook off her touch. "We have to find the sheriff. A killer cannot go uncaught, don't you know?"

Without a backward glance, he strode away, his long legs eating up the distance with every step. Phoebe turned to Letty but found the same bewilderment she felt in her friend's face. The doctor shrugged in evident helplessness.

Phoebe moaned and ran after Adrian.

Even after she caught up with him, she had to maintain a trot to stay at his side. Not that her efforts made any difference. As far as his response to her presence went, he could as easily have walked down Main Street all on his own.

Their passage elicited any number of quizzical looks from those who were out and about. The men just stared, but the women gasped and looked shocked. Surely the sight of the Widow Williams running after the new mine owner, with whom she was involved in a scandal already, gave them abundant fuel for their fire.

This wouldn't allay the gossip. In the eyes of those who wanted to believe the rumors, her actions would confirm the worst of Emmaline's accusations.

Phoebe did care about her reputation, but she couldn't put it ahead of this more pressing matter. Regardless of how Adrian's words had come out, how he felt about the matter, the truth remained the same. There was a killer in Hartville, and she had to make sure he was brought to justice.

She owed it to her dead husband, her newly adopted son, and the memory of that child's natural parents. She owed her Lord and Savior the righteousness to which He called her, to which He called His own.

She'd face her ruined reputation later.

Adrian entered the sheriff's office without the slightest ceremony. As though he owned the place, he faced Max Herman and said, "I've a matter for you, and it must be seen to immediately."

"Well, now, Mr. Gamble," Herman drawled. "It's right nice of you to come calling this fine day. We aim to please 'round here. Tell me. How're things going over to that mine of yours?"

The sheriff's sarcasm only made Adrian more tense. Phoebe noted the rigid line of his back and the flush that crept up his neck.

"That's what you need to investigate. There have been altogether too many deaths at the Heart of Silver Mine in the recent past, and today's is anything but an accident."

The sheriff bolted upright. "Today's? What's happened?"

"One of the Chinese men died, and Dr. Wagner says it was because of his use of opium."

"Opium," the lawman said, disgust in his voice. "So it's true then."

"You knew?" Adrian asked, his voice more ominous than before.

"We just suspected. None of the men would talk."

Adrian stepped up to the desk, planted his fists atop a messy stack of papers, and pinned the sheriff with his gaze. "You suspected but did nothing about it?"

The lawman recoiled momentarily, then recovered and mimicked the stance, doing his best to stare down eyes that stood about six inches higher than his. "What did you want me to do, shut you down? There ain't much I can do if no one's saying nothing real about it to me. 'Sides, it's only them Chinamen who use the stuff."

"The nationality of those who've been exploited doesn't matter one bit. Too many men have died. Didn't you think the cave-in last spring deserved investigation?"

The sheriff's mud-brown eyes remained steady. "What makes you think I didn't do my investigating?"

Adrian glared right back.

The sheriff's sigh gusted out. "I don't have much to bring to a judge when all's I know about's a cave-in at a silver mine. The roof made by blastin' away the rock just gave way. That's practically a daily happenin' in this part of the world."

Adrian whirled, dragged his hat off, and ran his hand through his dark hair. Phoebe watched his growing frustration with an impotence she hated. There truly was nothing she could do to help him.

He paced to the window and looked out on the rock face of the mountain from which his workers extracted the ore that had given birth to the town. Phoebe noted the intensity in his gaze, admired the determination in the set of his shoulders, shared the frustration on his face.

With a glance over his shoulder, he asked, "What do you intend to do about this latest death?"

The sheriff shrugged. "What I always do. I talk to folks who might could know something about it and try and get them to tell me what they know. I can't do much more'n that."

Adrian rounded on him. "You certainly can't just let it go like that. Not now. The men won't talk. They're scared. Right down to the last one of them. And I'd say they have every reason to be afraid. Not only is someone more interested in the money the Chinese miners pay for the opium than in their well-being, but he's also willing to kill to protect himself. You have a—"

He stopped the flow of angry words and closed his eyes. Phoebe took a step closer, but then he squared his shoulders again. His expression hardened as it had right before he turned from her at the miners' house.

"Sheriff Herman," Adrian said in a deadly cold tone, "you have a killer in this town. As the owner of the mine, I want to know what you're going to do about it."

The lawman tilted his head to meet Adrian's intense gaze. "I'll do my best, Mr. Gamble. That's all's a man can do." He crossed his arms over his powerful chest. "But now that you and Mrs. Williams are both here, I have me some questions for the both of you."

Adrian's gaze darted toward Phoebe, then focused on the back wall of the office, just above the sheriff's head. "What kind of questions?"

Dread, like a lump of lead, lodged in Phoebe's middle.

"A complaint's been brought to me about the two of you." The sheriff's eyes never wavered from Adrian's face. "Seems there's some as have their questions 'bout the death of that Chinese woman what you called your housekeeper." He turned to Phoebe. "The one whose kid you got now."

Phoebe cringed.

Adrian looked bewildered. "What kind of questions? Someone killed her and that someone likely thought she knew something that might hurt him."

Skepticism crept onto Herman's face, into his voice. "What're you talking about? What could she have known?"

"Mei-Mei's husband told John about the opium," Phoebe said. "I'm convinced that's why John went to the mine the day he died. I believe he wanted to get closer to the Chinese miners and perhaps learn who was selling the drug."

The sheriff tugged on his earlobe, then twisted his mouth in a humorless smile. "And there ain't nobody livin' what can say what's the truth."

Phoebe gasped. "Mr. Herman, are you calling me a liar?"

"No, ma'am, I ain't rightly so. I'm just saying what I'm see-ing." He turned to Adrian. "And seeing as we don't know much about you, I can't say I feel right about that death happening at your house."

Adrian flinched. A muscle twitched in his cheek. "Why would you connect Mei-Mei's death with my being new to town?"

The lawman's eyes narrowed. "It ain't rightly your being new to town what makes me wonder. It's that you ain't told nobody nothing much about you. How'm I to know y'ain't been carv-ing up folks or adding notches to your gun belt for the past few years?"

If Phoebe hadn't been watching, she might have missed Adrian's shudder.

"I don't have a gun belt to notch."

"Man don't need a gun to kill."

Adrian glared at the sheriff, then crammed his hat back on. "I wasn't in town when Mei-Mei was killed. I went to Rockton with Phoebe that day. I'd be happy to give you the names of the men we met while we were there."

"Might could help if you gave me the names of those who've known you a spell longer than you've lived here in town."

Adrian went to the office door. "Your business is to find who killed Mei-Mei, not to pry into my business."

"You must also find whoever is selling the opium," Phoebe added.

Adrian indicated that she should precede him. "Stop them, too."

"Seems to me," the sheriff drawled, "you've too much mystery to you for my comfort. There's more'n a mite I want to know about you to settle my questions. I don't cotton to dealing in the dark. And if you don't want to answer me, well, then I'll just have to get me them answers myself."

Adrian walked out, not waiting for Phoebe.

She glared at the sheriff. "You'd do well, sir, to stick to matters of crime rather than to let malicious gossips influence your opinion of folks."

The soft slap of wood against wood told her she'd managed to keep the door from slamming in her wake—but it had taken all her control to do so.

She stepped into the bitter, cold afternoon and noted how far Adrian had stalked in those few seconds she'd stayed behind. True, the death of the miner troubled her. And of course, Mei-Mei's death still weighed heavily upon her. But what troubled her most was Adrian's odd behavior.

It wasn't just his refusal to clear himself to the sheriff with a few simple answers. What truly confused her was Adrian's behavior toward her.

How could a man who'd kissed her with so much emotion then turn around and so coldly reject her efforts to reach out and comfort him?

His response to the sheriff's veiled accusation about Mei-Mei's death led her to think he hadn't heard any of the gossip. So that wasn't why he'd gone from tender and passionate to cold and abrupt.

To her dismay, his caresses had evoked in her a deeper response than she'd felt for John. She had loved her husband, but with a different kind of love than she felt for Adrian.

She had to acknowledge how intense her feelings for him had grown. And she wanted to share them with him. She also wanted to help him solve his problems, to encourage him during his moments of trouble, to know everything there was to know about him. But he didn't want the same thing.

Adrian seemed determined to keep his past to himself.

Why?

What was he hiding? For surely he had to be hiding something. Otherwise, he would have told the sheriff what he wanted to know, if for no other reason than to persuade the foolish man he wasn't some kind of criminal on the run.

Still, that didn't bother her as much as the changeable way he behaved toward her. Did Adrian care anything at all for her? His kindness and his kisses suggested that he did.

But his rejections? They made her wonder if there was nothing more than male self-indulgence in his passion. She needed to know.

Something soft and light landed on her cheek. She glanced up at the sky and saw the first snowflakes of the season. Although they looked tiny and sparkly at that moment, apprehension knotted in her throat. She'd heard so many grim descriptions of the severity of the Colorado winter that she'd begun to fear its arrival.

And here it was, on the same day Adrian made perfectly clear he didn't want her. The chill in the air was no greater than that in her broken heart.

She entered the store and saw him by the counter, speaking with Caroline.

"I'm so sorry I've been gone so long," she told the girl. "You'd best be on your way home. It's begun to snow, and I suspect your mama wouldn't be pleased with me if you caught a chill on my account."

Caroline picked up her soft blue wool wrap and peered out the front window. "Just some flakes out there, Aunt Phoebe. I'm fine, and Mama couldn't never be angry at you."

"You're a dear." Phoebe kissed the girl's cheek. "Thank you for taking such good care of my little one."

"He's sweet," Caroline said as she walked to the door. "I can watch him any time you want."

"I'll keep that in mind, especially since you have so much experience watching your brothers and sisters. Now, hurry along, my girl. I do know your mother."

An oppressive silence swamped the room. Phoebe glanced sideways and spotted Adrian by the hall door. The expression on his face was gentler than it had been all day, reminiscent of his tenderness toward Lee the other night.

She had questions for him, and if she wanted answers, it seemed this was to be the time to get them.

"I don't know whether to expect my four o'clock regulars or not," she said, "but since no one is here, I've a matter to discuss with you."

He sighed. "I can't promise to have anything of merit to say."

"It's not like that." She pushed her discomfort aside. "I need to know why you go from hot to cold every time we meet. And why you decided you didn't want to see me after . . ." She voiced a quick, silent prayer. "After we kissed the other night."

A blush colored his cheeks. "I haven't decided any such thing."

"You haven't even been to your office since . . . well, in days."

He averted his gaze. "I've been busy at the mine."

"Adrian, I'm not a fool, nor am I a child."

"I never thought you were either."

"Then please do me the courtesy of explaining why you've now kissed me twice, yet after each of those kisses, you've treated me as though I carried some dreaded disease. I need to know why you've done that. I need to know if . . ." She took a deep breath, then asked the most difficult question yet. "I need to know if my kisses have made you uncomfortable because I've been too forward or if I've offended or displeased you."

Off went his hat, and he rubbed the lines on his forehead. "It's not you, Phoebe. On the contrary. You're the sweetest, loveliest, kindest woman I know. Your kisses have meant the world to me."

She mustered a whisper around the knot in her throat. "Then why have you stayed away? Why did you push me aside today?"

Sadness spread across his face. "I did it for your sake. It's best this way."

"How?" she asked, and an unbidden sob escaped. "How can hurting me be good for me?"

"More than anything, I wish things could be different. But because I—" He closed his eyes momentarily. "Because I care for you, I have to stay away. It's the only thing I can do for you. And there's nothing more I can say."

He went into the hallway, and seconds later Phoebe heard his footsteps on the circular metal stairs. She hurried to the front door, put the small wooden plaque that read CLOSED back in the window, and headed for her apartment. The four o'clock regulars would have to find some other way to entertain themselves that afternoon.

If she hadn't been so familiar with the store, she would have fallen or at least stumbled. Tears made her blind.

The evening crawled by, and Adrian alternated between calling himself a fool and wanting to run downstairs, wrap his arms around Phoebe and Lee, and never let go. Since he couldn't do the latter, he focused on the former.

It was his fault matters had come to such an uncomfortable pass. He should never have touched Phoebe. But he was obviously too weak to do what was right for her, and even for himself. The lovely young widow had filled the empty spot in his heart with her warmth and caring, her gentle smile, her efficient manner. And there was something so perfect in the way she held Lee, how she tended to his needs. It was all Adrian could do to keep from rushing her right down to Pastor Stone, marrying her, and building a family with her.

207

But he couldn't do that. And so he'd hurt her. She thought her sweet kisses might have offended him, but to correct her mistaken impression could only expose her to unspeakable danger.

So he sat in his office, worn Bible in hand, unwilling to leave the building where she and Lee slept. He didn't want them at the mercy of a mere lock. Whoever had killed Mei-Mei hadn't let a solid door or its strong lock keep him from doing evil. Adrian feared little would keep the culprit from killing Phoebe if he realized how much she already knew.

He'd finally learned the true meaning of love, the truth behind a certain pertinent Scripture. He read it again.

Greater love hath no man than this, that a man lay down his life for his friends.

Adrian now recognized a fate worse than losing his life for doing what was right. It would be far worse if Phoebe was hurt when he might prevent it.

The storm that raged outside was no worse than the one that roared in Phoebe's head. Her thoughts chased one another, dizzying her with their circular path.

What should she do? What would be the right thing?

Should she stay in Hartville, keep her position at the general store, and somehow fight her feelings for Adrian? Should she try to find work in town? Who would hire her?

Should she leave?

Right then, the Shaker family at North Union and Eldress Clymena's wise and gentle ways looked appealing, safe, and protected. Lee would flourish in the care of the Sisters in charge of the children. She could even return to her old job at the children's dwelling and care for him.

But the fallacies in Shaker beliefs held her back. God the Father, Son, and Holy Spirit was her all and all. She couldn't go along with the heresy that named Mother Ann Lee the second coming of the Christ Spirit, and that in female form. Jesus of Nazareth, virgin-born Son of the Almighty, was her one and only Savior.

Once Lee slept in peace, Phoebe fell to her knees and cried out to her Father in heaven.

She would trust in Him.

On Sunday morning Adrian rose early, dressed, and headed for church. He needed to feel a part of something greater than himself. God's church offered him the sense of belonging he lacked in every other part of his life.

The two-day blizzard had been an exercise in self-control. Phoebe had brought him meals at the appropriate times, but she'd had nothing to say. She hadn't even met his gaze.

Which should have satisfied him, but his contrary heart only wanted more of her.

What was he going to do? Should he sell the mine and go back to living on the run? Should he stay and make peace with the strain between him and Phoebe? Could he continue to see her and not want everything she had to offer?

Dare he stay and gamble on having given his pursuers the slip? He hadn't forgotten his experience at the restaurant the day he took Phoebe with him to Rockton. He'd sensed someone watching them.

Each time she'd left the office, he'd fallen on his knees in prayer. He'd sought guidance in the Scriptures, and while he'd revisited many familiar teachings, he still hadn't found the answer to his most pressing questions.

He hoped Pastor Stone had some nugget of wisdom for him in the sermon that day, something for the man he'd become, for Adrian Gamble, owner of a mine full of troubles greater than he could solve and a heart full of love for a woman he couldn't have.

As he entered the sanctuary, the murmurs in the pews caught his attention. Usually, cheerful chit-chat resounded until Mrs. Stone played the first notes of the morning's opening hymn. Today, surreptitious and anticipating glances toward the altar and choir box flew on the wings of heated whispers.

Adrian took a seat in a pew near the center of the vast chamber. As soon as he did, he felt the scrutiny of all those eyes as though they were thousands of needles pricking his skin. The whispers grew to a sharp sibilance.

Then the organ's notes rang out. The choir filed in, Phoebe at her usual place in the center of the front row. Instead of dying down, however, the congregation's conversation took on a heated insistence. Adrian noted the fixed stares now leveled on Phoebe. He also noticed her dignified carriage, her shoulders straight, her head high.

Although her skin looked paler than the snow that now blanketed Hartville, determination burned in her blue eyes.

As he took in the bizarre spectacle, he heard a voice to his right. He turned and saw Naomi Miller next to that Ruthie McMiniver.

"Two days," Naomi whispered. "That's how long they spent locked up in that store together. And you thought that charade of a trip out of town plenty bad."

A sinking sensation hit Adrian's stomach.

"No, no, no," Ruthie said. "It's the murder of that poor Chinese woman that I think is the worst. I figure they must have done it together. You know, to get her out of the way so they could be together to . . . well, you know."

Rage roared through Adrian. How dare they? He and Phoebe were innocent of what those vicious women were saying. Was that the town's current topic of conversation?

He glanced around and found half the congregation staring at Phoebe, who tried stalwartly to sing God's praises, her voice as strong and sweet as ever. The other half stared at him.

What had he done to that decent, gentle woman? He'd only hoped to protect her from a killer, yet with his sincere effort, he'd managed to taint her reputation.

He took another look around the room and groaned. Her reputation had wound up in shreds. *How, Lord Jesus, am I going to get us out of this mess?*

How would he know the right thing to do?

15

Adrian's stomach churned as the citizens of Hartville continued to savage Phoebe's good name. All because of him.

While they had shared some moving embraces, they'd done nothing untoward. Yet these people, her supposed friends, neighbors and fellow church members, chose to believe the worst of her.

He couldn't help but wonder if the gossip was this virulent because of his status as an outsider who struck the townsfolk as mysterious and dangerous. Would the scrutiny be as judgmental if Phoebe were linked with an established, local man? Would the gossip be as unreasonable if he hadn't had to keep silent about himself?

By coming to Hartville, Adrian had sought relative anonymity to prevent detection by his pursuers. Yet it appeared that his attempt at discretion had backfired. He was now the most notorious man in town. Not only that, but as he'd tried to save himself, he'd injured an innocent woman, the woman he loved.

Would the curious have accepted him better if he'd provided every detail they wanted? Might that acceptance have tempered the heat of the gossip?

He didn't know. He just knew that the worst had happened. He'd hurt Phoebe. Again.

To make matters worse, Pastor Stone had chosen to preach on the merits of living an honest and forthright life, one that revealed Christ's lordship in the believer's thoughts, actions, and choices—one that needed no deceit or subterfuge.

Yet another boulder of guilt to add to the pile that weighed down Adrian's heart.

Bowing his head, he cried out in silence to his heavenly Father. How could he have lived a life like the one Pastor Stone described without consigning himself to what amounted to suicide? If he hadn't gone into hiding, the two surviving train robbers would have tracked him down well before this sickening day. Would accepting death at the hands of those two have been preferable in God's eyes?

A familiar Scripture returned to his heart. *Trust in the LORD with all thine heart; and lean not unto thine own understanding.*

Was that the root of the problem he faced now? Had he not trusted the Lord enough? Had he instead trusted his understanding of the situation too much?

He shook his head to clear his thoughts, no longer sure of anything. What else could he have done? Should he have waited for the vengeful men to appear at the door and take his life as he'd taken their leader's? Would that have been more honorable in God's sight?

No matter how he looked at his circumstances, the failure to act still struck him as a form of suicide, and he knew only God had the right to determine the place and time and means of a man's death. On the other hand, if the two crooks had caught up with and dispatched him, he would never have exposed Phoebe to the wrongful censure under which she now struggled.

You would never have met her either, never have held her, loved her, kissed her.

That would have kept her safe, but would that have been better? To go through whatever passed for his life without knowing love like he felt for her? Like she clearly felt for him?

He looked up to see the wet glitter of unshed tears in Phoebe's blue eyes. The mountain of guilt grew heavier yet. He'd done that to her. His refusal to explain his apparent rejection had hurt her; his attentions had led to the gossip and scorn that brought tears to her eyes.

Pastor Stone's sermon resounded with truth. Adrian had to give Phoebe an honest accounting of his actions. He had to be forthright with her, to bring an end to his elaborate subterfuge, at least with her. He would also have to trust in God rather than in his abilities and understanding. He had to believe that the Father wouldn't let her suffer just because she knew the truth of his past, just because she knew him.

He stood with the rest of the congregation for the final hymn. He knew what he had to do. And yet he was ashamed to admit that he didn't know if he could go through with what God called him to do.

He didn't know if he could relinquish all control of his circumstances and trust God implicitly from that day forward.

Lord forgive him that sin.

Through sheer force of will, Phoebe made it through the opening hymns. She wondered, however, in what kind of worship the congregation had engaged. It seemed they'd focused on her and whispered among themselves, avid and judgmental expressions on their faces. On occasion they'd shot equally condemning glares at Adrian.

Shortly after she'd begun her first hymn, his expression had changed. Since the volume of the buzzing had peaked at that same moment, the substance of the gossip was more than likely at fault for the shock and anger that had burst on his rugged face.

How could these people who claimed to be her friends, who'd comforted her through her darkest moments of grief, who'd come to know her better than even the Shaker Sisters had, think the worst of her? How could they think she'd indulged in a tawdry entanglement with Adrian? How could they spoil her memories of those loving and passionate kisses?

Phoebe squared her shoulders, held her head high, and forced her thoughts aside to listen to Pastor Stone. After the final hymn, she left the choir box with the others, put away her robe, and hurried to find Mim and Lee. The girl had watched the baby for her, and Phoebe thanked her in word and with a hug.

As she headed outdoors, she heard Mrs. Stone call her name. Instead of waiting, she ran from the house of God. She couldn't bear even sympathy at that moment.

With Lee held close to her chest, she hurried home. The urgency did not leave her until she stepped onto the boardwalk in front of the store. At the door she juggled the baby and her reticule, rummaged in the small bag's depths for her key. To her surprise, the door swung open as she searched.

"Come inside," Adrian said.

Phoebe's emotions rioted. The pleasure of his presence warred against mortification. He now knew what others in town said about them.

The internal battle kept her frozen in place until Lee began to whimper. Adrian reached for the child, and she mutely acceded. He took Lee in his arms, stepped aside to let Phoebe into the store.

"Hey, there, little fella. Don't tell me you've a nasty diaper again. Or are you just hungry?" He gave Phoebe a sheepish look. "Maybe he's both, like that other time."

The remembered embrace hung between them. Heat filled Phoebe's cheeks, and tears stung her eyes. She couldn't bear the misery and shame she felt because of the gossips.

With a prayer for strength and composure, she took a deep breath and headed for the hallway door. "I suspect he's indeed both hungry and wet. But you don't need to concern yourself with Lee. Since it's Sunday, I don't have anything else to take me from his side. I'll take care of his every need—"

"We need to talk."

His abrupt statement made a mockery of her forced normalcy. She reached for Lee. "You've said all that needs to be said."

He held the child tighter to his broad chest. "On the contrary. I've said nowhere near enough."

The strain of the morning caught up with her, and Phoebe felt tremors from her fingers to her knees. Her broken heart couldn't stand another devastating rejection. She had accepted his last one as final.

"Please. I . . . I need to be alone."

He opened the hall door for her. "You can be alone once I've said what I need to say."

Afraid she would fall, her legs too shaky to support her, Phoebe nevertheless stepped in front of him and entered her apartment. Seconds later she heard him close the door.

"I can't imagine what you have in mind now. Wasn't my humiliation at church sufficient for you?"

"That's precisely what's brought me here."

"What? Do you intend to kiss me again and then walk away for 'my own good'? Thank you, Mr. Gamble, but I'd much rather not."

He winced. "You have every right to your anger. I haven't treated you in a particularly honorable fashion."

"I'm glad you admit it."

"How could I not? I'd have to be made of stone to deny you've been hurt because of me."

She went to take Lee, but Adrian shook his head and placed the child on the bed. "I know how to change him. I do learn from experience."

"Am I supposed to infer something from that statement?"

"Yes. Between Pastor Stone's sermon and the misery my actions caused you, I've learned quite a bit."

Phoebe took note of his gentle touch when he opened the large diaper pin. He took great care to not hurt the child. She wished he'd taken equal care with her—

"I've hurt you." He sprinkled cornstarch on the baby's bottom, then glanced at her. "It was never my intention. You mean more to me than I can say, and I'd do anything to keep you from harm."

The sincerity in his words brought tears back to her eyes. But she kept her peace. If he finally wanted to speak, so be it.

"I came to Hartville under difficult circumstances, as you must already suspect."

He sounded weary, heavy laden. The lines on either side of his mouth looked deeper than she remembered, and his shoulders drooped.

She murmured a wordless acknowledgment.

"I'm a wanted man, but not in the way you—or the others—might think."

At her arched brow, he reddened and turned his attention to Lee. He again demonstrated great caution as he gathered up the ends of the diaper and pinned them. His large hands tugged on rubber pants, then he bundled the blue blanket around the child, brought him to his chest, and stood for a moment, clearly savoring the closeness.

"I've been on the run for a long time," he murmured, his gaze on Lee's little face. "My life depends on my staying out of sight, so to speak."

"You're awfully visible as the owner of the mine."

"Yes, but those who are after me don't know I'm here—at least I pray they don't. I've done everything possible to make sure they don't learn that the man they're after is me. That I'm here."

The strain got the better of Phoebe. "Just tell me what you've done. Why are these people after you? Who are they? Why do you fear for your life?"

She held out her arms, took Lee, and collapsed in her comforting, familiar Shaker rocker. "What you're hiding can't hurt me any more than what's happened in town already. I'm seen as the worst of Jezebels, and some call me a murderess, too. How bad can your story be?"

Adrian strode to the back door, reached for the knob, and then stopped. With deliberate effort, he turned and went back to the bed. "I can't run from you anymore. I never should have in the first place."

He opened the buttons on his coat and laid it across Phoebe's bed. He removed his hat and tossed it onto the coat. He rumpled his hair with a hand, closed his eyes tight, and thinned his lips. Lines appeared on his brow.

"Of course you're no murderess. Rather, it's me who's killed a man."

If she hadn't been seated, Phoebe would have crumpled to the ground. "I don't . . . know what I expected . . . I just never expected you to say that."

"That's why I never spoke about it. I've yet to meet the person who takes that revelation lightly."

"I can well believe it." Shaker teaching against violence, against the taking of human life, swirled in Phoebe's head. "Tell me everything."

He pulled out one of the two chairs at the table and sat in front of her. "I'll tell you everything from the beginning. But please don't ask me anything—"

He paused when she opened her mouth. "At least, don't ask until I'm done getting this out. If I stop, I'm afraid I'll never get to the end. And I have to."

She frowned at his request, but in the end realized she didn't have a choice if she wanted to know what had led to their current straits.

"Very well," she said.

He again ran his fingers through his dark hair, then rubbed his forehead and tightened a finger and thumb against the corners of his eyes. Keeping his head down, he began.

"My father fell ill nearly two years ago, and a great deal of the responsibility for his business fell on me. Our family owns a stove manufacturing company."

He swallowed hard. Phoebe leaned forward and reached toward him but then realized the foolishness of her action. She sat back and pressed a kiss onto Lee's forehead instead.

"I was honored and so proud that he'd asked me to visit merchants in Kansas and California in his place." A sad smile played on his lips. Then he shook his head and grew serious again. "Not long after the train pulled out of Kansas City, a trio of thieves forced the engineer to stop. They came into the dining car where I was, the obvious ringleader holding a gun to the poor man's head."

The earth beneath Phoebe seemed to shift. Evidently, this wasn't as cut-and-dried as she'd feared. She bit her tongue to keep from commenting and prayed for Adrian, as he suffered in the telling of his tale.

"When everyone in the car turned over their valuables to the two who held burlap sacks, the leader shot his captive in the leg—to show mercy by sparing his life, he said."

Adrian's mouth twisted as though he'd tasted something foul.

"The two with the loot ran off into the next car, but the one with the gun noticed the earrings an older lady still wore." He met Phoebe's gaze, and she read rage in his eyes. "Something snapped in me when that animal turned the gun on her."

Phoebe gasped, but Adrian went on. "It was wrong to terrorize innocent folks like that, but when that sweet lady—someone's grandmother, I'm sure—swooned and couldn't hand him the trinkets, I refused to sit there and watch. I jumped him."

"Oh, Adrian . . ."

"I startled him enough that he released the engineer, but then he turned the gun on me—"

"Oh no . . ."

He continued, immersed in the memories of the nightmare. "I wrestled him for the gun. I don't remember much after I got hold of the steel, but the shot slammed my gut and I went deaf for a moment. I felt something warm and wet run down my legs. I thought it was mine . . . I called out to the Lord, figuring I was on my way to eternity."

Adrian stood, scraped the chair against the floor, and paced the length of the room. He reminded Phoebe of the picture of a lion she'd once seen in a book.

"When all was said and done," he said, "the thief was dead." He kept silent for a moment, then came to her side and knelt, grasped her hand, and made her meet his gaze. "I was alive, and his gun was in my hand."

With her free hand, she took hold of his taut forearm. The knot in her throat began to melt, and she opened her mouth to comfort him.

He placed a finger on her lips. "I'm not done."

He told of the attempts the two surviving thieves made on his life while he traveled in California. He related his circuitous and furtive return home, as well as the cautious, deliberate steps he and his attorney had taken to declare him dead.

But when his voice broke at the mention of his mother's farewell, Phoebe's tears spilled over. She wept for the man she loved, a man who'd done the honorable thing one day, only to then watch the rest of his life become a true hell on this fallen world.

He'd felt the need to hide and to lie to stay alive . . . to protect the family, who could be used to get at him if his hunters suspected he still lived.

"They know," he said, his voice now hoarse, "that I'd turn myself over at any time if it meant protecting Mother or any of the others. Their thirst for vengeance doesn't seem to ebb."

A large finger caught one of the tears on Phoebe's cheek. He studied the moist drop. The strain on his features eased, and his eyes touched her with a look of pure love. He then stood and went to stare out the glass in the back door.

Phoebe also rose but went for the bureau drawer that served as Lee's crib. She put the infant to bed and again sought the Lord for courage. Unsure of Adrian's reception to her gesture, she approached and slipped a hand in the crook of one of his arms.

"Perhaps," she whispered, "you're too hard on yourself—"

"On the contrary." He covered her fingers with his. "That's not all I've done, and you know it. Because I put my own safety before everything else, I hid my identity and refused to answer questions about myself when I came to town. That gave birth to the wildest case of rampant curiosity I've ever seen. I gave the gossips good cause. And because of my silence, they kept so close a scrutiny on me that I tainted you."

Her cheeks heated again. "You didn't stay quiet only for you. You have a family to protect. That's hardly a selfish motive. And the gossip? Well, you didn't bring it about all by yourself. I was there when you kissed me. I could have refused, you know."

"But—"

"But that's the truth. I did indulge in those caresses just as much as you did. When one is a widow, such actions are viewed with a sorely jaundiced eye."

"But that's wrong."

"It is. As is the situation you're in. I could never ask you to put yourself in danger just to silence foolish, uncomfortable gossip. Your life is priceless, while the lies they tell are worthless."

Adrian's arms went around her, and Phoebe thrilled at his touch. She curved hers around him in turn, placed her head on his chest, relished the beat of his heart beneath her ear, the rise and fall of every breath he took.

"I love you," he whispered.

Her breath caught in her throat. Had he truly said those wondrous words?

Pulling back a tiny bit, she met his gaze, and the tenderness there told her everything she needed to know.

"I love you, too."

He brought his hand up to cup her cheek. Phoebe leaned into the caress. She closed her eyes, then felt him slip his hands into the loosened hair behind her ears. With gentle pressure, he brought her face closer until his lips touched hers. The kiss began as a tender, caring gesture that sealed their words of love. But then, as the seconds fled by, it warmed into something deeper, more passionate. Tremors of emotion, and indeed of pleasure and need, rose in her, and she returned his kiss with all the love she had in her heart.

Long moments of joy passed before Adrian pulled back. The look he gave her was one filled with sadness and longing.

"What—?"

"Hush," he said. "I've talked myself empty already. It was something I had to do, and there were things you had to know, but I can't talk anymore, nor can I answer any more questions."

She slipped from his embrace and, feeling awkward, turned toward the stove. As she stood there, unsure of herself, she withdrew her watch from her pocket. To her surprise, it was nearly two o'clock. The retelling of Adrian's tale had taken longer than she'd realized.

Back to him, she said, "I roasted a chicken yesterday, and there's plenty left. Please say you'll stay and share a meal with me."

During the long silence that ensued, she feared he'd refuse. Then he replied. "If you insist . . . I mean, if you'd like, even though someone somewhere might again consider it improper."

Phoebe walked to the icebox. "That's something I'll have to deal with, but I can't do it right now. You've finally told me what I needed to know, and because of it, you haven't eaten yet. It's the least I can do . . . and I'd really like to."

"Then I'll stay."

In a short time Phoebe set a savory spread before them. As

they gave thanks for their food, as they ate, and especially as they chatted about Lee, the strain between them evaporated. They enjoyed the chicken, potatoes, peas, and fresh bread. The hot tea she served soothed them further, and by the time the baby awoke, the sense of rightness she'd experienced the first time they'd shared a meal had returned.

As she fed Lee, Adrian insisted on bringing a stack of firewood inside. "You shouldn't have to dig it out from under all that snow each time you need to stoke the stove."

She studied his face and said with a smile, "You're a good man, Adrian Gamble. Don't you dare let that guilt you carry tell you anything different."

The sweet, sad look again appeared on his face. "And you, Phoebe Williams, are a wonderful, godly woman. Don't you let those hateful biddies make you forget that."

She blushed, wondering if God truly saw her as wonderful or even as the kind of woman He'd called her to be. But it wouldn't do to argue and spoil the lovely afternoon.

"It's dusk already," Adrian said after he'd set the wood in a neat pile beside the stove. "I'd best be on my way so you and Lee can rest."

She wished he didn't have to leave, that they had the right to stay together, to be the family she so longed for. But they couldn't. First and foremost because Adrian had never voiced that same longing she felt. He'd only said he loved her, and that could mean a multitude of things.

She held out his hat. "Thank you for the wood. And even more, for your honesty today."

"It was long overdue, and the very least I could do seeing how much trouble I've caused you."

She couldn't deny it, since his secrecy had fanned the flame of gossip, so she said nothing.

"I'll be coming to the office in the morning," he said as he drew open the door. "Good-night."

"Good-night, and the Lord's blessing be with you."

His eyes widened, and Phoebe saw him swallow hard. His lips curved into the start of a smile, and she thought she saw a moist gleam in his eyes. She read once again that deep longing she'd spied before. Everything in her urged her to reach out to him, but she'd already done that too many times and been rebuffed. She didn't want another rejection, not after he'd finally let down his guard around her, not now that he'd finally confided in her.

He surprised her by coming closer. "Phoebe . . ."

But that was all. He turned on his heel and left, closing the door behind him.

The loneliness that for so long had haunted her returned.

"Lord," she whispered, "you're the God of widows and orphans. Please fill the void this little innocent and I feel."

As he left Phoebe's warm little home, Adrian again felt the world's cold, lonely grip. Each time he bid her farewell, the emptiness inside him grew greater and his need grew stronger. He trod through the silent street, forcing his way into the icy wind, surrounded by the gloom that forecast yet another winter storm.

At 8:00 a.m. sharp, Adrian stepped onto the boardwalk at the corner of Ore Road and Main. He was just six doors away from the general store, and anticipation burned in him. Phoebe was only six doors away.

Eyes fixed straight ahead, he saw her step outside to sweep last night's snow from in front of the store.

"Would you just look at that brazen hussy," a woman said from across the street.

Emmaline harrumphed. "You'd think she was as pure as the

driven snow—if even a decent widow can be called that. And goodness knows, she's not decent by half."

Adrian froze in his tracks. Phoebe's movements grew erratic and the color leached from her face, but she continued with her task.

"I'll have you know," Ruthie added, "I saw him leave her place in the dark—last night. No shame, I tell you. Such debauched goings-on must be stopped."

"Really, Ruthie?" another woman asked. "You really saw him leave late at night?"

"I'd never make up something like that."

"Jezebel!"

"Strumpet."

From there the epithets worsened. Phoebe's face turned the color of marble, and her blue eyes blazed with a brittle light. She seemed fragile, more vulnerable than he'd ever seen a woman look . . . except perhaps the elderly lady to whose aid he once sprang.

Still, with her characteristic mantle of dignity, Phoebe straightened her spine, held her shoulders back, and tipped up her chin. She then turned and went back inside the store.

Unable to move, to even utter a rebuttal to the assault, Adrian felt like the greatest coward alive. Fear kept him from voicing anything that might ease the situation. Then again, he didn't want to unmask and become visible to a pair of vengeful killers, to renounce the foolish hope of someday seeing his family again, of holding Lee any time and all the time, of spending day after day at Phoebe's side.

As he stood, he watched Letty march up the street, approach the gossips, and give them a piece of her mind. In what seemed like seconds, they scattered and she made a beeline for the store.

Never in his life had he felt so useless, so worthless.

"Son," Pastor Stone said at his side, his kind voice in sharp contrast to Adrian's self-loathing, "you need to act. You can do something about this."

"What? What could I do that wouldn't make matters worse?"

A caring arm reached across his shoulders, and Adrian thought of his late father. Surely this wasn't what that loving man had wanted when he'd urged Adrian to care for and protect the wife he would soon make a widow, the younger son and daughter who'd soon be orphaned, the sister who'd never married and would lose the brother she'd always leaned on.

"What could I possibly do?"

"Marry her, son. No one can say another word against her once you make her your wife."

For a moment Adrian's heart soared with hope. Then reality crashed down around him. "I can't."

"Why ever not?"

"Because, Pastor Stone, I love Phoebe too much to do that to her. I won't marry her, not because I don't want to, but for her sake."

The reverend opened his lips, and Adrian continued to avoid the man's questions. "You'll have to trust me. It's best for her if I don't."

Nothing had cost Adrian so dearly, not even leaving his family, as uttering those words.

16

The pastor stared at him for a long, uncomfortable moment, then bid him farewell. Adrian nodded, aware that his words hadn't been enough.

Neither had doing his best been enough to ensure the life he really wanted.

There was, however, something more he could do. He'd recently contacted a Pinkerton agent he knew, and he hoped the man would track down the source of the opium. He needed to urge the agent to a faster pace. Lives hung in the balance.

He had, however, another difficult task to accomplish. Phoebe would see it as a betrayal, but it was his only way to protect her.

He chose to address the most difficult matter first.

Inside the store, he felt its four walls close in on him—just as his past was closing in as well. His present looked bleak, and as for the future? He couldn't see much of one.

As he approached the counter, he heard Phoebe's exquisite voice lifted in song. But unlike the other times he'd heard her, this time she faltered, the flow of the lyrics broken by sobs. Lee's whimpers filled in some of the gaps.

"Phoebe," he said, knowing he was about to hurt her. "I'm so very sorry about what happened out there."

She turned, and although she held her head high, she did nothing to hide the tears that bathed her cheeks. "You saw."

"Yes. And it sickened me. It's my fault they've slandered you. You've done nothing wrong."

She looked away. "I'm not blameless, Adrian. I let my feelings for you override my common sense."

Once again her honest confession of love humbled him. Adrian's only regret was that he couldn't promise her a future filled with that kind of love. Instead, he had to bring even their present to an end.

"What I now realize I must do—" He struggled over every word. "—is difficult and painful. Mostly because I'm again about to hurt you. I see no other way out of this. Your safety and well-being are my main concern."

He'd known his words would alarm her, but he'd wanted to give her the opportunity to brace herself. He realized how well he'd come to know her when he saw her stand tall and meet his gaze.

"I don't see how hurting me can be in the interest of my well-being, but nothing about the recent past has been understandable."

"Again, I take responsibility for that."

"Nay, you can't. At least, not for everything. You didn't own the mine when the accident took place."

"True, but your other troubles are because of me." He swallowed hard and prayed for courage. "I hope someday you'll understand why it's best for you to find other employment—"

She gasped and blanched.

Adrian nearly lost his nerve. But he had to go on. He had to make sure she suffered no further harm from contact with him.

"As long as you live and work here, they'll link you to me. And that's the reason for the scandal. Please believe me. I'd much rather it be otherwise, but we must put a proper distance between us. Only then will the gossip end. Only then will they stop their slander."

Without losing an ounce of dignity, Phoebe nodded, her skin paler than ever. "Very well," she said in a faint yet firm voice. "I'll vacate the premises within the hour and make arrangements for the removal of my larger belongings."

"That won't be necessary. Please, do take the time you need. I understand you'll have to find lodging, other work . . ."

He let his words die off. They sounded absurd. He'd just thrown her out, and in nearly the same breath, asked her to linger at his side.

She rounded the counter without a sound.

Adrian felt ill. Where she should have sent insults his way, called him every sort of cad—if not much worse—Phoebe only graced him with a look of aching sadness, one that made him crave another glimpse of her glorious smile. But that was not to be. His words had ended that possibility.

She disappeared into the hallway, and with her went all of Adrian's wishes. Wishes he should never have made.

He'd again taken necessary measures, and again his life had changed as a result, as it had on that train. Both times, it had been for the worse.

Please, Lord, please. Don't let me fall. Please help me leave this room without another moment of shame.

She felt Adrian's gaze at her back until she slipped into the hallway, and although something inside urged her to argue, to fight his decision, she knew better. What more was there to say?

The situation couldn't stay as it was.

Putting distance between them did seem the logical answer. And Phoebe couldn't think about the future. No telling what she'd do if she began to wonder how she'd keep Lee fed, clothed, and sheltered. She'd always trusted her heavenly Father, but only with her life. Now she had an innocent child.

Did she trust Him enough?

She leaned back against the door to her apartment. *Into your hands, Lord, into your hands I commit this little boy . . . and myself.*

As unhappy as Lee had been all morning long, Phoebe knew she couldn't work with him in her arms. She changed his diaper and bundled him against the chill outside, then donned her cape. She needed to know her child was safe and cared for as she saw to their immediate future.

She practically ran to the manse, in the hope that Mrs. Stone would be available. The pastor's wife opened the door, took one look at Phoebe, and let out a cry.

"Come in, dear." She reached for the baby. "Tell me what's wrong."

The moment Lee left her arms, Phoebe began to shake. The trembling grew so violent that she couldn't even form words. Tears rolled down her face, and nausea rose up within her.

"Mim! Mr. Stone!" the pastor's wife called. "Hurry, please."

As Phoebe's knees buckled, Mim took Lee and hurried back up the stairs. The pastor arrived as the girl reached the top floor. Mrs. Stone wrapped an arm around Phoebe's waist.

"What's happened?" Pastor Stone asked.

Phoebe parted her lips to explain, but only a sob escaped. Pain clutched her heart and left her speechless. She waved ineffectually, her fingers icy and shaky.

"Fetch Letty," Mrs. Stone urged her husband.

"I'll be but a moment." Foregoing outer garments, he ran outside.

Mrs. Stone led her a few steps farther, but Phoebe couldn't tell where they were going.

She sat at the older woman's insistence, then noticed they'd gone to the parlor. The sofa yielded under her, and the cushions' welcome comforted her.

"Go ahead, dear," Mrs. Stone urged, "cry it out. Sometimes it's the very best remedy. Once that storm passes, one can look at one's troubles more dispassionately."

That was unlikely. Phoebe had nowhere to go, no means to earn a living, a tiny child to care for. And winter had arrived. The train came to Hartville only when the weather allowed it these days, and the recent blizzard had made the rails treacherous. She wouldn't be leaving town any time soon.

In what seemed like seconds, the pastor returned with Letty at his side. The doctor hurried to Phoebe's side. "Are you ill?"

Phoebe shook her head. The knot in her throat tightened.

"Is the baby unwell?"

Again Phoebe only mustered a mute denial.

"Please tell me what's happened. How can I—we—help?"

After long, shuddering breaths, Phoebe regained control of her tears, if not her broken heart or her situation.

"I . . . Adrian and I have agreed . . ."

Had they? Had they agreed? Or had he simply fired her? She hadn't done more than accept his decision. Could she have done anything else?

"Go on," the pastor said.

Letty took Phoebe's hand and pressed warmth into her cold flesh.

"We feel it's best if I find employment elsewhere," she said. A sharp pang accompanied her words, and she gasped at the pain.

"What?" Pastor Stone's kind features took on an angry cast. This was the first time Phoebe had ever seen him display anything other than benevolence or concern. "Has that man taken leave of his senses?"

Phoebe clamped her lips together and shook her head. She offered a brief prayer, then went on. "It's for the best. I should have sought new lodgings as soon as he arrived. In hindsight, I know how unseemly it is for an unmarried woman to live in a bachelor's building. He spends a great deal of time in his office, and that gives rise to the appearance of impropriety."

"Appearances aren't reliable," Mrs. Stone said.

"They're not," Phoebe agreed, "but as a Christian, I have to make sure I don't dishonor my Lord by any action others might misconstrue."

"Phoebe," Letty said. "You can't let a gaggle of gossips mandate your life. That's worse still."

"I'm not letting them determine my life. I'm just waking up to the truth I've ignored. A woman's reputation, her good name, and her clear, consistent witness are her most prized possession. I've let the Lord down with my carelessness."

Pastor Stone paced the room, his hands clasped behind his back. "I sincerely doubt that. And I agree with Letty. You can't let evil set aside all the good you do and the way you live out your faith. Don't forget you need only God's approval. He's the one who knows your heart. Not those who want to judge you. The Almighty is our one true judge."

"I clouded my witness when I let my emotions overcome my common sense. I can't find even the suggestion of wisdom in my behavior."

"Why? Because you fell in love with a man?"

Phoebe blushed, and although the heat came from embarrassment, she welcomed the easing of her earlier chill. At least now she felt alive.

"You . . . I mean, I don't . . . I haven't—"

"Don't," Letty said. "Don't deny your feelings for Adrian. There's nothing wrong in loving him. Neither of you is married, and were it not for this silly gossip, you might be planning a wedding instead of making a muddle out of an already unpleasant matter."

Phoebe winced. Yea, were it not for the gossip and Adrian's past they might indeed have been planning a future together.

"The scandal exists, and I can't ignore it. Besides, additional circumstances make it impossible for us to be together."

Letty made an impatient sound that to Phoebe sounded very

much like a snort. "I think you've read your Bible often enough to know that with God, nothing is impossible—nothing."

"But—"

"But nothing," the pastor cut in. "Letty's right. Our God had Moses part the Red Sea, He gave Sarah a child in her old age, He gave a young virgin girl a child. Our God let that baby grow into the man who suffered the cross for everyone's sake. Then after Jesus died God raised Him from the dead to fulfill ancient prophecies of the Messiah. Nothing is impossible for the God we serve."

Tears again stung Phoebe's eyes. "Well, then I'll just trust God to provide for the baby and me. That won't be difficult. I've always placed my faith in Him, since I've never had anything material to count on. I know that in His own good time the Lord will find me a new position and shelter."

Letty stood. "Employment won't be a problem. I need a nurse now that my practice has grown so much. And Shaker knowledge of medical matters is legendary. You have valuable experience, don't you?"

"All the Sisters and novices took rotations doing the work needed to sustain our Shaker family. I have had experience with the sick, but for the most part I worked in the children's dwelling."

"There's no one else in town with that much experience," Letty said. "And during our conversations, I've learned how well versed you are in the healing properties of various herbs and medicinal plants. You'd be an asset to my practice."

Phoebe wished she could put faith in Letty's words. But she knew the doctor's generosity and had experienced her willingness to help right after John's death. She had no alternative.

Although still wobbly, she stood. "I appreciate what you want to do for me, but I can't accept charity. I'm sure my presence would harm your practice."

To her astonishment, Letty laughed. The Stones joined in, and Phoebe wondered what kind of foolishness she'd uttered.

"I'm afraid," Letty began, "that you need to remember recent Hartville history, that scandal I caused shortly before you arrived. At that time, no one came to my clinic besides Mrs. Stone, Randy Carlson, Daisy, Mim, and the occasional miner or carpenter who was too ill or injured to care who doctored him. The Lord saw me through, and with His continuing help, we can weather anything."

"Yes indeed," Mrs. Stone said. "Phoebe was likely too new to town or too busy when she and John first arrived to have given much notice to the hubbub. You'd do well to give her some details, Letty dear."

The pastor smiled. "There's no time like the present, Mrs. Stone, so I'll leave you and Letty to fill her in. I'll see to the matter of a new home for Phoebe and Lee. I'm sure someone has empty space to share."

Phoebe looked from face to face, afraid that they'd soon lose their faith in her. They'd change their minds once they realized the seriousness of her situation and the measure of the townsfolk's moral outrage.

She had to think about the future. It grew more evident each minute that the future would take her far from their midst. She couldn't let her ruined reputation taint them. It was bad enough that John's widow had become the talk of the town—no one remembered the good he'd done in the ministry. These days they only spoke of her scandalous affair.

Later that evening, Phoebe and Wynema showed a pair of brawny young men where to put the boxes they'd brought to the Howard home from the apartment behind the general store.

"I still think you've taken leave of your senses," Phoebe said. "You don't need me to muddy the good name of your photography business."

Wynema sent Phoebe one of her surprisingly wise looks. "Don't you think they spend their fair share of time tearing me to bits? Although they come here when they want a likeness of their little darlings or their dear departeds, they certainly don't spend time or effort befriending me. I'm that odd, unwomanly creature who dares to do a man's trade."

"That may be, but they're not questioning your morals or your adherence to the Ten Commandments."

"Give them time."

Wynema went to develop her latest batch of photographs in the pantry she'd converted to that purpose. Phoebe went with Lee to the large bedroom that had once belonged to Mr. Howard. Although the widower had come to Hartville to make his fortune in silver, he'd soon found it more advantageous to open a shop to fix damaged mining tools and any other implement that might need repair. His tinkering had earned enough to build a comfortable, solid home for himself and his eccentric daughter. He'd succumbed to influenza a year ago this past fall.

The young men who'd helped Phoebe move had brought her rocker into the room, and once she'd changed Lee's diaper, she took up its familiar rhythm and soothed the little one to sleep.

She had no idea what to do next. She didn't have many marketable skills other than those she'd gained while running the general store. Hartville had only one such emporium. Rockton's mercantile was a small family business with abundant offspring to keep it staffed. In a town the size of Hartville, work would not be offered, not when most considered her unsuited to decent dealings.

Lee gave a sweet sigh and nuzzled into the crook of Phoebe's neck. Her heart welled with love for the child God had given her. Surely the Father wouldn't entrust her with this tiny angel if He didn't plan to provide for them. Over the years she'd come to recognize how mysterious the Almighty's ways could be. She couldn't presume to know or even to try to guess how He might ensure their days. But she would indeed cling to the many promises He made in His Word. As He asked, she would seek first His kingdom and wait for Him to add to her life all those things she and her child would need.

She knew no other way to live.

She would trust in Him.

Adrian had heard the bustle of activity in Phoebe's apartment, but he hadn't had the courage to run downstairs and offer to help. He feared that just by seeing her, he'd lose his resolve.

That would put them back where they'd started. The town's self-righteous gossips would continue to heap all their ugly accusations on Phoebe. He couldn't subject her to any more of that.

And, if he was brutally honest, he couldn't do it to himself either. He feared that the hotter the talk grew and the longer it persisted, the more likely it was to spread beyond the borders of Hartville. That could draw the attention of those who sought him. Then anyone linked to him would be in as great a danger as he was.

He refused to risk Phoebe and Lee.

He didn't want more danger for himself.

He didn't feel he'd yet accomplished even a fraction of what God had for him to do on this earth. Did that make him selfish? Was it wrong?

He didn't know, and so far, the Lord continued to keep His counsel. Why couldn't God speak more clearly, more loudly? Why did he struggle to discern the Father's will? How did others hear the voice of the Almighty so clearly? Why not him?

Adrian prayed daily—even hourly. He read chapter after chapter of Scripture each night, and he waited. He'd been seeking heavenly guidance ever since the train.

Still, he hadn't identified any particularly wise leading from above. Oh yes. He had taken one Scripture verse to heart recently. He was trying to lean only on God's wisdom and all-seeing knowledge, but so far all he'd perceived was his own meager understanding of the circumstances.

Heavy footsteps on the iron stairs dragged him from his morose musings. He didn't know many who would breach the metal monster Hart had installed to guard his privacy.

Daisy had the day she'd persuaded Adrian to let her visit the mining company's office under the ruse of an interview. And during the recent blizzard, Phoebe had brought him his meals. He didn't think either woman would seek him out after what he'd done earlier that day. Besides, these footsteps indicated someone larger, heavier. It seemed his visitor was a man.

At the knock, he said, "Please come in."

The door opened to reveal Eric Wagner. The seriousness on the newspaperman's face brought additional tension to Adrian's already taut muscles.

"To what do I owe this visit?" he asked, hoping the strain didn't show in his voice.

Eric leveled a piercing stare at Adrian. "If you gave your most recent actions consideration, you'd know without having to ask."

Adrian couldn't hold the perceptive glare. He looked down at the papers on his desk. "I couldn't let her stay where her character would be misjudged any longer."

"That's awfully convenient—put her out of work and home rather than taking things into your own hands and putting them to rights."

He rose, his anger growing. "What right do you have to come to my office and accuse me of such cowardice?"

Eric crossed his arms over his chest. "I find it interesting that you use a word I haven't. Could the accusation come from your conscience?"

"You don't know the particulars of my situation, and I assure you I did what had to be done. It's best if Phoebe and Lee stay far from me. I'll have you know it took more courage to send her away than it would have to keep her by my side."

"So you admit you love her."

"I never said that."

"No, but only a man who loves a woman would be stupid enough to think it in her best interest to deny their love and push her away."

Something in Eric's words made Adrian look up. "You speak from experience."

"That's what gives me the right to make you see the truth. You have greater strength in the face of trouble when you have the one you love at your side. Especially when you both base your love on God's promises."

"But you and Letty aren't under a threat."

"We might not have threats against us, but we've faced our share of trouble." Eric's expression softened, and Adrian sensed him trying to reach out, to share the benefit of his experience.

He wished he could trust it.

Eric clasped his hands behind his back and continued. "I lost my first wife a number of years before Letty came to town. I blamed myself for her death and that of . . ." Sadness crossed Eric's face. "That of our unborn son. I felt unfit to love a woman and refused to endanger Letty or any child we might have by loving them as much as I'd loved Martina. I believed I'd failed my first wife because I'd loved her too much. I did everything I could to keep Letty at a distance."

"Your concerns don't sound unreasonable."

"That's because you're still blind to the gift God has given you. You're refusing His blessing and thinking you know best."

Adrian drew in a sharp breath. Could this finally be God's response?

No. The town newspaper's owner didn't strike Adrian as

a particularly heavenly messenger. In fact, he came across as judgmental and intrusive. Besides, what he said appealed too much to Adrian.

"So," he said, "you now consider yourself an authority on matters of the heart."

Eric narrowed his eyes and opened his mouth.

Adrian cut him off. "Tell me, what do you think you'll gain by confronting me like this? What's in this for you? I don't see much of a newspaper story in my private affairs."

Eric leaned on Adrian's desk. "I have nothing to gain, certainly not a story for the paper. I'm here because my wife is angry and distraught over the shabby way you treated her friend."

"I resent that—"

"Resent whatever you wish, but that doesn't change facts. You turned Phoebe and an infant out of their home. You also fired her from the job that provided their living."

Eric's glare pinned Adrian, and all his doubts gained strength. He didn't know what to say.

He didn't have to speak. Eric had plenty more to offer.

"As a Christian," he said, "I abhor cruelty. From where I stand, what you did to Phoebe is unreasonably cruel. You hurt her to appease a handful of nasty gossips. Does that make sense? Does it strike you as something God would honor? Can you see our Savior acting likewise?"

Adrian's stomach plummeted. Put in those terms, he appeared as cruel, cowardly, and craven as Eric said.

"What would you have me do? I sent her away to protect her life. There are those who won't hesitate to hurt her if they realize how much she means to me."

His words had an effect on Eric. "Why don't you just tell me what you've been hiding ever since you came to town? It might make things better. I find it best to let the sun shine on everything."

"I don't rightly reckon Mr. Adrian Gamble's any too keen on

telling anyone what he's been hiding," Sheriff Herman said from the open doorway.

Adrian turned. His blood chilled when he saw leashed rage in the lawman's eyes. He hadn't noticed Herman's arrival, but he didn't think forewarning would have helped.

"Pull out your trusty little black book, Mr. Wagner," Herman continued. "Looks like we got us a real juicy story for the *Hartville Day.* I'm here to arrest a train robbing killer. One who's gone so far's to change his name and all."

Dear God, help me.

"You have it all wrong." His voice sounded rough, raw, even to him. "I didn't rob a train. You have the wrong man. I just tried to save an old lady—"

"That's what they all say." Herman rounded the desk and grabbed Adrian's right hand. Before he could react, the sheriff clapped a manacle on his wrist.

"Wait! You're wrong—"

"Save it for the judge, Mr. I Don't Rightly Know Who You Are. I'm sure he's gonna want to hear every last little old lie you choose to weave for him."

As Sheriff Herman dragged Adrian from the room, he caught a glimpse of Eric's face. The anger burning the newspaperman's gaze said it all.

Adrian had betrayed his trust.

He was on his own; he and his God.

Help me, please, Father. Help!

17

Phoebe hadn't thought her heart could break any further. But that was before Sheriff Herman arrested Adrian for train robbery and murder.

Had he told her the truth? Or had she swallowed a well-woven tall tale?

How could she fall in love with a killer and a thief?

Had love blinded her to the truth? She didn't want to believe that. She remembered Adrian's earnestness, his intense regret when he'd told her about the event. Had he lied?

She hadn't thought so then.

But now the sheriff had arrested him. She'd seen it with her own eyes. Surely the lawman wouldn't have acted without cause.

After the young men had finished helping her move, she'd returned to the general store for a final look to make sure she hadn't forgotten anything important. As she'd stepped onto the boardwalk at the corner, the door had swung inward, and, while the cowbell still clanged, Sheriff Herman had dragged Adrian outside. Manacles had bound the two men at the wrist, and the shame in Adrian's face had cut deep.

Adrian had given her an anguished look. "I didn't rob that train . . ."

She'd stayed frozen for long moments and watched the lawman, Eric Wagner, and Adrian march down Main Street toward the center of town. If she hadn't used the post for support, she would have crumpled, just as she did the day she'd emptied Mei-Mei's armoire.

In the time since his arrest, ten long days by now, the gossip had exploded. No one had a single good word to say, even those whom Adrian kept on the payroll despite his incarceration. He'd asked Douglas Carlson to run the mine, and he'd enlisted Pastor and Mrs. Stone to man the counter at the general store.

Phoebe hadn't budged from the Howard home. The moment she showed her face in public, she'd once again become the object of scorn. She didn't have the strength to cope with that.

Wynema related the pertinent details of Adrian's circumstances. It seemed Sheriff Herman had sought the help of other sheriffs, police officers, and even a handful of Texas Rangers he knew. One of his contacts recognized Adrian from the photograph Herman had sent. Wynema wouldn't forgive herself for taking the likeness.

The two women discussed Adrian's retelling of the facts at length. Wynema believed his version and, as her hurt eased to a dull ache, Phoebe once again sensed he'd told the truth.

She doubted a ruthless thief and killer would care whether the miners who depended on the Heart of Silver Mine kept their jobs. She didn't think a hardened criminal would care if the general store closed and its customers could no longer meet their needs.

And she doubted a man of low character would have Douglas continue to pay the sum he insisted was due little Lee.

"Here you are," Wynema said later that afternoon. "Mr. Carlson gave me this."

As she had the week before, Phoebe took the envelope and questioned the accusations leveled against Adrian. She remembered his concern for the baby when he'd changed his diaper. And she still suffered from his determined, if misguided, attempt to shield her from scandal.

She wondered if he'd considered the law as great a threat as the robbers.

She called up her courage. "Wynema? Are you busy for the next hour or so?"

The photographer thought a moment. "I only had one appointment this morning. What do you need?"

"Could you please watch Lee? He won't be much trouble, since he's sleeping right now, but he might wake up before I get back."

"Where are you going? I thought you'd decided to hide here for the rest of your natural life."

Phoebe blushed. "I hadn't decided that, but since I also haven't decided what to do, I don't think it prudent to give the tongue waggers any more ammunition than they already have."

"So . . . have you now plotted the rest of your future? You seem to have pondered the matter long enough and then some."

"Nay. I've only recognized my failure to do right by Adrian."

"Oh?"

She winced at the interest in Wynema's face. "The Lord showed me how wrong I was to jump to conclusions without speaking with Adrian first. I owe him at least that before I render judgment."

"I'm heartily glad you've seen reason. It's for that reason—and only that one important reason—that I'm willing to watch that poor mite. I've no experience with anything but my cameras and photographic paraphernalia, and I might pose him greater danger than if you left him alone."

Phoebe smiled. "I doubt it. You always sell yourself short. But I do appreciate your help. I promise I won't be long."

Wynema surprised her with another of her sage looks. "You don't have the stomach for the ugly air of self-righteousness blowing out there. You won't be gone long. You'll be back and, more than likely, before your little one awakes."

Not ready to debate her intestinal fortitude, Phoebe donned her cape and faced the world. As she hurried down Creekside Lane, she prayed and didn't leave room for any disturbing thoughts that tried to take shape.

But when she reached Main Street and stepped onto the boardwalk, she couldn't so easily dismiss what she saw. Every step she took inspired someone to move aside and give her a wide berth. Her neighbors seemed to think she might taint them with scandal or immorality or some other kind of scurrilous stain.

She approached the jail with a measure of relief. But when she grasped the latch on the door, a wad of spittle landed inches from her right foot. Revulsion clawed up her throat, and she looked for the culprit.

No more than ten feet away, Stan Fulton stood next to Naomi Miller, mockery in his gaze.

"Harlot," Naomi muttered.

"I see you're still seeing to your lover's needs," Fulton commented, a sneer now in the place of the mockery.

"Shameless," the laundress added, then with great, deliberate intent, she showed Phoebe her back.

Fighting to maintain her dignity, Phoebe opened the door and walked into Max Herman's office. The sheriff looked up and gave her a curious look.

"I reckon you're wanting to see that Gamble fella," he said.

Phoebe nodded but didn't speak.

"Well, little lady, if you'll come this way," he indicated the door behind his desk, "you can see him. Can't be giving you much time though, seeing as he's a prisoner waiting on the circuit judge to come soon's the weather lets him."

"I don't need much time. I've a child awaiting me."

Again curiosity lit the sheriff's dull brown eyes, but to his credit, he didn't indulge it.

He jangled a metal ring laden with large black keys. "Follow me, then."

Moments later she faced Adrian. Thick iron bars separated them. The anticipation in his gaze vanished the moment he realized who'd come to visit.

"Why are you here?" he asked. "This is no place for a lady like you."

"You must be the only person left who considers me a lady."

"Yet another sin," he muttered and averted his face. "You haven't told me why you came."

"I had to." He gripped the bars that bound him, and she placed a hand over his. "I need to hear the truth. I need to know . . ." The knot in her throat tightened. "Oh, Adrian, please tell me what's what."

A fierce light glowed in his dark eyes. "Phoebe, I came clean that day. I didn't rob the train. And the man I killed . . . well, he was about to hurt that old lady. I—I couldn't let him do it. Even now, after all that's happened, I'm not sure I'd act differently if I had the chance. I couldn't just stand by."

She covered Adrian's other hand. "Then why? Why would Sheriff Herman jail you? Who's accusing you?"

He shrugged and slipped his hands from under hers. He stepped back and turned away. "From what little Herman said, I suppose the authorities think I was part of the gang. They believe I thought the other guy would cheat me out of my cut, so I killed him for his."

"Did you?"

He sent a sad look over his shoulder. "I just told you I didn't. Can't you believe me, Phoebe? Even you?"

His quiet question touched her heart. She studied his dear face and thought back to the day when he'd confessed. She'd sensed the sincerity in his words that day. And, heaven help her, she sensed it again today.

"I do, Adrian. I don't know why, but I do believe you. I suspect you're as honest as the dawn and as generous as the vein that runs through your mountain."

A sheen appeared in his eyes. "Thank you. You can't know what that means to me."

She lowered her gaze to her hands. "Perhaps I do. Don't forget, I've been wrongly accused as well."

"Yes, but not of theft and multiple murders."

"Multiple?"

He laughed without humor. "Didn't you know? They've also charged me with Mei-Mei's death."

She went light-headed, but this wasn't the time for a case of the vapors. Adrian had been wrongfully jailed. Since he couldn't do anything about his situation while behind bars, then she'd have to prove him innocent. Somehow. She didn't know how, but she had to persuade his accusers of his innocence.

Phoebe couldn't let them hang the man she loved.

"Now you listen to me." She took hold of two bars, wishing she could transfer her determination to him. "You can't just give up. You're innocent, and you have to fight this. I can't do it alone. There must be something, information to clear you or someone who'd vouch for you. Please tell me. I can't leave you here without hope."

"I lost all hope the day I killed that man, Phoebe. Don't you understand?"

"I understand that a wrong is being done, and in no way does it right what you did."

"Robert Andrews," he finally said without much conviction. "He's a Pinkerton. I contacted him weeks ago about the opium problem. A few years ago he worked for my father on a company matter. He also helped me set up my demise."

Phoebe caught her breath. He'd confided in her. Perhaps he harbored more hope than he dared confess.

"Thank you for your trust," she said. "I won't let you down."

Eyes dull, expression bleak, Adrian looked defeated, desolate. "You could never let me down. No matter how this turns out. What you've given me is more than I dreamed I'd find. If only . . ."

When he fell silent, she waited, hoping he'd finish his thought, but he didn't. Heartened anyway, she asked how to contact the man.

Adrian referred her to a ledger in the mansion and told her Douglas would let her inside. "Please don't do anything dangerous."

His anxiety made Phoebe agree where she wouldn't have otherwise. "I'll be careful. All I intend to do is telegraph Mr. Andrews. At the very least, he needs to know what's happened. Perhaps he'll help me set you free."

Adrian bid her farewell, clearly doubtful of that eventuality. Phoebe had no alternative but to leave.

She didn't, however, do it silently. In the front office she faced Sheriff Herman. "He didn't do it."

The lawman arched a brow.

"He didn't. He didn't steal a dime."

"You don't say, little lady?"

"I've yet to tell a lie, Mr. Herman, and I believe you know that. Adrian Gamble didn't kill Mei-Mei, and he didn't hold up any train."

The man's impassive expression goaded her further.

"He didn't." She'd say it over and over again until everyone believed her. "And about that other death?"

"Yes . . . ?"

She held her head high. "It was an accident. The man was a thief, and Adrian jumped him to protect an elderly woman. The gun went off as they fought. That, you'll agree, is an accident."

"Well," the sheriff said as he scratched his chin, "at least he told you the same tale he told me. We can give him credit for being a consistent crook."

Anger threatened to blind Phoebe. "Someday, sir, you'll have to ask forgiveness for your accusations. I'd suggest you compose your apology while I find the proof."

"What you gonna do, little Shaker lady? Ask one of your spooky spirits to help you?"

Phoebe stood tall. "Nay, sir. You have it all wrong. I'm not a Shaker. I never signed the Covenant. I couldn't. I left the Shaker family that raised me because I couldn't accept their heresies. You see, Sheriff, I'm a Christian, and I only follow Jesus. All the help I need will come from God Almighty Himself."

In the ensuing silence Phoebe took her leave.

On her way home Phoebe saw a group of miners headed toward the east end of town. Fulton led the crowd.

"Hey, Stan," one miner called. "You won't go changin' yer mind once we get there, now will ya?"

The foreman laughed. "Nah, Lowery. I promised you two rounds on my dime, and I mean to come through."

A rowdy cheer rang out.

Phoebe shuddered. The trouble that crowd might make didn't bear thinking on. Especially since they seemed intent on a drunken revel.

"You're mighty cheery," another miner said.

"Sure am."

"What we celebrating?" asked a third.

Fulton preened. "I'm back in charge now that that lawyer man's taken up the books again. He knows nothin' what goes on in a mine."

Some of the men cheered again. Some looked concerned. All continued on their journey.

Against her better judgment, and despite Adrian's warning, Phoebe chose to follow. She stayed to the boardwalk while the men marched down the middle of the road. She might learn something that could help Douglas run the mine as it should be run instead of in a way that unduly benefited Stan Fulton.

A couple of the doubters exchanged whispers. Then one of them said, "I can't say as I know Gamble well, but what d'ya have against the guy?"

The foreman's face turned ruddy. "Ain't got anything against Gamble. Not rightly. But he doesn't know more than the lawyer, and he's made all kinds of stupid changes."

"Like the stuff he bought for the Chinamen?" asked another man.

Fulton shrugged. "That don't make a difference. It's that sticking his nose in the shaft and telling me how to run a mine. All them poles he wanted me to add to shore up the roof—or so he said. Ain't nothing wrong with our roof."

Again a few of the men put their heads together. Phoebe strained to hear, but to stay concealed she had to keep a distance between them.

"Hey, Fulton!" another whisperer called out.

"What d'ya want, Carmichael?"

"You can't argue but what we had that cave-in back in June. Mr. Hart and that preacher fella died. So did a bunch of the Chinamen. Maybe if we'd had them poles, nothing woulda happened."

Phoebe ran ahead of the men to get a look at Fulton's face. She cast a look over her shoulder and gasped at his murderous expression.

"So a bunch of squinty-eyes and a nosy preacher died. What of it? Hart's dying didn't do nothing to keep you from getting paid, did it? Besides, who's to say them poles he's already had me put in won't tickle something they shouldn't and bring the whole thing tumbling down? You can't go messing with what works just to keep a bunch of foreigners happy."

A vise closed on Phoebe's lungs. She couldn't draw breath, but not because of her rapid pace. Fulton's disregard for life shocked her. She'd never known anyone as callous or as hateful. Perhaps she could persuade Douglas to let the foreman go.

"You mark my words," Fulton added. The crowd turned onto East Crawford Street, where saloons and billiard halls and other unsavory establishments ruled. "If anything happens down to the mine, it's on account of that fool easterner's fool notions. He can't even keep himself out of jail, so how do you expect him to run a mine?"

He pushed open the batwing doors of a brightly lit emporium and disappeared inside the raucous cave. The others followed. Phoebe leaned against the nearest building to catch her breath.

After Phoebe telegraphed Robert Andrews, she spent days in anticipation of his response. But inactivity didn't suit her; it never had.

Buoyed by Wynema's gentle bullying and Letty's unflagging support, she soon joined the Stones at the general store. She didn't care if she was no longer on the mining company's pay roster. She needed to keep busy. And Lee was young enough that he still slept a great part of the day.

Despite the presence of friends, the days that followed were the most difficult of Phoebe's life. Everyone who entered the store immediately focused on her. Whispers and shocked glares were the order of the day. Praying for patience and extra doses of love for others, she treated everyone with kindness, greeted them cheerfully, and served them efficiently.

She also took the opportunity to broadcast Adrian's innocence.

"You know, Mrs. Stone," she said as Ruthie gawked at her from mere inches inside the door. "It's only a matter of days before the Pinkerton man arrives with proof. Mr. Gamble is innocent on all counts."

The first few times she'd done that, the pastor's wife had looked at her strangely but hadn't commented. By now, however, she'd joined Phoebe's campaign.

"I know, dear," Mrs. Stone said, "and when he does, there'll be many whose ears will go red from embarrassment. It's a pity how some are led astray by baseless rumors and partial truths."

"Oh, indeed." Phoebe appreciated Ruthie's discomfort.

Then Mrs. Stone gave the gossip a calculating look. "There's also those whose cheeks will burn when they withdraw the false-hoods they spread about you. Gossip is never a reliable source of information."

Phoebe gave her friend a chastening glare, but then, when Ruthie spun and rushed out, she relented. "I should scold you, you know."

"And I should scold you for letting them shame you and for hiding away."

She blushed. "Well, I'm no longer hiding."

The door slammed open and the ever-present cowbell clanged. "Aunt Phoebe!" Caroline cried. "Oh, Aunt Phoebe, hurry. Mama says to meet her at the mine."

"What's wrong? Has there been another accident? A cave-in?"

Caroline's eyes grew wide as saucers. "I don't rightly know, but I think it's another accident. She said nothing about a cave-in, but she says she needs you. Please, run!"

Phoebe did. Just outside the mineshaft, the crowd of mill-ing men obstructed her approach. Silence reigned despite their number.

"Dr. Wagner!" she called.

"I'm here," her friend replied from inside the group of miners.

As if by an unseen hand, the crowd parted and let Phoebe

through. She prayed for mercy when she saw Tong Sun motionless in a pool of blood.

"Is he . . . ?"

Letty nodded. "I'm afraid so."

Phoebe averted her gaze. She'd never seen so much blood. "What happened?"

"He had just finished his shift and was on his way out of the mine," Letty said. "The crossbeam brace for the roof gave way. It crushed his skull, but he stumbled this far before collapsing. At least, that's what the men say."

Phoebe looked around. The miners nodded.

"Was anyone else hurt?" she asked.

"No." Stan Fulton pushed forward, shoving men out of his way. "Only the squint—"

Letty's glare cut short the insult.

Fulton didn't have the decency to look ashamed. "He's the only one. And even he wouldn't've been hurt if that fool easterner hadn't made me force another pole under the beam. That opening didn't need no more support. The pole must've unbalanced everything. It's his fault, that Gamble guy in jail. You can add another killing to his name."

Phoebe's stomach lurched. "Mr. Gamble never hurt anyone, and he bears no blame in this man's death. If he insisted on the pole, why, then he must have had a reason."

"I hear say," Fulton said, his voice a taunt, "that he killed a train engineer and an old lady when he didn't get a big enough haul."

"That's not true," she cried. "You have it all wrong. When the train robber threatened the woman, Adrian jumped him. The gun went off between them."

Letty stood. "I agree with Mrs. Williams. Mr. Gamble is not the violent kind."

"Oh, and Mrs. Williams is an expert on Mr. Gamble, ain't she?" Fulton sneered. "I'll bet she's got herself some mighty intimate knowledge of him. Nobody's going to believe a killer's slut—"

"You don't have to believe anyone," a stranger said from just beyond the circle of mesmerized miners. Everyone turned.

"I'm Robert Andrews, with the Pinkerton Agency," the tall man said. "I have proof to support Mr. Gamble's version of the event. He didn't hurt a soul. You have only to believe the evidence."

Although Mr. Andrews's arrival relieved her, Phoebe felt the shame Stan Fulton's crass words left behind. She'd done what she'd set out to do. She'd brought the Pinkerton to town, and Adrian's name would soon be cleared.

Her name, on the other hand, was irredeemably smirched. She couldn't stay here any longer. She couldn't expose Lee to the scandal surrounding her. She had to go far from these people who accused her of base acts.

She had to go home, where she probably shouldn't have left.

In North Union she'd once again know the peace of Shaker life. She didn't have to practice the Shaker faith. She knew God, His Son, and His Holy Spirit. All she wanted was the safety she knew while growing up.

She was going home.

❦

Max Herman turned the key in the lock to the prison door. He didn't offer an explanation, and Adrian wasn't about to ask for one. Perhaps the circuit judge had arrived.

When the sheriff didn't clap the manacles on his wrist, Adrian arched his brows in query, but Herman had no response. The lawman led him from the jail.

Eric Wagner extended his hand. "You're the man of the hour." Adrian stared at that broad palm and then raised his gaze.

"I owe you an apology," the newspaperman said. "Please forgive me for doubting you."

He took Eric's hand. Then an arm around his shoulder made him turn. Robert Andrews gave him a rueful grin.

"Sorry I took so long," the agent said. "I had to extricate myself from a sticky situation after I received Mrs. Williams's telegram. And I had to make certain everything was in order."

"I understand, Robb."

"Ahem."

Adrian turned to the sheriff. The man's ears had turned the color of mulberries. "I . . . uh . . . er . . . I owe you one, too," Herman said. "I reckon from what this one's saying, you're even a hero after all."

"Hardly that."

"You saved that old woman's life, didn't you?" the sheriff asked.

"And in the doing, I killed the robber."

"Guess he got himself his just rewards."

Eric stepped forward. "I suspect you'd like a bath and a decent meal, and maybe not even in that order. You're free, you know. You can go home."

"Free?" He glanced at Andrews.

The agent shook his head. "Not completely."

"Then that means . . ."

"Yes," the Pinkerton said. "It means that with the inquiries Sheriff Herman here put out, your hunters will likely catch your scent."

Adrian took a breath and met his friend's gaze. "Then there's only one thing to do. I'll have to keep running. I hope you'll help me again."

Robb nodded. "You can count on me."

Eric took hold of Adrian's arm. "But you can't mean that. Why don't you wait? We can help, perhaps even set a trap for them. What you suggest is no kind of life. Have faith. God will provide—"

"Running is my only hope," Adrian said. "And now, if you'll excuse me, I have one last thing to do here in Hartville."

Adrian ran from the building to Wynema's house. He had to thank Phoebe for her help.

And bid her farewell.

18

"What do you mean, she's gone?"

Wynema smacked her fists onto her slender hips, pushed a hank of messy hair out of her eyes, and glared right back.

"What do you mean, what do I mean? She's gone, Mr. Gamble. I came home to an empty house when I returned from photographing the town's latest corpse. She didn't even leave me a note."

He'd come to say good-bye, and he'd known it would be difficult, but finding her gone cut deep. She'd known he was about to be freed, yet she hadn't bothered to wait.

He ran a hand through his hair. "Have you any idea where she might have gone?"

"No, but if you read the letter she left you, you might."

"Why didn't you give it to me at the start? Where is it?"

With a defiant glare, the photographer withdrew a crumpled envelope from a pocket in her skirt. "Here."

Adrian called on the good manners Mother spent years instilling in him and dredged up a perfunctory "Thank you."

The young woman didn't reply but crossed her arms and continued to stare. He glowered back, hoping she'd relent and give him a measure of privacy.

She didn't. Instead she said, "Well? Aren't you going to read it?"

Exasperated, Adrian capitulated but said, "It's private, you understand."

"Yes, but you must tell me where she's gone. It's the least you can do, seeing as I didn't open and read the letter. I could have, you know." For the first time, her brave façade slipped. "I'm worried about her . . . and Lee."

"This is ridiculous," he muttered, then tore open the envelope.

Phoebe's note was brief and direct, quintessentially her. In just one concise paragraph, she told him she wished him well and hoped he would do the same for her. Now that his innocence was established, he could stop running, settle in Hartville, and work his mine. She, on the other hand, couldn't stay with a storm cloud of scandal above her. She'd gone back home, where she and Lee would be cared for and loved, where they would both find peace.

Had it not been for the smudged signature, Adrian might have believed Phoebe's calm words. The blot looked suspiciously like a fallen teardrop.

"She's gone back to the Shakers," he told Wynema.

"I don't believe it. Phoebe didn't cotton to their religious ways one bit. Are you sure you read that right?"

Adrian met and held Wynema's contrary stare. "Yes, I read it right. She said she was going home. The only home she's ever known is that North Union place near Cleveland."

The young woman tipped up her chin. "That's not one bit true. Phoebe often said Hartville was her first and only home. If she's gone back to the Shakers, she's done it out of either fear or . . ."

As she paused, her defiant expression wavered. "Out of heartbreak." She trembled but then stood tall and donned her fiercest glare again. "So there. Now what are you going to do about it?"

Wynema was right. Phoebe had left with a broken heart. She'd also left in fear of the continued attacks of the gossips. But none of that mattered as much as her safety. No matter where she went, she'd be in danger. If the men who were after him learned how much he loved her, no pacifistic Shaker utopia would ever protect her.

He gave in to the inevitable. "I'm going after her."

"Well, it's about time you got some sense into that head of yours, Mr. Gamble. Go! Don't waste another minute. And hurry back with her. This is where she belongs."

The photographer's words rang with truth. Phoebe belonged in Hartville. Adrian would make sure she knew it. He'd bring her back to her home. Then once he knew she was safe, he'd vanish from her life.

Adrian Gamble would die so that Phoebe might live in peace.

Anticipation grew as the train ate up the miles of track between Colorado and Ohio. As exhausted as she was, Phoebe nevertheless couldn't wait to see Eldress Clymena again, couldn't wait to walk up the steps of the large dwelling house, couldn't wait to sit down to another abundant, tasty, silent Shaker meal.

She needed the peace that underscored Shaker life.

At the Cleveland railway depot, she used the last of her money to hire a buggy for the eight-mile ride to the North Union colony. The odd look the grizzled driver gave her didn't surprise her. Most of the world's folks thought Shakers unusually strange.

She pointed out her carpetbag to the driver and climbed into the rig. Lee had awakened before the train pulled to a stop, and although she'd fed and changed him, he hadn't fallen asleep again. She hoped he didn't cry all the way out to North Union. The taciturn driver didn't look particularly forbearing.

When they had about four miles to go, Phoebe leaned forward to look at the land she'd left five years before. Things had changed. Magnificent dwellings now lined both sides of Euclid Avenue, and their fantastic gardens teemed with fountains, gazebos, ornamental trees, and shrubbery of varied heights shrouded in snow. The most jarring sight of all, however, was the electric streetcar running down the street.

Unsettled by all the development, Phoebe wondered how the North Union society felt about the modernization. Then she remembered how the Shakers had maintained their peculiar way of life for a century, how they'd eschewed what some called progress, and her concern diminished. She knew what awaited her in the Valley of God's Pleasure, as the Brethren called their small town.

She sat back in the uncomfortable seat and thanked the Lord for the safe trip home. She also asked Him for strength in the days to come. She figured she'd need it to adjust to Shaker ways after her long absence. She especially asked her heavenly Father for the right attitude toward the religiously misguided Brothers and Sisters.

"We're here, lady," the driver said soon enough.

Every ounce of the fatigue she'd denied crushed down on her. She could scarcely move to disembark from the buggy. Once she stood by the side of the road, she took a good look at her surroundings.

What she saw rocked her very foundation.

This couldn't be the Center Family colony at North Union. It couldn't. She glanced back across the road to Cleveland and gasped. What she could see of the East Family's colony looked even worse.

Once-immaculate buildings now showed surprising wear and disrepair. Some looked vacant. The window glass had been broken out, and holes revealed where rotted boards had fallen away.

She couldn't imagine either Elder Samuel or Eldress Clymena tolerating these conditions. As she walked toward the large dwelling house, the hub of Shaker communal life, Phoebe took care to avoid the deepest drifts of snow. Her horror knew no end when she spotted the large and once beautiful meeting house. Its dilapidated condition made it look as though the Shakers had left it to the ravaging of rodents, weather, and time.

When she left, this local society had numbered only thirty or so, far fewer than the two hundred it had counted about thirty years earlier. And although many of the Brothers and Sisters were elderly, Shakers always worked hard, even through their later years.

This skeleton of her former home troubled her. Was Eldress Clymena gone . . . dead? How did the others fare? How about Sister Rachel Russell? And did Sister Harriet Snyder still take such care in writing her articles for the Shaker publication, *The Manifesto*?

Fear took hold in Phoebe's heart. She increased her pace, and then when she could no longer control her anxiety, she pressed Lee closer to her bosom and broke into a run. She hurried to the dwelling house. She knocked on the front door.

A stranger answered. "May I help you?"

Phoebe's senses reeled. She fought to keep her wits about her. "Eldress Clymena, please."

"Goodness, child," the woman replied. "Them Shakers been gone for right on to four years now. They sold some of their lands back in 1889, and we've leased this place since a bit less than that."

They'd sold the property one year after she left. Phoebe couldn't believe that the village she'd left to assume the position of elderly Mrs. Carmichael's companion could have died so quickly. Yes, five years had gone by, years during which she'd helped her employer through her last illness, met and married John, and come to Hartville only to become a widow. Still, it didn't really seem possible that all she'd known for so long had vanished during that brief time. Things must have been far worse than she'd realized for the Brethren to dispose of the land they loved. Phoebe thought about Lee. She'd had such happy hopes for his future among the caring Shakers.

"Where did they go?"

"I'm not sure, child, but I think I heard tell as some went down to another of their towns by Dayton way. Some say the others took to that Union Village place near Lebanon."

"No one's left . . ."

"Are you ill, girl?"

"Nay, not really. Only heartsick."

She turned and descended the stairs slowly, taking in the desolate landscape that once was a prosperous, bustling village. The fruit trees looked as though they'd gone wild, and even the outlines of the gardens were no longer visible under the blanket of snow as they had been in the past. More than likely, they'd fallen victim to undergrowth.

Phoebe glanced toward the nearby Mill Family's colony and felt still more alone, something foreign when she'd lived among the members of the three Shaker settlements that made up North Union proper.

"Lord God, where are you?" she whispered. "I'm all alone, I've a child, and we need you."

She sobbed and made her way through the drifts of white toward the once-proud mill. The crossing took her a while, since the snow was deep in places and she didn't want to wake Lee. He finally slept again.

Despite the difficulty, Phoebe remained determined to visit the place where she'd often played while growing up. The large stone building had always intrigued her.

She heard the river's chortles before she reached the mill itself. Although a crust of ice had formed over the water, the happy sound still filled the silence. She would have taken a seat on one of the boulders near the water's edge, but the snow made that impossible. She took refuge inside the mill.

Only then did she surrender to her emotions.

"Lord God, what would you have me do now?" She sobbed. "All I wanted was to come home, but there's none to come to anymore. How will I raise this child? Where am I to go? Where will I find a home? Should I follow the others to Union Village or Watervliet? Or are you telling me a Shaker village isn't for me? If so, then where do I belong?"

As the enormity of her loss hit her, Phoebe's legs gave way. She fell to her knees on the cold stone floor, and sobs ripped from her chest. Hot tears scalded her cheeks as her cries became utterances of despair.

All her effort had been for naught. She had nothing to come home to. She had no home. She had nothing at all.

Had it been possible, Adrian would have pushed the train down the rails. His urgency stemmed from either guilt or fear. He didn't know which, but he didn't take the time to think it through.

He had to find Phoebe soon.

When the train finally stopped at the railway depot in Cleveland without incident, he allowed himself one heartfelt sigh of relief. He was close. Only a short ride now separated him from the woman he loved.

He found a tolerable conveyance for his trip to North Union, and even when the horse took up a steady trot, his need to hurry didn't abate. He doubted it would have even if he'd been able to sprout wings and fly.

As they traveled the eight or so miles the driver said separated North Union from Cleveland, Adrian saw wealthy homes down both sides of the street. This part of town could hold its head high beside any great city he'd seen in his travels. Even the riches of New York wouldn't put it to shame.

Then they stopped. After Adrian paid the man, he turned and studied Phoebe's fabled Valley of God's Pleasure. What he saw didn't match the glowing word pictures she'd painted.

An air of shabbiness and neglect surrounded the buildings on either side of what the driver had called Shaker Center Road. Others fared worse. Instead of the thriving community he'd expected to find, the forlorn structures revealed varying degrees of decay. Some were obviously empty.

He followed the road, hoping it might lead him to Phoebe. Up ahead a vast white structure leaked out a river of smoke from its chimney. Adrian made for that beacon of habitation. Before he reached it, however, he made an alarming find.

A substantial carpetbag nestled in a snowdrift, and although he had no reason for his certainty, he knew it was Phoebe's. He paused only long enough to pick up the case, then redoubled his intent. Soon he reached the large building. He ran up the front steps and rapped his knuckles on one of the two side-by-side front doors. Phoebe had said the Sisters used one, the Brothers the other.

"Yes?" asked the middle-aged woman who opened the door on the left.

"Phoebe," he said, his breath a series of exerted gusts. "I'm . . . looking . . . for Phoebe."

The woman's brow furrowed. "Can't say I know of no Phoebe. None by that name lives around here."

"She no longer lives here, but she's traveled a long distance to get here. She must be here somewhere." He showed the woman the carpetbag. "This is hers."

She shook her head, then narrowed her gaze and peered around him into the wintry-gray world outside. "Maybe she's that girl with the babe."

"Yes, Phoebe has a child. Where are they?"

"Can't tell you that, but a woman with a little one stopped by earlier today, looking for them Shakers that used to own this place. Called it the Valley of God's Pleasure. I sure can't see why they'd do that, since it's just as hard and no more pleasure to work this land as any other I've known."

Adrian thanked her but didn't stay to discuss the ethics of

hard work Phoebe said the Shakers espoused. He had only one thing in mind, and that was finding her and Lee. He had to make them safe.

Beyond that, he didn't know what he'd do . . . other than disappear once again. Adrian Gamble was about to die a quiet, unobtrusive death. It was the only way he could see to escape the fate two robbers intended for him.

He walked through the well-planned village, searched the vacant buildings, called her name. Sadness joined his anxiety, a feeling of hope lost, of work gone for naught, of time running out for a peculiar, gentle folk.

He got no response regardless of where he went.

In those buildings that still showed signs of habitation, he inquired after Phoebe, but no one else had seen her. Nevertheless, he redoubled his resolve and plowed on through the snow. She'd come home only to find that home no longer existed.

He could only imagine how she felt.

From her vivid description, he identified the smaller cluster of even more decrepit buildings a short distance from the Center Family grouping as the East Family colony. There, Phoebe had said, novitiates lived until they learned Shaker ways and faith and were ready to sign the Covenant, that agreement by which they pledged their lives to the community.

It looked desolate.

She'd said another colony existed to the west of the Center Family—the Mill Family, she'd called those who lived and worked there. Her fond description of the efficient flour mill, its enormous wheel powered by the flowing river, gave him hope he'd find her there.

In the west the sun was setting, and without its benevolent warmth the evening turned colder still. He had to find them before anything happened to them.

He soon spotted the mill. Its stone walls stood in better condition than the wooden-frame ones of the other structures, although the roof showed signs of collapse. The sound of running water spoke of the power that once had turned its wheel. As he admired its elegant, simple lines, the russet glow of sunset outlined the crumbling building. A sound inside the structure caught his attention.

Urgency impelled him forward and into the vast doorway, yet caution made his movements stealthy and discreet. Moments later he thanked God for the care He'd led him to take. Twenty feet away a familiar feminine figure struggled against an equally recognizable masculine one. To one side, a second male held Lee in one arm. With his free hand, he held a gun against the child.

Adrian froze.

His past had caught up to him. He'd endangered two of the people he loved most. He had to do something, yet he was unarmed. He saw no other alternative but to surrender and hope his pursuers would take him in trade for Phoebe and the child.

He had to trust God. There was no other way.

"Let her go."

The two robbers turned toward him, and he prayed for strength, not just for himself, as he faced a certain death, but also for Phoebe. Seconds later the Father made clear he'd heard Adrian's plea.

Phoebe wrenched free in her captor's momentary distraction. The thief who'd held her rounded on Adrian. "So you've quit hiding, coward."

Instead of an understandable fear in the face of this man's intent, Adrian experienced pervasive peace.

"There are more important things in life than saving my skin," he said. "Give her the child. You have me now. There's no reason to hold onto either of them anymore."

The robbers hesitated, and Adrian feared they'd deny his request. They knew that Phoebe and Lee meant the world to him, otherwise they'd never have followed her. Only Phoebe tied him to this obscure and abandoned Shaker village in Ohio. If they thought they'd benefit further from threatening the woman and child, they'd surely have no compunction about holding them captive for a time.

"Well?" the gunman asked the other.

His partner shrugged.

The gunman held Lee out to Phoebe—but only after he'd turned the gun on Adrian. She took the child and held him close.

As evidence of good faith, Adrian stepped closer to the two who'd spent so long searching for him.

"Adrian!" Phoebe cried. "Don't—"

"Go," he said. "Everyone is waiting for you in Hartville. That's where you and Lee belong."

"Isn't this the touching scene?" the man who'd held her taunted.

Baby in her arms, Phoebe approached. "I can't go back. Lee deserves better than to grow up in the shadow of scandal. I'll follow Eldress Clymena to Watervliet."

"You sure don't look like one of the plain Shaker nuns," the other robber mocked. "Besides, they aren't supposed to have kids."

She continued to ignore the men, but instead of moving away from her captors, she stumbled and fell against the gunman.

"Now!" she cried.

Adrian could have throttled her but instead took the chance she gave him. He had to; he could be no less courageous than she was.

As Phoebe sprawled over the dazed thief, the baby at one side, Adrian recognized the opportunity before him. He called on the Lord and acted in those precious few seconds. He lunged at the man. As his fingers grazed the weapon, the thief lunged back.

Adrian felt his worst nightmares had sprung to life as he wrestled another train robber for a loaded gun. The man's greater size

266

left Adrian at a disadvantage, and his opponent seized control of the firearm. This time, however, Adrian refused to let fate or evil succeed. He fought with everything he had. Uncommon strength filled him, and seconds later he grasped metal warmed by the thief's hands.

With a final, powerful twist, he wrested control of the pistol from his foe and in turn found himself threatening the man. As though from a great distance, his senses hovered over the scene before him. Was that him? Was he ready to pull that trigger should Phoebe or Lee be threatened again?

He hoped he never had to find out.

"Run, Phoebe! Go home. The Stones are worried. Letty, Randy, and Wynema are waiting for you."

When she didn't respond, he gave himself a second in which to glance her way, certain that in that blink of an eye, his captive could again become his captor. What he saw nearly brought him to his knees.

In the last rays of sunset, Phoebe was locked in battle with the other, her smaller frame no match for a man's greater power. Just then, as if to announce his objection to being separated from his new mother, Lee began to wail.

Adrian saw movement out of the corner of his eye. He turned to his opponent and aimed right for his heart. "I've never purposely hurt another soul, but if you come any closer, I will."

"You killed my brother," the man said. "So don't go saying you haven't done anything wrong."

Upon hearing those words, Adrian saw the events of that long-ago train ride in a fresh, new way. This man's accusation had done what volumes of comforting words from family and friends couldn't do. The Lord had evidently found this cruel, sin-filled man a useful vessel to reveal truth.

"I didn't kill him," Adrian said, certainty now in his heart. "Your brother was ready to kill a helpless woman for her money and jewels. I couldn't let that happen, not without trying to stop him. The gun went off between us, and I'll never know if it happened by accident or if he tried to kill me."

Then Phoebe moaned. He turned toward her cry. So did his prey.

In that final moment, she pushed against her enemy's broad chest, and either fear or courage, miracle or maternal need, gave her greater strength. The man's breath whooshed out, and he stumbled. He staggered backward, fighting for balance, but instead dropped. The robber fell out of the opening in the stone wall. He vanished from sight.

A crash announced his landing on the ice.

Phoebe collapsed to the floor, sobbing. A pair of uniformed policemen ran into the mill. Adrian relinquished both the weapon and control of his foe.

"I'm glad you're here," he said on his way to Phoebe's side, "but how did you know to come?"

"A Sheriff Max Herman from some lost corner of Colorado wired us," the older officer said. "We contacted the Pinkertons, who verified what Herman said. It looks like we got here just in time."

Adrian wrapped his arms around Phoebe and pulled her close to his heart. "Go ahead," he whispered at her temple, pressed tender kisses on her soft skin. "Cry. Cry it all out. Goodness knows you've reason to weep."

Between sobs, she said, "Please . . . send someone to help him . . . it's cold. He . . . may be hurt."

Adrian's heart swelled with love for this kind, gentle woman. Only a loving soul could care about the fate of one who'd tried to kill her.

"Hush. He doesn't matter anymore. The authorities will see to—"

"His funeral," a third officer cut in as he came inside the mill.

Phoebe cried like a wounded animal.

The officer read her emotions correctly. "No need to fret like that, madam. We saw what happened as we hurried over. He must have hit a rock as he fell. He's dead, and he'll never cause you harm again. Are you quite all right?"

She nodded.

Lee shrieked, and Adrian reached for the child. He placed the baby in his mother's arms and held them both in his embrace.

Fierce emotions tumbled one over the other, but Adrian didn't let them blind him.

"God saw us through," he said, wonder in his voice.

Phoebe shook her head and raised wet, wounded eyes to meet his.

"Perhaps He did you, but He had nothing to do with my . . . my violent act."

"What do you mean?"

Her turmoil showed in her tear-bathed eyes and cheeks, her furrowed brow. "I—I killed a man . . ."

"No, love," he said in his gentlest voice, "you didn't. He chose a path of destruction when he picked up that gun as a means to an end. He lived by it and he used it—more than once, I'm sure. His trip down the road to perdition brought him to you and Lee. What do you think would have been your fate if you hadn't fought back?"

"That doesn't change facts," she said, her voice raw from sobbing. "I pushed him, and now he's dead. I . . . took a man's life. I sinned against God." She closed her eyes and, he supposed, prayed for forgiveness.

She went on. "I took God's place, as if I hadn't already sinned enough in Hartville. There I put myself in compromising positions, but this is worse. Mother Ann Lee was right, at least in this regard. Violence has no place in a Christian's life."

Adrian drew a deep breath. "Weren't you the one who told me I didn't kill that other man? Didn't you say it was no more than an accidental death?"

"Yea, but—"

"Listen to me. This is the same. You had a greater goal at heart. You were fighting for Lee."

"And for you . . ."

Her love, despite the terror he'd brought to her, humbled him. "We both have one thing in common, one more thing we must do."

She turned watery eyes to him.

"We must hand our guilt to Jesus, the one who, at the cross, ransomed us. I turned my enemy over to the police, and now we must surrender that guilt to God."

"It's not like that—"

"It's exactly like that. Although I'll admit you've been dealt a more serious blow than I have."

"Oh?"

"You came to the home where you knew nothing but love and found it no longer existed. There's nothing you can do about the disbanding of your Shaker family."

Another sob rent her, and Adrian brought her head against his chest and pressed a kiss on her silky hair. "In contrast, I chose to leave my family and home."

Her surprise reminded him how little she knew about him. "When I staged my death, I did so to protect a mother, brother, sister, and aunt. I left them, fearing for their safety, and began a life of shadows and flight."

"Mr. Gamble," a policeman called from the entrance to the mill. "We've finished here. Won't you be needing a ride back to town?"

"In due time," he said. "I'm sure we can find someone kind enough to take us to the depot. We've a train to catch to Virginia before we return to Colorado."

"Virginia?" Phoebe asked.

Adrian nodded. "You need to meet your future family—"

"What?"

He felt his cheeks flush. "Well, they'll be your new family as soon as you do me the honor of marrying me."

"You can't marry me. I'm embroiled in the foulest scandal—"

"With me, don't forget. And I have it on excellent authority that the most expedient way to silence the gossip is to marry you."

She frowned. "You can't throw away your freedom just to put an end to my discomfort. That's not fair to you. You deserve—" Her voice broke—"a decent, loving wife, one who's free of any stain."

"That woman is you."

"Of course not. Have you lost your wits?"

"On the contrary, I finally have them in my grasp. I wasted too much time on fear and lack of trust. Centuries ago Jesus bought our freedom on the Cross of Calvary. Remember the Gospel, Phoebe. Once we believe, our sins are washed away, and we're free of stain."

"But—"

"Wait. I'm not done." He cupped her cheeks in his hands and forced her to meet his gaze. "We must trust God. Do you doubt His power to change the minds of a handful of spiteful cats?"

She wavered.

"Do it, Phoebe. Take hold of the freedom He gives. Make me a happy man, and together we'll give Lee the family he deserves."

Renewed tears flowed down her cheeks, wetting his fingers.

"Don't cry," he said. "Not now. Let's instead thank God for what He's given us, for His mercy and strength in our times of trouble. Let's pledge ourselves to Him . . . and to each other."

Hope came alive in her eyes once again, just as it had when he'd first met her.

"I love you, Phoebe, and I know you love me. Be my wife. Please be mine."

On the breath of another sob, she replied, "Oh, Adrian. If you're sure."

"Not me, Phoebe. God. He's sure. It was His grace that brought us here today. Let's carry it with us every new day we live."

"Yea, dearest man. Let's."

Epilogue

Weeks later Adrian entered the sanctuary of Silver Creek Church, his mother's hand in the crook of one arm, his sister Priscilla's in the other. He'd just handed his newly adopted son to Mim, and he intended to savor every second of this Sunday worship service. He didn't expect anything unusual. In fact, it was that ordinariness that he most anticipated.

His brother Stuart brought up the rear, and as they reached the middle pews, he leaned over. "Where do you normally sit?"

Adrian gave him a rueful smile. "I'm afraid my life in Hartville never was normal. Whatever we choose today will likely become my norm."

A man called out his name. Adrian turned and smiled. Douglas Carlson sat, as always, next to Randy, and the couple waved him over.

"Mother, I've some friends I want you to meet."

As he said those words, Adrian marveled. He'd thought he'd never see his mother again, and yet here he was, introducing her to the Carlsons. Earlier he'd introduced her to the Stones, the Wagners, Sheriff Herman, and even to the contrary Wynema Howard, with whom he'd established a truce. The always-perceptive Amos down at the livery now knew his whole family and a great deal about him.

His mother patted his forearm. "I can't wait, son."

She closed her eyes for a moment and then met his gaze, the gleam of tears in his eyes. "I never thought I'd see you again, had given you up for dead, if not in fact, then at least to me. Here I've met the woman you'll marry in days, I've held your first child, and am now meeting those who cared for you while we were apart. It's nothing short of a miracle."

"Indeed," he said around the knot in his throat. "God is gracious, isn't He?"

Priscilla, no longer a child, smiled impishly. "I think so. He's brought me to a new world, one far more fascinating than the parlors of Virginia. I've a notion to take up residence in Hartville, brother mine."

"Pity the men," Stuart muttered.

Adrian smiled. Joy gave him a benevolence he'd never known. "Perhaps we can work something out. But come. Let's take our seats with the Carlsons. The choir is about to enter, and I assure you, you don't want to miss a single note of Phoebe's songs."

As the four of them sat, his mother leaned close. "I should hope it's the teaching you don't want to miss."

His cheeks again heated. "Of course, Mother. We can always count on Pastor Stone's inspired sermons. It's just that . . . well, you'll see. Here's the choir."

At the sight of his soon-to-be bride, Adrian's heart took flight. She was lovely, and she'd promised to spend the rest of her life with him. He couldn't wait.

Sweet, joy-filled notes flowed from the piano keys beneath Mrs. Stone's gifted fingers. A moment later Phoebe's voice joined in the praise.

"'Tis the gift to be simple . . ."

With the lyrics of the earnest Shaker hymn, she once again captured the attention of every congregant, even those who spoke ill of her for weeks.

No one could question her love of God, just as none could ignore this gift He'd given her.

When the rest of the choir joined their voices to hers, Priscilla whispered, "You were right. Phoebe has the voice of an angel."

As Adrian had expected, Pastor Stone spoke bluntly to those who'd transgressed against Phoebe by indulging in idle gossip and repeating untruths. More than one neck in the gathered flock bore the red stain of a guilty blush.

"Instead of carrying tales," he said, "Christians should use their voices as they were meant to be used. Raise them in songs of praise to our God and King."

Before long, the pastor ended the sermon. "I've a few announcements today," he said. "Some are sad, others more joyful.

"As many of you know, one of the Chinese miners died recently. While his death was originally deemed accidental, it has now been proven otherwise. As were those of Mr. Hart, Pastor John, and the eighteen others who perished with them. I've decided to hold a service in their memory."

To Adrian's dismay, Emmaline snorted. Would the woman never learn?

Pastor Stone leveled a reproving stare on his contentious sheep.

"I'm relieved to announce," he added, "that these killings will be the last. Sheriff Herman and Mr. Andrews, the Pinkerton agent, produced enough proof to put Stan Fulton behind bars for his crimes. All his crimes."

The pastor met Adrian's gaze. The opium trade would no longer be plied in Hartville now that Stan Fulton's days would be spent in jail.

"Finally," Pastor Stone said, "it's my honor to announce the upcoming nuptials of our beloved soloist, Mrs. Phoebe Williams, and our esteemed mining company owner, Mr. Michael Adrian Gable. I'm sure you understand the change to his family name. He will now resume its proper spelling. But he'll still go by Adrian, since he has grown used to it and wishes to honor his late father by bearing his name."

A number of parishioners turned and smiled. A few stared. Mercifully few leveled unpleasant glares, and those . . . well, Adrian would leave them to the Lord.

"If you'll all stand," Pastor Stone said. "Please join Mrs. Williams in the doxology."

"Praise God from whom all blessings flow . . ."

Despite the many voices raised in song, Adrian heard only one. He met Phoebe's gaze, and what he saw there brought moisture to his eyes.

"I love you," he mouthed.

Her blush told him she'd read his pledge.

"She sings with her heart," Eleanor Gable whispered.

"No, Mother," he said, his gaze never leaving the face he so loved. "Phoebe praises God with the song of love He placed in her soul."

Ginny Aiken, a former newspaper reporter, lives in Pennsylvania with her engineer husband and their sons. Born in Havana, Cuba, and raised in Valencia and Caracas, Venezuela, she discovered books at an early age. She wrote her first novel at age fifteen while she trained with the Ballets de Caracas, later to be known as the Venezuelan National Ballet. An eclectic blend of jobs, including stints as reporter, paralegal, choreographer, language teacher, retail salesperson, wife, mother of four boys, and herder of their numerous and assorted friends, brought her back to books in search of her sanity. She is now the author of eighteen published works.

Spring of my Love

Coming in February 2005

Excerpt from

Spring of My Love

One glance at the slight growth of grass on his land told Jeremy Johnstone that this year would be worse than last. When he'd bought his spread two years ago, he'd known his future depended on one thing: water.

The languid little river that meandered around the southern border of his property swelled each spring with snowmelt. This past winter, as well as the one before, had brought little snow-fall—a couple of big storms had covered everything, and the icy temperatures had kept the snow on the ground. But it hadn't amounted to much in the way of water. Spring's rains had been more absent than not. Now, in late June, the banks of the river looked like dirty old china, cracked and crumbly.

Jeremy tugged off his hat and used his red handkerchief to sop up the sweat from the relentless morning sun. Not quite ten o'clock yet, and the temperature was high enough to roast a steer on the run. Where was God when a man stood to lose his very last dime on account of a dry sky?

He craned his neck to better glare at the blank blue bowl over-head. Not a cloud to be seen anywhere. A sigh of exasperation ripped from him, and he slapped his hat against his thigh. Small puffs of dust spread upward and outward from the denim and straw and once again made obvious his difficult position.

A ways behind him his herd made dispirited sounds. They'd been hunting for fresh pasture with little success. He'd already spent a fortune buying feed, and he couldn't afford to hire enough men to drive the herd up north to richer pastureland. Not if he wanted to see his ranch through another winter. If only he had a more abundant water source nearby.

Well, the source was abundant. But by the time the water reached his little river, large amounts had been diverted into other tributaries. Tributaries like Rogers Creek.

He'd heard tell Old Man Rogers was tough as rawhide. Wouldn't surprise him if it was true. The crusty codger would have to be to live through all Jeremy heard tell he had.

Oliver Rogers, if folks were right, was a true western original. Jeremy hadn't met the man, but he'd been told the fellow came out west as a baby-cheeked boy. They also said he'd done as much as Kit Carson and was a real mountain man, maybe even the last one left in Colorado.

Jeremy had also heard tell the old man had died.

Rumor had it he'd passed on in the early winter—he hadn't been seen in town since late fall. If rumor was anything to go by, then by all means, rumors in Hartville carried extra weight. He'd never known another place so prone to gossip, even though Pastor Stone spent much of his pulpit time preaching against the sinful habit.

Jeremy had always held that rumor sprang from a root of truth.

If that was so, then who was manning the ranch? Old Man Rogers's wife had died a while back, and they'd only had a freckle-faced, carrot-topped girl. Had the daughter left the ranch? Was she now living in Hartville? He sure hoped she wasn't stupid enough to try to run the spread on her own. If nothing else, livestock needed more than the soft hand of a big-eyed miss.

Then again, Old Man Rogers had never gone in for cattle.

Jeremy spat in disgust.

Sheep.

Who in his right mind would fill the notch in the Colorado mountains with an army of the pasture-shearing beasts? Maybe all that rough living had addled the man's mind. Otherwise, why would he have brought those woolly menaces out here?

To think that clear, fresh water was being wasted on nothing more than curly, fatty fur. Cattle. Now they were more worthy creatures—not to mention horses. Especially Jeremy's cattle and horses.

He'd wager the daughter was ready to sell by now if she hadn't already done so. He hadn't heard tell anything about a sale. He'd only heard rumors of the father's death. Surely, word of Rogers Creek changing hands would have reached his ears by now. If it had happened at all.

Had Oliver Rogers really died?

Pastor Stone said he hadn't done a funeral, and Jeremy had heard tell the Rogerses were devout and faithful Christians despite the old man's wild youth. Repentance and reform must have been Mrs. Rogers's underpinnings.

Jeremy squinted toward the green crotch between the two peaks—Rogers land. It lay just beyond his, abutting on the foot-hills to his north. And, more importantly, the main tributary of his water source, Rogers Creek, blessed the soil in that valley. His livestock needed the pasture those baaing beasts were surely destroying. He needed to fatten up his animals. He had to sell well this coming fall.

His future depended on it.

If he didn't realize a decent return on his two-year investment, he'd be sunk.

Broke.

Finished.

He had to make Old Man Rogers's daughter see reason. His money would bring him a better return if he used it to buy another source of water. She had to sell. A girl couldn't run a ranch, certainly not if she'd moved into town. The only reasonable solution to her dilemma was the same as his. She simply had to sell.

To him. And in time to do his cattle some good.

Jeremy had to move fast.

The Sunday following his decision, Jeremy rode out to the Rogers ranch after church let out. He hadn't seen that distinctive shade of Rogers red among the bowed heads of the faithful at Silver Creek Church. Sure, Hartville counted more than just one redheaded resident, the hardest to miss being the wife of the town's lawyer. Mrs. Miranda Carlson was tall, green-eyed, and, some said, a real firebrand. Her hair, though, reminded him more of old, fancy wooden furniture.

Rogers red was more the color of a ready-to-eat carrot—orange, if a man was honest, and Jeremy fancied himself a stand-up sort.

Because of that honesty, he allowed himself a moment to take into account the likelihood of disaster. The worst that could happen was that Old Man Rogers would greet him at his place, none too happy with whatever excuse Jeremy cobbled up for the visit. He couldn't very well try to buy out the man who'd cleared that land and worked it for years. There'd just be no reason.

Not that he wished anyone dead, of course. He just had a distinct need. And Angel Rogers, as the old man's girl was called, might be able to help him—if Oliver Rogers had indeed died.

Jeremy offered a prayer as he approached the Rogers ranch. Then details of his surroundings began to register. The place was tidy, with its solid log cabin and the barn a ways off to his right. A horse stood at the rail of a modest corral, and a couple of chickens pecked the ground just on the other side of the circle. As he approached, the old steed shook its head and snorted, sending the chickens scattering with much feather fluttering and loud clucking.

To the left of the cabin, a sizeable garden, lush with young vegetable plants, gave promise of upcoming bounty. Behind the garden, up the broad green slope of the foothill, he spotted the much-despised white blobs—Rogers's sheep. To him, they looked more like a lice infestation than livestock.

To his dismay, they also looked healthy and well cared for, as did the horse, the chickens, the homestead, the bovine who'd just stuck its head out the barn door . . . and the skinny, denim-trousered, plaid-shirted, double-braided, pitchfork-bearing redhead at its side.

"What do you want, mister?" she asked.

Jeremy arched a brow at her contrary tone of voice. "I'm here for a neighborly visit with your pa. Is he around?"

The tautness at the corners of her mouth hinted at her discomfort . . . or could it be grief?

She jabbed the blunt handle of the pitchfork toward the back of the property. "He's out that-a-ways right about now."

"Then I'd best head on over so we can have us a nice talk."

Her hazel eyes darted in the direction she'd indicated, and she came closer, the tines of the fork pointed at his knee. "I don't think so, mister. It'd be a sin to disturb him. So you just state your business, and I'll be sure to tell him all about it later on."

Before he could object, a sheep appeared at her side and butted its furry head against her thigh. Without a look at the animal, she patted its cream-colored topknot. "Back up, Snowball. I'm busy."

Snowball wasn't about to be put off. The sheep lowered its head and laid into the girl's leg again, this time with a more serious purpose. Angel's knee buckled and she stumbled. As she tried to regain her balance, the pitchfork waved in the air above her head, and Jeremy feared for her safety. If she dropped the nasty thing and tripped on the handle, there was no telling what kind of harm she might do.

He dismounted and hurried to her side but reached her as she righted herself, her grip on the implement as sure as before.

"Maybe you ought to put that thing down before you do yourself some pretty bad damage—"

"You stay right there, mister, and no one will be getting any damage done."

Although Jeremy didn't know if she'd actually go through with her threat, the jab she gave the fork seemed plenty serious to him. He backed up a step.

Snowball, who didn't seem to be patient at all, shoved Angel again, and this time she couldn't stay on her feet. The pitchfork flailed again, and Jeremy knew an opportunity when he saw it.

"For crying out loud, girl," he muttered and closed his hand on the fork's substantial wooden handle. "I'm not here to hurt you. You're only in danger from yourself and this crazy thing."

Her big hazel eyes widened and her nostrils flared. "You'd best be gone, mister. My Father won't be taking too lightly your bothering me. It'd be a sin if you didn't heed."

Again Angel's odd way of talking caught Jeremy's attention. This was the second time she'd brought up the matter of sin. Then again, seeing as how she'd grown up out here alone with her ma and pa—most recently with only the old man—maybe she'd picked up his way of talking. Especially since he was said to have done more than his fair share of sinning in his adventurous youth.

The girl put Jeremy in mind of a high-spirited, unbroken filly. He took care to use his best horse-breaking voice. "Easy there, girl. I'm not here to hurt you or sin against you or your pa. I'm your neighbor from down south of you, and figured it was right about time I stopped by and say how-do."

"Well, then, mister, now you've done just that. You can be on your way, and I'll be sure to tell Papa about you. Thank you much for your . . . neighborliness."

The faint tremor he spied as she raised her chin told him there was more here than he could see or hear. "I just—"

"Baa!"

Before he knew what had happened, he'd landed on his behind, his legs waving useless in the air, the sheep's nose right in his face.

"What kind of folk are you, anyway?" he asked when he'd raised up onto his elbows. "I've heard tell of those who keep guard dogs, but you people are the first I've known with a guard sheep."

To his amazement, a giggle escaped her mouth.

At the same time, her eyes sparkled and a peach tint spread under her cinnamon freckles. Jeremy could hardly believe what he saw before him. Despite the manly clothes, plain waist-length orange braids, and boyish bravado, Angel Rogers was a very pretty girl.

She came to his side, retrieved her pitchfork from where it landed when he fell, and hugged the cantankerous Snowball. "The Lord works in mysterious ways, I always say."

Jeremy shook his head and picked up his hat. "I'm as Christian as the next fellow, but I've never thought sheep instruments of His grace. They're more like curses upon His creation."

Angel's good humor vanished. "I'll have you know, sheep are indeed part of God's creation, just as much as you and I are. He loves them, and you'd do well to pay them the respect they deserve, if for no other reason than that He made them and put them on this earth."

The flashes of green in her changeable eyes told Jeremy he'd have to at least pretend to tolerate her flock if he was ever to have a chance at talking with her father.

If the man was still alive.

He stood and crammed his hat back on to shield his eyes from the glare of the sun. "Hey, you can't blame a fellow if he isn't particularly disposed toward a critter that just sent him flying onto his . . . er . . . well, you know."

A twinkle replaced the sharp shards of color in her eyes. "Couldn't miss how you landed, mister. And it may just be a good idea if you take it as fair warning to you. We do well for ourselves here, and we don't cotton to strangers wandering about our property. None of us do—not even the animals."

Raising his hands in surrender, Jeremy took a step back. "I didn't come to wander. I just came to be neigh—"

"I'm not deaf, mister. I heard you the first time. You came to be neighborly, and like I told you up front, you've been neighborly enough already. I'm sure my father will see your gesture as he should. So you can just turn yourself right around and head back home. We're much obliged for your effort and all."

She was a wispy thing, all flowing lines and slender frame. But Jeremy now knew the delicate package contained a will of iron . . . and carried a wicked weapon in that pitchfork of hers. He'd never been dismissed quite so thoroughly in his twenty-six years, not since his Aunt Gertie—Lord rest her orderly soul—last scolded him for one of his adolescent pranks.

There wasn't much a man could do in this situation. "Since you've made your wishes plain, ma'am, then I guess I've no choice but to be saying my farewell. Please give your pa my regards."

"I'll do just that—"

"Baa!"

The wail carried a world of pain with it. Angel cast Jeremy a warning glare, then spun and ran to the barn. She never eased her grip on the pitchfork.

He considered this sudden twist. Should he leave and avoid further riling the girl? Or should he see it as God's helping hand in his time of trouble? Maybe he could help Angel with whatever was wrong with that suffering animal and at least show her he wasn't her worst enemy.

Even if her pa might see him as just that.

Jeremy called on the Lord for . . . well, he didn't quite know what for, but he did know that without heavenly help he was unlikely to succeed in anything he undertook. His adolescence and Aunt Gertie had taught him that much.

In the doorway of the barn, he blinked at the change in lighting. The moment of blindness gave him the chance to listen keenly. From somewhere in the far right-hand corner of the dark structure, he heard Angel's voice. Sweet, gentle murmurs gave it a softer quality than he'd heard up until then.

"Easy, Maggie. Easy, now."

Another pain-filled wail tore the air.

Even though Jeremy had no patience for sheep, he didn't have it in him to ignore an animal's misery either, and that was just what this creature's call told him. Once his eyes adjusted to the shadowy barn, he approached.

"What's wrong with her?"

Angel turned her head and gave him another scowl. "I told you to go, mister. We don't need you here."

This time, he ignored her words and knelt at her side. "My name's Jeremy Johnstone, not mister. I'd be right honored if you'd call me Jeremy. If you don't feel easy doing that, then Mr. Johnstone's fine with me."

She turned back to the sheep.

Jeremy peered at the animal. Despite his inexperience with sheep, he'd spent years around livestock at Aunt Gertie and Uncle Frank's farm, and his last two years had exposed him to any and all circumstances of a creature's life. This ewe was having herself quite a time of birthing.

"Is the lamb coming out backward?"

Angel nodded.

"Have you tried to turn it?"

Another nod.

Her wordless responses were fast eating up his patience. "Well?"

She shrugged. "Well, nothing. I couldn't turn it. It's too big and she's too small."

The sob that hitched her voice at her last word told Jeremy more about Angel Rogers than anything he'd observed until then. The ewe's suffering was breaking her heart, and, quite possibly, she was also dreading its probable death if birth didn't happen soon.

"Look, Miss Rogers, I might not know much about sheep, but I've helped many a cow, horse, and a couple of dogs birth their young ones. I'd like to help. It'd be a crime if I didn't even try."

The big hazel eyes studied him over one shoulder while a

graceful hand swept over the laboring ewe's swollen side. Jeremy held his breath. Where was the girl's father at this critical moment? Had Old Man Rogers gone off and left her to handle all by herself what was plainly going to be a rough time?

Highly unlikely.

With a growing sense of certainty, Jeremy felt that Oliver Rogers had indeed passed on not too long ago. Angel was alone on the ranch. As he watched the sheep convulse with another contraction and heard Angel's indrawn breath, Jeremy realized how defenseless she was.

And how brave.

She needed help, and somehow his need of water had brought him to her side at just the right moment. He knew what he had to do.

"Where's there water and good, strong soap?"

"There's a bucket near the door," she said, her voice soft, husky, "and I've a cake of Fels Naphtha soap right by it. Towel's hanging off a nail above it all."

Jeremy folded his shirtsleeves out of the way, sudsed and rinsed his forearms, and dried off. Moments later he returned to Angel and her sheep. "What's her name? Sunny, did you say?"

"It's Maggie."

"All right, then, Maggie it is." He reached a hand toward the animal. "There, there girl. Everything's all right. I'm just going to check to see if I can give the good Lord a hand today."

Angel gasped and turned, her eyes wide and warm with splashes of gold. Jeremy met that gaze and knew this moment would remain forever branded in his memory.

He prayed he could rise to the challenge, even though he wasn't certain what that challenge really was. What mattered most right then?

The life of a sheep?

Easy access to fresh water?

Or the trust of a lonely, vulnerable woman?